"Son," the president said. "What in the name of Moses is going on in this country?"

Weigand, his pipe clenched tightly between his teeth, said, "Mr. President, it's a Depression."

"A Depression?"

"Yes, sir."

"*What* is a Depression?"

"Well sir, I've been reading up on it. We haven't had one since 1939. Before our time, of course. What usually happens is that businesses fold, millions of people lose their jobs and go on relief—"

"All right, I think I get the idea. But how do you get rid of them?"

Weigand had been afraid he was going to ask that. "That's a good question. . . ."

World traveler, expert observer of the human condition, Mack Reynolds has been a world famous Science Fiction writer for more than two decades. In fact, of all the writers published in the leading SF magazines, *Galaxy* and *If*, a poll conducted among the readers put the stories of Mack Reynolds consistently higher than any other. Perhaps it is because his stories have an uncanny way of discussing *now* the questions that will concern everyone ten or twenty years later.

Mack Reynolds is the author of more than two hundred SF short stories, novelettes and novels. Many of them have been published by Ace Books and more will be published in future months.

Depression or Bust

by

Mack Reynolds

ace books
A Division of Charter Communications Inc.
1120 Avenue of the Americas
New York, N.Y. 10036

FOREWORD

The way the computers checked back on it later, it all began in the home of Marvin and Phoebe Sellers, 4011 Camino de Palmas, Tucson, Arizona. Marv Sellers, at 7:30 p.m., on a Friday in May was going over his income and his outgo. It had taken him a good hour before he came up with his history shaking conclusions.

"Phoebe," he said, "there can't be no other damn way of working it out."

"How'd you mean, Marv?" She was heating up three dinners, one Mexican, one Chinese, one Italian, in the electronic cooker.

"That new deep freeze'll hafta go back. What the hell was wrong with the old one?"

"Why, Marv, you know we had that old deep freeze nearly onto three years. The new ones got a lot of improvements. It was into all the ads, on the Tri-Di and all."

"Old one wasn't even paid for yet," Marv said. "What new improvements, for crissakes?"

"Well, the old one was colored white. Nobody has a white deep freeze any more."

Marv said, "Anyway, we gotta send this one back to the store. We just can't stretch out the payments, what with the house and the car and the furniture and swimming pool and that there vacation we took, rocket now, pay later."

"They ain't going to like that over to the store."

"Then they'll hafta lump it."

Harry came around to Jim Wilkins and said, "Boss, I just got a call from Marv Sellers. Says he can't keep up the payments on that deep freeze he bought a few weeks ago."

Jim Wilkins thought about it. He looked around the shop, darkly. "Listen," he said. "Call the distributor up in Phoenix and tell him to cancel that order for three new freezers. We're overstocked in here."

He turned on his heel and entered his small office. He was in a vile mood and the cancellation didn't help any. He sat down and thought about it for awhile, then switched on the phone and dialed.

When Bill Waters faded in one the screen, Wilkins said, "Listen, Bill, I'm going to have to postpone that Buick Cayuse air-cushion."

Waters argued for awhile. "I think you ought to reconsider. You realize these new models have nearly a thousand horses under the hood? And built low? Did you hear the one about the guy thought it was raining out but he was only parked under a policeman's horse?"

Jim Wilkins sighed and said, "See you later, Bill."

Bill Waters flicked off the screen and turned to his secretary. He said, "Balls."

"I beg your pardon?"

"You heard me. Miss Harding, write to the Denver office and cut back our allotment. Oh, two cars a month in each line."

"Gosh, Mr. Waters, all on account of one cancellation?"

He looked at her. "I can sense a trend. Jim Wilkins must be taking a beating in that appliance store of his. Cars'll be next. I don't want to be overstocked."

He sat there for awhile. Finally, he switched on the phone again and dialed. When the screen lit up, he said, "Frank, I've been thinking about that new house. I think we better shelve it for the time being."

Chapter One

Weigand Patrick slouched on through the door of Scotty's office, fumbling in his jacket pocket for his tobacco pouch. He slung one leg over the corner of her desk and began rubbing a quantity of the rough-cut in his left hand with the thumb of his right.

Scotty, without looking up from the paper she was perusing, said, "Get your ass off my desk."

Weigand Patrick let his eyebrows go up. "I beg your pardon?"

"Get your ass off my desk," she said.

Weigand said, "You're pleasantly red-headed, got pleasantly blue-green eyes, and are built like a brick outhouse. It's a criminal shame that as nice a chunk of meat as Scotty McDonald doesn't put out."

"You're the world's most inept seducer," Scotty told him. "Given any finesse at all, and you would have had me in bed months ago."

"I've been trying for years."

"I haven't had the time, until these past few months."

"You'll wake up, one of these days, so old and wrinkled nobody around'll want to lay you," Weigand Patrick told her.

"A fate worse than debt," she snorted, going back to her report.

He said plaintively, "You practically promised, back during the campaign."

"We were in too much of a rush those days," she said, not looking up.

"Every night you went to bed, didn't you? I was perfectly willing to go along."

"I went to bed to sleep."

"That's a hell of a thing to waste time on in bed."

Scotty said, "I suppose there's some purpose in you being here besides practicing what is without doubt the lousiest approach to deflowering an innocent virgin known to the history of seduction."

"Virgin yes, innocent, no. You are the least innocent virgin in the tradition of virginity," Weigand told her. "How about a date? I mean *the* date. Finally made up your mind. Screw your courage to the sticking place as old Lady Macbeth had it. You don't seem to realize that you're in your mid-twenties. Ten years shot to hell. Some three thousand six hundred and fifty rolls in the hay wasted."

He produced a corncob pipe from another jacket pocket and fingered the rubbed tobacco into it. He brought forth a kitchen match and struck it beneath the desk and held it over the tobacco.

She twisted her mouth skeptically. On her it looked fine, the mouth being wide and good. She said, "You want I should have started when I was fifteen?"

"When they're old enough, they're big enough and when they're big enough, they're old enough," Weigand recited. "*I* started when I was fifteen." His face took on an overdone nostalgia. "She was a healthy little minx who'd been at it for years, at the age of fourteen. We were necking on her back porch and she asked me if I had ever played Inspection."

"Inspection," Scotty said.

"That's right," Weigand nodded very seriously. "Derived, I suppose, from the military short-arm inspection. Well, you'll never believe this but——"

"Spare me," Scotty growled. "Listen, Weewee Patrick . . ."

He flinched at that. "You *promised*," he protested.

10

". . . what in the hell do you want?"

He took the pipe from his mouth. "Well, if you must know, the Sachem sent for me."

"Oh." She looked at a pad to the left of her typer. "It's not on here. He has Secretary Bollix scheduled for three o'clock."

Weigand looked at his watch. "What's a Secretary of the Interior compared to the Sachem's alter ego, his *eminence grise*, the power behind the throne?"

"Ha," she said. "If you're going in, you'd better get underway. He and Bollix are going to go over that latest Far-Out Society bit of his. Project Porpoise. They've finally got those poor porpoises to the point they can really communicate with them. So the project is to lick the world protein shortage, put the porpoises to work out in the oceans riding herd on tremendous schools of whales. Whale meat tastes like beef, so they say. Now I've heard everything."

He unslung his leg from the desk, stood erect.

His voice had lost some of the banter. "How about the date, Scotty? It's in the cards. It's meant to be."

She looked at him and pursed her lips in thought. She took a deep breath. "All right," she said.

He whistled, a hiss of a whistle. "You mean it?"

"Yes. Yes, I guess I mean it."

"At my apartment?"

"I suppose so," she sighed.

"Whew! When? I'll have champagne. I'll have the caterers bring in the most elaborate . . ."

"Tonight," she said ruefully. "If it's not tonight, I'll talk myself out of it again. Why don't you ask me to marry you?"

"Why buy a cow, when milk's so cheap?" he said earnestly, as though really wanting to know. "Besides, you wouldn't want to marry me. I'd be a lousy provider.

I'm so improvident I can go into a revolving door and come out two dollars the poorer."

"Get the hell out of here," she growled at him. "You'll have Old Chucklehead on your neck. When he summons someone on his staff, he vaguely expects them to show up—sooner or later."

Weigand headed for the sanctum sanctorum. "He's already probably forgotten," he told her over his shoulder. "When I was a kid, my mother told me any American could become president, and I'm beginning to believe it. Now, don't forget, tonight's the night."

"I won't forget," she said. "It's probably the biggest mistake I've ever made."

"Bring a sleezy nightgown," he said, his hand on the doorknob. "No, on second thought you won't need it."

"What is it Chief?" Weigand said.

"Sit down, Son," Horace Adams told him, and before the other had lowered himself into one of the heavy leather chairs, "You find more time than I can to keep your ear to the ground. What in the name of Moses is happening in Cleveland? In fact, what's happening everywhere?"

"Why particularly Cleveland?"

The president took up a report and waved it. "We just got this hurry-up call asking for financial assistance to keep their soup kitchens going. What's a soup kitchen?"

Weigand Patrick reached for his tobacco pouch, even as he said, "Actually, not a very good term, under the circumstances. It goes back in time. What's happened in Cleveland is that they have this emergency food program. Those on their uppers can request free meals from the city."

"Is it that bad in Cleveland?"

"I'm afraid it is, Mr. President. And this project is just too much for them. You see, they tied it in with another program, to come to the relief of some of the delivery services, trucking concerns and so forth that were having a bad time. So instead of having to stand in line, at the soup kitchens, the food is delivered to each home."

"Well, what's the crisis?"

Weigand Patrick was packing his corncob. "Evidently, those on relief rebelled against the diet. Everybody's weight-conscious these days. They lit into City Hall demanding a low carbohydrate, high protein diet. You know, shrimp, steak, asparagus, artichokes, avocados, that sort of thing. Elections were coming up, so the city father capitulated."

For the moment, President Adams was in his own field of understanding. He said, "Well, that makes sense."

Patrick shrugged, searching for matches in several pockets. "Yes, sir. But the city treasury was already low, all taxes and other city income being down. Consequently, they're calling on the Federal government for aid."

"Craminently!" the president snapped. "Don't they realize how much money we're going through as it is? Don't they realize how much it costs to be liberating Mozambique, containing Finland and conducting a police action in the Antarctic? Not to speak of the moon colony."

He picked up another report and waved it at his press secretary. "That's not all. That's not all by a damn sight. What's going on in Denver? They want money too."

"They ran out of local relief money and the unemployed drove on city hall."

"Drove on city hall?" the president scowled.

13

"Yes, sir. In the old days, people with a beef used to march on city hall, carrying banners and so forth. These days they drive."

"Oh." The president remained silent awhile, his face working as though in hard thought.

Which surprised Weigand Patrick. Presidents were not expected to be particularly bright anymore. This one had possibly the best public image, the most appealing Tri-Di television personality of all time, and a superlative hand shake.

"Son," he said finally. "What in the name of Moses is going on in this country?"

When Weigand got his pipe to fuming, he exhaled the smoke from his mouth and said, "Mr. President, it's a Depression."

"A Depression?"

"Yes, sir."

"*What* is a Depression?"

Weigand clicked the stem of his pipe against his teeth. "Well, sir, it's been a long time. I've been reading up on the matter the past few days. Checking it out. In the early days they'd call one a Panic or a Bust, but after a time they must have realized it didn't help get out of them by using that sort of terminology so they switched to Depression. Even that had too negative a connotation so after the big one, 1929 to 1939, they called them Recessions. Finally, some brain came up with Readjustment or Rolling Readjustment. But we haven't had a real blockbuster since 1939. Before our time, of course."

"But what *is* it?" In sudden irritation, the Chief Executive added, "What do you burn in that damned thing, soft coal?"

He slipped the pipe apologetically into a side pocket. "Well, sir, do you know the term geometric progression?"

The President had been involved in campus politics

14

at the time mathematics were being handed down, but he made a point of never admitting ignorance about anything.

Weigand Patrick understood the expression on the other's face. He said, "A geometric progression is when you go 2-4-16, uh, sixteen times sixteen would be, uh, 256. And so forth."

His ultimate superior was looking at him blankly.

Weigand shifted in his chair. "Well, sir, a depression is the opposite of that."

The other was still blank.

Weigand said, "Sir, take Los Angeles. It starts as a small city. Some people come out to retire, liking the weather. They have houses built. The contractors haven't enough construction workers to do the building so they offer premium wages and attract employees from back East. These like the looks of L.A. and decide to remain, which involves building more houses and apartment houses and stores to supply their needs. All this calls for more materials, cement plants, brickworks. It calls for more gasoline stations, more newspapers. More everything. A boom is on. More people arrive to get in on it. Money flows. Bars go up, nightclubs, nice restaurants. Boom begets boom. People making lots of money want luxuries. Car dealers go into business, swank hotels go up to house the businessmen coming to town.

"Little people get into the act too. They've twenty thousand dollars or so to invest in a small business. Largely, they go into things they know nothing about. A retired restauranteur starts a chicken farm. A retired farmer opens up a little restaurant specializing in Chinese food; he's a Swede. While they're building their restaurants or chicken farms, or Drive-In Tri-Di theatres, or whatever, they spark the boom still more."

The President said, "Yes, yes."

Weigand Patrick fished his pipe from his pocket unconsciously and pointed the stem at his superior. "Well, Mr. President, you can probably see it coming. The bust. The depression. Some of these little businesses fold. The empty buildings are up for lease. The construction workers go on unemployment insurance and cut back on their buying. They stop patronizing restaurants, beer joints and Tri-Di theatres. So a lot of these places fold or at least cut down their staffs, causing more unemployment. People stop buying new cars. The local agencies fold or cut back. People start leaving town to go back to living on small farms where they can at least grow their own gardens. Meanwhile, Detroit cuts back car production, which means cutbacks in steel and all the other things that go into cars. Detroit lays off a hundred thousand employees or so, and steel lays off the same. The farmers begin getting less call for their products and farm prices skid. The farmers stop buying everything from kitchen appliances to Joy perfume."

"All right, all right. I get the picture. It pyramids backwards," the President said.

Weigand winced but said, "That's about it, Chief."

The President's face worked in thought again, to the fascination of his press officer. Finally he said, "Why, this could be awful. Craminently, it's interfering with my Far-Out Society, the most fabulous society of all history."

Weigand Patrick clicked the stem of his pipe against his teeth. "Yes, sir, it'll do that. And all our aid programs. It's going to be difficult to keep shoveling all that money abroad."

His superior said plaintively, "How did they get rid of them in the past?"

Patrick had been afraid he was going to ask that. He

said, "Well, it's a good question. Roosevelt, who inherited the classic of all times, tried various things, most of which the Supreme Court kicked out. Like the NRA, which was supposed to mean National Recovery Act but, to most businessmen, meant Never Roosevelt Again. Then he figured on sending prices up by shooting pigs in the Middle West and pouring kerosene on potatoes up in Maine. He put all the juvenile delinquents into the CCC where he paid them to range around the woods supposedly planting trees and so forth. It's debatable whether they trampled more than they planted. Then he brought beer back."

"Brought beer back? Where'd it been?"

His press chief suppressed another wince. "He'd inherited Prohibition. But, of course, all that great experiment did was put the booze income into the pockets of the hoods, such as Al Capone. The government needed the taxes, so they brought back first beer and then liquor. That, of course, threw a lot of honest bootleggers out of work and they started robbing banks and kidnapping the few remaining citizens who had any money."

The President stared at him. "He sounds drivel-happy."

"Well, yes sir. At the time, a lot of people thought so. But, on the other hand, some thought him the greatest politician ever to come down the pike."

"Oh, they did, eh?" President Adams went through his thought processes. "I suppose there's a lot of political popularity to be won by a President who gets the nation out of a hole like this."

"Yes sir. I suppose there is. Roosevelt was reelected three or four times."

"Three or four times? That's illegal!"

"Roosevelt was pretty popular. He wowed them in California by paying the farmers to chop down their fruit trees."

The President was wide-eyed. "What did that accomplish?"

"Well, sir, it evidently made sense to Roosevelt and his brain trust. They wanted to send the price of fruit up. It seems as though there were some fifteen million unemployed and a lot of people hungry and . . ."

The President held up a hand. "Hold it, Son, you've lost me already. What was this about a brain trust?"

Weigand told him about the brain trust.

The President thought about it. "Hmmmmmm," he said. He thought about it some more.

Finally, he flicked a switch and said, "Fred?"

Fred Moriarty's voice came tinkling in. "Yes, Mr. President."

There was a petulant note in the chief executive's voice. "Why doesn't anybody ever tell me anything around here?"

Predictably, there wasn't any answer for that.

"I've decided I need a brain trust," the executive head of the United States of the Americas told him. "See about it."

"Yes, Mr. President. A brain trust."

The President flicked him off and turned back to Weigand. "What are you doing tonight?" he demanded.

Weigand said, "I've got a date, sir."

"Well, you can take her along."

Weigand looked at the other warily. "Yes, sir. To where?"

"To the party at the Soviet Complex Embassy."

"But I've been to a party at the Soviet Embassy. You eat caviar and smoked sturgeon and you drunk toasts to

18

peace and coexistence and togetherness until you fall down."

The President tapped the side of his nose two or three times with the forefinger of his right hand. It was his gesture indicating a sly performance on his part, with a connotation of inordinary wisdom being utilized. And it was one of the crosses his press secretary bore.

"That Nick Stroganoff, or whatever his name is . . ."

"Stanislov," Weigand said. "The new ambassador from the Soviet Complex."

"The CIA has passed on a couple of items about him. One, he doesn't hold his liquor any too well. Two, just before this appointment he was connected with their space program."

"So," Patrick said.

"So we want to know just how many men they plan to plant in their moon colony. If it's more than our eight, we're going to have to boost the size of our colony."

"I thought eight was all we needed. Two physicists, two astronomers——"

"Not if the Russkies send up more than eight." The Chief Executive shook a finger at his press secretary-cum-Man Friday. "A lot of people don't seem to realize, Son, that this race into space is still on. It all started back when Eisenhower was informed by the CIA that the Russkies planned to orbit an artificial satellite during that Geo-whatever-it-was year.

"Ike had some quick fellas on his team. Before the Russkies could announce their plan, *we* put on a special TV broadcast announcing that *we'd* orbit an artificial satellite in 1957. When the Russkies came out the next day and said they also were going to send one up, everybody laughed. It was our first space triumph."

Weigand Patrick said, "The trouble was, up to that

point we hadn't done any work on any such project."

"No, but we started right away. Of course, the son-of-a-bitchin Russkies got their sputnik up first. Then they had several other firsts, like the first dog up, and the first man, and the first orbit around the moon, the first woman, the first three men at a time, the first space walk."

The Chief Executive looked pained. "Finally we caught up. But you know, Son, somehow nobody—Eisenhower, Kennedy, Johnson, every administration since the space program began—nobody seemed to lay any plans for what we'd do once the moon was reached. The whole thing just stopped there."

He tapped himself on the chest modestly. "It was up to me. The space race continues. We've got to beat the Russkies by putting a bigger colony up there than they have."

"Yes, sir," Weigand sighed. "What's that got to do with me going to the May Day party at the Soviety Complex Embassy?"

The President shook a finger at him. "Strogonoff——"

"Stanislov."

"Whatever his name is. He'll get drenched. He practically has to. It's unpatriotic for a communist not to get smashed on May Day. You'll be around. You'll get the conversation around to the Moon colony. Maybe he'll drop a hint."

Weigand Patrick sighed again. "All right," he said.

Scotty's voice tinkled, "Mr. President, Secretary Bollix is here."

"All right, send him in." The President added vaguely to Weigand Patrick, "What in the name of Moses was it he wanted?"

Patrick unwound himself from his chair, fishing for pipe and tobacco pouch.

He said, "Your Far-Out Society. He probably wants to discuss that idea of yours, turning Wyoming into a National Park, putting all the remaining Indians in it, outfitted with their old equipment, bringing back the buffalo, and so forth."

The other's face lit up. "Ah, yes. The final solution of the National Park question. A big enough National Park to hold *all* the tourists. What do you think of the basic idea, Son?"

Patrick said unhappily, "I think the Indians would wind up scalping every car load of tourists that came through."

The President looked at him bleakly. "Let me know tomorrow how the party came out, Son."

Chapter Two

Marv Sellers came into the house from the back, the way he always did when he returned from work. He threw his hat on the kitchen table in disgust.

Old Sam looked up from where he sat in his rocker before the kitchen Tri-Di set and said, "What's wrong, boy?"

"Where's Phoebe?"

"She ain't home from work yet."

"Well, the contractor just laid me off. Me and eight of the other guys, fer crissakes."

"What happened?"

"Ahhh, the house we were going to be working on, the guy wanted it changed his mind. That Bill Waters over to the Buick agency. Business must be bad. Well, it's me for rocking-chair money for awhile. But you can't make ends meet on a hundred a week unemployment insurance." He grunted disgust. "We'll hafta send back that new couch and easy chair Phoebe bought."

The old man said, "Lucky you still got the old ones out to the garage. Business bad, eh? I'll hafta talk that over with the boys in the park in the morning."

Marv opened the refrigerator for a plastic of beer. "Glad Phebe's working," he muttered. "Don't know how long it'll be before I get onta another job."

He flicked the top off the plastic with his thumb and took a long drink. He took the container away from his mouth and scowled at the imprinted label.

"What a slogan," he muttered. "*It's the Water.* It's the water, all right, but I'd rather have beer with some alcohol in it, fer crissakes."

Old Sam said, "You think beer'll ever come back? In the old days, we usta have beer with some body into it. It was kinda darker and you could taste the hops. It was richer and stronger. Then some New York wisenheimer come up with the discovery that maybe men drank more of the beer than dames but women bought it, usually down to the ultra-market. So he figures they better slant the ads to the womenfolks. So they come up with slogans like *light beer* and *dry beer*. What the hell's dry beer, and whatdaya want with light beer? Beer supposed to be rich. This stuff now, they can put it back in the horse. Folks now don't know Schlitz from Shinola."

"Sure, sure, gramps," Marv told him. "But you can't stand in the way of progress."

"Progress?" Old Sam said disgustedly. "Back when I was a youngster, we usta have a brew in Boston called Pickwick Ale. Yes, sir, the Poor Man's Whiskey, we called it. A nickel for a schooner. Three schooners and you was drenched. High we usta call it then. Three schooners and you was high as a kite, we called it. They usta have free lunch in those days. Stuff like potato chips and cod fish balls."

"Best part of the cod fish," Marv muttered.

"What?"

"Nothing."

Phoebe came in and put down a heavy bag of groceries she was carrying, and Marv told her about being laid off. She was her usual placid self.

"It's not important," she soothed him. "You'll have another job in no time at all. But meanwhile it takes a little thinking. We'll have to retrench, like they say." She laughed sourly. "This would have to happen on the night I wanted you to take me to June Perriwinkle's restaurant. Now I think I just better cook something here."

"Well, that's one good thing," Marv snorted. "I can't make a meal out of those teeny-weeny hotdogs she serves."

"Shucks," Old Sam told them, "when I was a boy, all we could afford was hotdogs and hamburgers. Everybody eats high on the hog these days. Least they eat expensive. Somehow, it don't taste the same."

Phoebe said, "Well, we'll be eating lower on the hog for awhile. I'll have to start doing some of my own baking."

Chapter Three

When Scotty McDonald returned from the ladies' powder-room, where she had left her coat, Weigand Patrick's eyes bugged. She ignored his stare.

He hissed, "One of your tits is out."

"Mind your language," she murmured. "It's the latest style. The Agnes Sorel revival."

"The *who?*"

"Agnes Sorel, the mistress of Charles the Seventh."

"Never heard of her. But if she ran around like that——"

"She was one of the most beautiful women in history."

Weigand darted his eyes around. "None of the other women have a tit showing."

She couldn't have cared less. "It's the latest thing in Paris. The Gaulle has banned it, or tried to. Not even the hereditary president of Common Europe can ban a new style."

"Holy smokes, you better not show up at the office in that get-up. The Sachem would bite the tip of it off as you walked by."

Scotty snorted her scorn. "I had all that out with him back when he was governor. He'll never lay a hand on me again. But the fashion doesn't apply to day wear. It's formal."

"Formal!" Weigand muttered. "Well, come on. Let's go and snag a drink. I've got a suspicion that you're going to wow 'em tonight. The men, at least. Stay out of the ladies' room. They'll lynch you. I wonder if Nick Stanislov has got a load on yet. The quicker he gets potted and I get him around to the Moon colonies, the quicker we can ditch this party and get over to my apartment." He leered at her.

"Huh," she said. "I haven't been to an embassy party for months. There's no hurry to get to your place."

"That's what you think."

An Italian appropriated Scotty for a dance before she'd had a chance to knock back even one of the Stolichnaya vodkas that were being passed around in wholesale lots by a full platoon of servants.

Patrick looked after her. He muttered to himself, "I'm going to have to watch that Wop. I've got her all keyed up to the sticking point. But I want to be sure *I* do the sticking."

Somebody said, "I beg your pardon? Ah, Mr. Patrick."

Weigand Patrick turned. It was young Frol Krasnaya, one of the *Pravda* men. Weigand said unhappily, "Hi, Frol. Nice turnout."

The Russian journalist was looking after Scotty and the Italian attache. "Quite a dress," he said, blinking.

Weigand Patrick tore his own eyes from the pair. He didn't like the way the Italian was jiggling. It didn't look as though it was called for in the type of dance they were doing. A waiter went by. Weigand put out a hand and grabbed a drink.

Frol Krasnaya made a half gesture with his own glass. "To Peace, Mr. Patrick. I am sorry the President couldn't make it."

Weigand grunted. "If the President came to a Russian May Day celebration, he'd lose a million votes. You have to remember, you people are still our prime bogy-men."

The other smiled regretfully. "And you are ours. I suppose every nation must have a bogy-man. It keeps the people from thinking about their real troubles."

Weigand looked at him. "You've been reading Machiavelli, Frol."

The young Russian newspaperman chuckled. "The Romans had the axiom long before Machiavelli was ever born. When you fear trouble at home, stir up war abroad."

Weigand took down half of his water-clear drink, then looked into the glass accusingly. "Holy smokes," he complained. "Haven't you got something to mix with this liquid H-bomb?"

Frol Krasnaya said, "We Russians have a few axioms of our own. One is that the only thing that mixes with vodka is more vodka."

The American press secretary grunted at that. "Listen, Frol," he said, as though only half interested. "What's the latest scoop on the Moon colony?"

"Moon colony?" the other said warily.

"Ummmm. I heard somewhere that you were going to increase your personnel at the moon base."

"Ah, you did? How numerous is your own group of scientists—if that is what they are—on Luna, Mr. Patrick?"

"Search me," Patrick said. He should have known better than to try to get anything out of Krasnaya. The *Pravda* man was young but not particularly stupid. However, he was anxious to get out of here. Scotty's half-bared chest wasn't conducive to allowing him to forget the original manner in which he had planned to spend the evening. And the sooner he got away from this party. . . .

He said to Krasnaya, "Where's the Ambassador? We got here a bit late. I haven't seen him yet."

"Comrade Stanislov is over there in the library with some of the, ah, more prominent guests."

Weigand Patrick looked at him.

Krasnaya said hurriedly, "Of course, he would wish the President's press secretary to join him."

"See you later, Frol," Patrick said. He shot one last agonized look in the direction of Scotty, and headed for the library. Scotty had been appropriated by a Rumanian. A Rumanian in military uniform, his waist so pinched that he must certainly have been wearing a corset. He was kind of jiggling too. Weigand wondered vaguely if it was a new dance step, or simply Scotty.

There were a round dozen guests with Nicolas Stanislov, most of them of ambassador or consul rank. As he approached, Weigand wondered what they were discussing so animatedly. The President's police action in the Antarctic? The liberation of Mozambique? Perhaps,

26

hopefully, the Moon colonies. If he could just get the Russian on that. . . .

He came up and most of those present nodded at him and some murmured his name, but Stanislov, who was speaking, wasn't interrupted. They all hung on his words.

He was saying, "This worker was employed in a pickle factory in Kiev. He had worked there for a good many years and finally he confessed to his wife that he had acquired a compulsion, a sort of, ah, neurosis. No? The fact was, he was fascinated by the idea of sticking it into the pickle slicer. He got to the point of thinking about it night and day. Finally, one day, he came home pale, obviously upset. His wife asked him what had happened and he told her the Comrade factory manager had fired him. 'Why?' she demanded. He said, 'Well, you know, all these years I've had this compulsion to stick it in the pickle slicer? Well, today I did it.' His wife stared at him, aghast. 'How are you?' she demanded. 'I'm fine,' he said. She was surprised. She said, 'Well, then, what happened to the pickle slicer?' 'Oh,' he said, 'they fired her too.'"

The assembled diplomats laughed.

A waiter went about with a fresh tray of vodka glasses. Each must have held a good three ounces, Weigand decided. He shot a look at the Russian Ambassador from the side of his eyes. Good. The man already looked slightly blurred around the edges. He'd evidently been drinking toasts since the early hours of the party.

Weigand Patrick held up his glass. "To the Moon colonies!" he toasted.

Everybody knocked back their drinks, bottoms up. Weigand followed suit and turned to Stanislov. Too late.

The Mexican Consul was saying, "Have you heard the one about Manuel and the American tourist?"

No one had heard the one about Manuel and the American tourist. The Mexican launched into the story, while Weigand groaned inwardly.

"This American tourist had a date with his wife at the fountain in the middle of the Zocalo, the town plaza. His watch had stopped and he didn't know what time it was and he was due at two o'clock. As he hurried along, he recognized Manuel stretched out prone on the grass, taking a siesta. Next to Manuel was sprawled his burro, also out like a light. The American occasionally had Manuel and his burro haul wood for the fireplace and other tasks. He stopped now and said, 'Hey, Manuel, what time is it?' Manuel opened one eye after a moment. He said, 'Senor, as you know, I am a poor man. I do not have a watch. However . . .' He reached out slowly toward the burro which was so sprawled that his scrotum projected behind him through his hind legs. Manuel took up the animal's testicles and hefted them. He said, 'It is ten minutes to two, Senor,' and closed his eyes again. The American tourist stood there for a long moment, looking at him. He hurried on toward the fountain and when he got there, he found his wife. As an afterthought, he said, 'Dear, what time do you have?' She looked at her watch and said, "Five minutes until two.' He thought about it for a minute. Finally, he said, 'Wait here. I'll be right back.' He returned to where Manuel was still sprawled and said, 'Hey, Manuel. What time is it now?' Manuel sighed, opened one eye again, reached over and hefted the burro's scrotum once more. He said, 'Senor, it is now two o'clock.' The American tourist looked at him for a long unbelieving moment. Finally, he cleared his throat and said, 'Look, I've heard about a lot of different ways of telling time. Sun dials, hourglasses, water clocks, all sorts of things. But, well, I know you Mexicans have some, well, sort of mysteries, going all the way back to the Aztecs. Things we, well, white men don't understand. But, well, I never heard of telling time by weighing a burro's testicles. Listen, I'll give you ten pesos if you'll tell me how you do it.' Manuel opened both eyes but still didn't stir. He said, 'Senor, it is very simple. When I lift the burro's balls out of the way I can see the clock in the Cathedral.'"

All laughed.

Ambassador Stanislov stopped a passing waiter who presented a tray of vodka glasses.

Stanislov turned to Weigand and said, his glass high, "To the President of the United States of the Americas."

Everybody knocked their drinks back.

Everybody looked at Weigand Patrick.

He cleared his throat and reached for another glass. "To Andrei Zorin, Number One of the Soviet Complex!"

Everybody knocked back their drinks.

Pierre Dusage, Ambassador from Common Europe looked slightly miffed.

The Mexican Consul reached out quickly and picked up a third vodka. "To The Gaulle and Common Europe!"

Everybody knocked back their drinks.

Weigand Patrick coughed gently and began to say, "Now the Moon——"

But the Israeli cultural attache was saying, "Did you hear the one about the British oil prospector in the Arab States?"

Evidently, nobody had heard that one.

"Well," he said, "it seems that this oil prospector was driving a caravan of camels loaded down with oil-drilling equipment. He was working on a deadline and was making the best time he could across the desert. Eventually, they came to an international border between two of the small Arab States. Here they were stopped. The customs official declared it was impossible to let the male camels in the caravan through. It seemed they

were very proud of their camels in this country and
didn't want inferior breeds coming in and possibly crossing. The Britisher was up in the air but the Arab was
adamant. Only if all the male camels were castrated
would he let them past. But the Englishman argued,
the nearest vet must be five hundred miles away. He
couldn't possibly take the time to send for him. The
Arab shrugged hugely. 'But,' he said, 'there is no need
for a vet. It is very simple.' And he took up two bricks
and came up behind the nearest camel and smashed
the animal's testicles. The Englishman went pale and
clutched his stomach. 'Oh, no,' he said. 'Oh, no. I can't
bear it.' The Arab looked at him, surprised. 'What is the
matter?' he said. The Englishman said, 'Oh, no. I can't
bear the thought. The pain!' 'But,' the Arab said, 'there
is no pain.' The Britisher stared at him. 'No pain!' The
Arab shook his head and held up the two bricks. 'Only
if you get your thumbs between the bricks.'"

All laughed.

A new waiter came up.

Weigand Patrick was beginning to feel the last round
of toasts, but good. He looked owlishly at Nick Stanislov
who was obviously also feeling no pain.

The Indian Consul said, "We have toasted the President, Number One and The Gaulle. I now propose a
toast to everlasting peace between them all."

Everybody knocked back their drinks.

Ambassador Stanislov took up another hooker of vodka
and held it high. "Not only peace, but cultural coexistence."

Everybody knocked their drinks back.

Everybody stared at Weigand Patrick. He could begin
to feel the fog rolling in, but he took up the new glass
the servant proffered.

"Uhhh," he said. "To the Moon colonies."

"We did that one," the Mexican Consul protested in a slur. "I wish this were tequila. I can drink tequila all night."

But everybody else had knocked theirs back.

Ambassador Dusage looked embarrassed. He said, "We have forgotten to toast President Cantinflas, of Mexico."

Everybody knocked that one back.

Weigand Patrick could quite distinctly feel the fog rolling in now.

However, the Russian was talking to him. From far, far away his voice said, "Ah, you are interested in the Moon colonies, Mr. Patrick?"

"Sure . . . sure am . . ." Weigand could hear his own voice from away, far away. He didn't quite seem to be in control of it, but he could hear it. "Sure am . . . Moon colo-kneed. I mean . . ."

The fog was swirling higher.

The Russian was saying. Well, he was saying something.

. . . hydroponics . . . complete self-service, self-sufficient . . . closed aquarium . . . true colony . . . glory of Soviet space . . . eliminate need for freight transport . . .

The fog rolled all the way in.

For a brief moment, the fog rolled out again, in swirls.

Weigand Patrick was in a hovercar limousine. One of the White House limousines. Scotty was driving. Her coat was back on. He was subjected not to the Agnes Sorel revival style.

He shook his head and tried to say something.

"Shut up, you drunken sot."

He was mildly indignant. "What do you mean, drunken sot? What other kind of sot is there? Besides . . . besides, I did it for my country."

31

"Great. Just what was accomplished for the U.S. and A. by passing out into the arms of the Common Europe ambassador?"

"Good ol' Pierre," Weigand slurred. "Always in the middle. Dependable in emergency. Where we going?"

"Where we started out for. Your apartment," she said bitterly. "I had to get one of the Polish attaches to help me drag you out."

"Good," he said. "Tonight's the night, eh Scotty, ol' girl. Tonight's the night."

She snorted.

And the fog rolled in again.

When the fog rolled out, partially, he was seated on the edge of his bed, in shirt sleeves, pants and socks.

Scotty was hunkered down before him, tugging at his pants legs, snorting and muttering incoherently.

"Hey," he said. "Take it easy."

"Shut up," she told him. "Ha! The great lover. Casanova, Don Juan, Errol Flynn. Ha!"

The fog rolled in again.

When the fog rolled out, it was morning. Well into the morning. He was in bed, in his own apartment. He was dressed in nothing save his undershorts.

He looked hopefully at the place next to him. But nobody was there and the pillow showed no signs of anyone having been there.

Weigand Patrick groaned pathetically.

Chapter Four

When Marv Sellers returned home after sitting around with the others at the union hall, he was surprised to find Phoebe there. He looked at his watch, then remembered that it had stopped and that he hadn't wanted to spend the money for repairs.

He opened the refrigerator door and peered in hopefully, although he was well aware that there hadn't been any beer for a week, and that he had checked to make sure he hadn't missed one last plastic every day since that sad milestone.

Marv grunted disappointment and said over his shoulder, "What the hell you doing home, Phoebe?"

Phoebe Sellers made her mouth into a bitter moue. "Fired," she said.

"Fired, for crissake!"

She said, "The company's big item here in Tucson was distributing all these gadgets like. You know, nuclear back scratchers, electric toothbrushes, automatic Martini stirrers, that sort of thing. Evidently, people finally got around to the fact they could do without them. So the company folded. Even Mr. Edwards' gone on relief."

"Oh great," Marv groaned. "Now we're both unemployed and all our payments coming up."

Phoebe tried to surface her basic optimism. She said, "Look, Marv, we can sell the car. It's only a year and a half old and nearly paid for. We'll get several thousand dollars for it."

"Oh yeah. You oughta see all the used cars on the lots."

"We won't sell it through a dealer, we'll put a ad in the paper."

He said, "What'll we do without a car? I need it to get to work . . . if I get a job."

Old Sam had come in. He chuckled, almost happily. "Gettin' to be like old times," he said. "I usta ride to work on a bike, when I was a kid. More fun than a car."

"Knock it, Gramps," Marv growled. "And it's no use looking in the refrigerator. There ain't no beer, and there's not gonna be no beer. Too damn expensive."

Nevertheless, Old Sam peered into the box, duplicating the hopeful expression of Marv a bit earlier. He grunted disgust and made his way over to his rocker.

"We gotta do something about that," he said. "Especially with the hot weather coming up."

Phoebe shook her head and began making preparation of a sparse evening meal. "No beer, Gamps, it just ain't in the budget."

Old Sam said thoughtfully, "In days past, my old man usta make his own beer. Had all these crocks, brewing away. Way I remember back to it, he usta figure it cost him something like two anna half cents to make a quart." Sam chuckled. "Sometimes he made the stuff too strong or somethin' and it blew the bottles up."

Marv looked at him. "That's the trouble," he said. "You'd hafta buy bottles and all." But there was a thoughtful element in his voice.

Sam said, "I saw a whole lotta bottles over near to the city dump. They don't use 'em much nowadays. When I was a boy we got everything in bottles. Milk, beer, everything. All these plastics and crap like that came later."

"I'll bet," Marv said.

Old Sam said, "Heh, heh, lot of things to remind you of the old days."

"Listen, what else d'you need besides bottles?"

Bill Waters flicked off his phone screen and muttered "Balls."

Miss Harding flinched only slightly. "I beg your pardon, Mr. Waters?" Actually, she was by now long familiar with the expletive.

"Balls," he snorted. "Balls. You've heard the old saying, *Balls, said the queen, if I had them I'd be king.*"

Miss Harding was taken aback. She said, "Yes, sir."

"That was old man Benington cancelling the only order we've had for over a month. And I figured that was the one sure sale coming up. He's the only man left in town with enough money in his sock to buy anything more expensive than a used fart."

She ignored the latter part of that and looked distressed. "Why, that's terrible, Mr. Waters. He was just here the other day and was so definite about needing a car."

Waters growled, "He bought a used car from some damn bricklayer who sold it for less than half price. How can I compete with that sort of thing?"

"I don't know, Mr. Waters. I . . . I heard the new models aren't going to have any chrome at all. Bring down the price. Possibly that will be an inducement."

"That's right," he grunted in disgust. "So there's a crisis in the chrome industry. They've laid off something like five thousand men. Which means exactly five thousand families more not in the market for cars this year. And everything's air-cushion hovercars this year. No tires. You know what that's done to the rubber industry up in Akron?"

"No sir."

"Well, use your imagination."

He came to his feet, prowled over to the watercooler and located the sole remaining paper cup they had been using the past several days.

He drew himself a drink, knocked it back stiff-wristed, as though it was gin, and drew another. The bottom dropped out of the cup, at long last soaked through, and the water dumped into the wastebasket below. He stood there for a long, suffering minute.

Miss Harding said brightly, "By the way, Mr. Waters. We seem to be out of typewriter ribbons. I need one for my machine."

He snorted deprecation of that remark. "Fine. But even if I had the money for such items as typewriter ribbons, I don't know where you'd buy any. Did you know Keefer's stationery store just folded up? Who needs stationery these days? There's so little business correspondence, I'm surprised the post office doesn't call it a day."

Miss Harding said, "There're other stationery stores, further downtown, sir." She thought about it for a moment before adding cautiously, "I think."

He came to a sudden decision. "Well, that cancellation is the straw that broke this ruptured camel's back. Notify the men out in the shop that I'm closing."

She looked both distressed and sympathetic. "The usual two weeks severance pay, Mr. Waters?"

He laughed bitterly. "Where do you think I'd get it, Miss Harding? My father-in-law's offered me a job as delivery boy for his delicatessen. He's fired the two he used to have. Wants to keep the job in the family."

Chapter Five

Weigand Patrick ambled into the office of the President's personal secretary, the inevitable corncob, which was his own pet affectation and distinctive mark invariably used by the political cartoonists, slung from the side of his mouth.

Scotty didn't look up, but she said, "How did the

press conference go? Did Old Chucklehead wow them?"

Weigand said, "There wasn't any. Fred and I tried to brief him but he was afraid to face the music. I went over to the press lobby and told them the President couldn't be present because he had a headache and Samuelson from the *Times* said he didn't doubt it, and Harrison from *Newsweek* said no wonder."

"So then?"

"So then I offered to answer any questions and they looked at me for awhile and finally they began telling limericks."

"Limericks?"

"Listen to this one. Simak, from the *Guardian.*"

"There once was a man named Durkin,

"Who was always jerkin' his gerkin.

   "Said his wife, one day,

   "Deprived of her lay,

"Durkin, you're shirkin' yer ferkin' by jerkin' your
     gerkin, you bastard."

Scotty looked at him. "That doesn't scan, and besides, it doesn't even rhyme. Bastard doesn't rhyme with Durkin."

"A critic," he protested, fishing matches from his pocket.

Polly Adams wandered in vaguely and said, "Hello, Weigand, hello Miss McDonald. You haven't seen Hilda, have you?"

Weigand Patrick slouched to his feet, from where he had been perched on the side of Scotty's desk, and took his pipe from his mouth.

"Good afternoon, Mrs. Adams," he said.

Polly Adams said archly, "Oh, do call me Polly, Weigand. After all these years."

Scotty said, "I haven't seen your Social Secretary for

days, Mrs. Adams. The last time was during the reception for the Congolese Ambassador. She was, uh, rather fed up with all the poison pen letters."

Polly Adams looked about the office, as though in faint hope. "I'm surprised you don't have a bit of a bar in here, Miss MacDonald. Such an important little office, the President's personal secretary."

Scotty said, "Mrs. Adams, if I had a bit of a bar in here, half the people that got in to see Old Chuckle . . . , that is, the President, would be smashed. Half the people that go through this office, are still nervous about meeting the President. Well, nearly half these days."

The butler entered through the door the First Lady had used only moments before and stood politely.

Weigand said, "Hello, William."

Polly Adams turned to the newcomer. "What is it, William?"

The butler announced, "Madam, the ladies of the Potted Planters Gardening Society are here."

"The who?"

"The Potted Planters."

"Already, at this time of the day?"

"Yes, Madam. Should I see about tea for them?"

"Tea?" Polly said vaguely. "Do they look like the types that blast? No, no William, you're apt to overdo. I suggest from your description of the state they're already in, that you serve Planter's Punches. Ummm, and William . . ."

"Yes, Madam?"

"Put a stick in them."

"Yes, Madam."

William, his aplomb visibly shaken, about faced and more or less staggered out.

The First Lady, somewhat brightened, said, "Oh, dear, another society to greet. However, it's so important for Horace. I suppose I'll have to entertain them."

When she was gone, Scotty and Weigand looked after her emptily.

Scotty said, "Why didn't you say something?"

"What? But that reminds me. The boys have been writing some snide remarks about Polly listing to starboard, almost everytime she shows up in public. I'll have to plant the story that she's got a pierced ear drum. Throws off her sense of balance."

Scotty snorted and got up and went over to one of the businesslike files that lined one wall of the tiny office.

Weigand blurted, "Holy smokes, what's happened to your clothes?"

She smirked at him over her shoulder. "You like this outfit?"

"Like it? Where is it?"

"Don't be prehistoric. It's the latest thing from Common Europe. London. They call it the Minuskirt."

"Minus skirt? You mean you're going around like that on purpose?"

"Of course, silly." She started back for her desk, a folder in hand. "You can't see anything that you can't see on any beach."

"I can see anything, on any beach, what with these new bottomless bathing suits. What's that got to do with it?"

She sniffed contempt of his opinions. "Besides, I can tell you like it by the expression of your pants."

"Keep your obscene cracks to yourself, Scotty Mac Donald. However, I'm glad to see you're a red head all over."

"Now who's making obscene cracks?" She looked down, doubtfully. "Besides, you're a liar. They aren't *that* transparent."

"Listen," Weigand Patrick said earnestly, "that brings something to mind. When are we going to do that bed scene?"

"What do you mean it *brings* something to mind? When was your mind ever clear on the subject?"

"Well, I'll tell you one thing, it's not going to be as long as you run around in outfits like that. No wonder the textile industry is in the biggest slump in history. How in the hell can they sell any women's clothing when you broads are reunning around without skirts and with bottomless bathing suits?"

Scotty decided to ignore him. She looked at the schedule on the desk top. "Isn't Old Chucklehead expecting you?"

"Look, you oughten to call the Sachem that. He's the President of the United States of the Americas."

"Yes, and I'm his personal secretary and have been for years and if there's anybody who knows what to call him, it's me."

"All right, all right." Weigand Patrick began heading for the door to the presidential office. "However, let's get together on that big defloweration scene."

"Ha!" she snorted after him. "After what happened the last time?"

"I can explain that."

"You can explain anything, you demi-buttocked Casanova."

The oval study on the second floor of the White House was empty. Weigand Patrick looked around in mild surprise and fished in his jacket for his pipe. He wondered if his ultimate superior had snuck out the back way

40

again, in that silly disguise of his, to get smashed and play poker with some of the lobbyists and hangers-on who had taken up residence in Greater Washington when Horace Adams graduated from governor of his state to Chief Executive. The Secret Service boys had one hell of a hassle finding him the last time.

However, at that moment Weigand Patrick spotted a figure standing alone on the second-story back porch. He pushed open the glass door and stepped out onto the cool and sunlit erpanse and joined the other.

"Chief," he said.

The President turned. His handsome face was unhappy, and obviously in thought, which was as ever in itself of passing surprise to his press secretary-cum-special-assistant.

Horace Adams said, "Son, Jimmy just reported on the latest polls. Did you know my popularity rating, my public image, has sunk to a new low?"

Weigand Patrick said, "I didn't know what was possible, Mr. President. I thought it was already as low as it could get."

"They've got a new system, evidently," the President muttered lowly. "For the first time in history, a president's popularity is being rated in negative percentages."

"Negative percentages?" Weigand said, scratching a match and lighting the corncob.

Horace Adams was disgusted. "Evidently, in the old days the polls would indicate that, say, 55% of the public approved the way you were handling the administration. If you were lucky, it might get up to 75% or if things were going bad, it might drop to as low as 35% during something like the Bay of Pigs, or the U-2 overflight, or the Asian War. But this is the first time we've had a negative number from a poll."

Weigand Patrick closed his eyes in pain.

The President said accusingly, "What in the name of Moses do you smoke in that thing, shredded army blanket?"

Weigand put his pipe in his jacket pocket and followed his superior back into the presidential study.

Horace Adams took his place behind his desk. His eyes went down to his feet and he snorted. "You'd think after all these years, you wouldn't be able to see those holes from the golf shoes. I wish I played golf. Anything to get out of here. Have you ever seen the statistics on the amount of time Ike played golf while he was holding down this job?"

"No," Patrick told him. "And you don't really want to get out of here, Sir. Which brings up the matter of the next election. We're going to have to start thinking about that."

"I have been thinking about it. Smogborne thinks we ought to call a moratorium on it."

Weigand winced. "A moratorium?"

"Because of the emergency. The country's in an emergency. Call off the election, until it's over."

Weigand leaned forward. "Look, Chief. The country's been in an emergency since Roosevelt. He was the first president to come up with the advantages of an emergency. This, that and the other thing had to be postponed until the emergency was over. Special taxes were levied to help take care of it. Evidently, the emergency never ended, certainly the taxes never did. If it wasn't a depression it was a new war, either cold or hot, or a missile lag, or the red-threat, or whatever. By this time, the Chief Executive has taken over every power Congress used to have, except kissing babies. But this is a new one, declaring a moratorium on the next presidential election."

The presidential expression amounted to just short of

a pout. "Well, what's the difference?" he grumbled. "Craminently, Son, you know very well there hasn't been any difference between the Republicans and the Democrats for the past ten elections or so. Why go through the routine of pretending there is and holding a campaign?"

"Well, Chief, the public likes to have the optical illusion dangled there before their eyes. Periodically, they like to take one figurehead out and put a new one in. They don't particularly care, evidently, whether the new one is any different. They just like a change."

"Well, let them change something else. I've got the Far-Out Society to worry about."

A small light flickered on the desk and Horace Adams scowled at it and said, "Yes?"

His Appointment Secretary's voice said, "Mr. President, you are scheduled for the meeting with the brain trust."

"Oh, yes, of course. Thank you, Fred." He came to his feet. "Let's go, Son."

Weigand Patrick followed him through the outer office, where Fred Moriarty dropped in behind the procession, and down the hall to the Cabinet Room.

The others were already there, seated about the horseshoe-like Cabinet table. The President muttered some sort of a greeting, when they came to their feet, and took his place at the head. Weigand Patrick sat immediately behind him to his left, and Fred Moriarty behind him to his right. The professors, economists, sociologists and psychologists sat about in a circle, dimly reminiscent of King Arthur and his Round Table.

The President had on his Tri-Di personality—to begin with. He said brightly, "All right, uh, . . . you."

Weigand Patrick leaned forward and whispered, "Leland Markham, Harvard, economist, recently published *The New Unaffluent Society*."

"Yes, yes," Horace Adams muttered, and aloud, "Your report, Professor Markup?"

Patrick whispered, "Markham," but was ignored.

Professor Markham shuffled his papers in full stereotype. He said, a hurt quality in his voice, "Our road-building program didn't exactly turn out the way we thought, Mr. President."

The President scowled. "Why not? It was a natural. Put men to work all over the country building the roads, mining the needed materials, asphalt, cement, everything. You had it all worked out. Very impressive charts. Computer reports, everything."

The professor cleared his throat apologetically. "Yes, sir. It was all right as long as we were *building* the roads on a crash basis. It is what happened afterwards we didn't anticipate." He cleared his throat again. "The fact is, these newer, wider roads enabled the truck companies to move freight faster and hence with fewer men and trucks. Since the roads are so straight and strong, it also enabled them to use larger trucks. Now fewer drivers are needed, and since there are fewer trucks, less mechanics. Besides that, the competition had crowded out various railroads and resulted in the remaining cutting down their daily freight car loadings. The long term result has been greater unemployment."

The President groaned softly. "I'll never end this confounded depression and get my Far-Out Society underway," he complained. He turned to the next intellectual looking type.

Patrick leaned forward, "Doctor Smyth. Winchester Smyth, physicist and engineer. Stanford. The dam project. New water for irrigation, new hydro-electric . . ."

"Oh, yes, yes," the President muttered. He turned to the other, "Well, Doctor?"

The other expressed discomfort. "I am afraid my report has similarities to Professor Markham's."

The President turned off what remained of his Tri-Di personality and said coldly, "You were pretty happy about it as I recall."

"Well, yes, Mr. President. As a temporary make-work project, building the dam employed tens of thousands of men, and even a good many women office workers."

"What could possibly go wrong?"

"Well, when the dams were completed, they opened up wide areas of former desert to agriculture. As you know, given water, desert areas can prove fabulously fertile. Also, these areas were so flat they particularly lent themselves to automated farming." The doctor shook his head mournfully. "There's been a double result. We're producing more surplus farm products than ever, but at the same time the smaller farmers are being driven to the wall because they can't compete."

The President closed his eyes for a moment, in pain. He muttered accusingly, "Why couldn't we have built the dams where there wasn't any water?"

When there was no immediate response to that he said, "Anything else?"

"Well, yes, Mr. President. There was another side effect. The new dams, with the very latest hydroelectric generating equipment have released so much additional power that several projected nuclear power plants in those areas have been cancelled. At this stage they couldn't compete with water power. It has . . ." he hesitated before breaking the news ". . . led to the dismissal of several thousands of construction and nuclear power workers."

"Craminently," the President complained. He thought about it for awhile, causing all to drop into a surprised silence. Finally he said, "We could sabotage the new dams. Blow them up some dark night." He looked at his appointment secretary. "Fred, what department of government would that come under?"

Fred Moriarty said apologetically, "Mr. President, I don't think there is a department devoted to blowing up government projects. We would have to form one."

Horace Adams glared around the table. "Does anybody have any *good* news?"

Somebody rustled papers and said meekly, "I have a report here that the Bull Durham Company is booming."

"Bill Durham?" the President said.

Weigand Patrick leaned forward. "A roll-your-own cigarette company, Chief. The, ah, tailor-made cigarette companies aren't doing so good. Neither are liquor companies, and the breweries. With taxes so high, and pay falling off so fast, everybody's making bathtub gin and homebrew."

One cheerful faced type chirped, "Well, here's one from the plus side of the ledger, Mr. President. We've finally got every men jack of the military forces back home, and most of them out of uniform. Had a bit of trouble in some of the special officer clubs, PX stores, and officer housing communities, in such countries as Germany and Spain. They threw up barricades. Had to send in the paratroopers to root them out, but it's all finished now. It will cut literally billions from our expenditures and free the money to use to fight the depression."

"Money, we can use," somebody muttered. "Some of our plans, originally evolved to solve world problems at bargain basement prices, are running into financial escalation. Project Porpoise, for instance. We thought

46

that once we got the herds of whales going, the cost would be minimal."

The President glared at the speaker. "What's wrong with Project Porpoise? That's one of my favorite Far-Out Society operations. Feed all the underdeveloped countries with whale meat."

The other cleared his throat, apologetically. "It seems, Mr. President, that the porpoises are demanding full pay. The same pay the average cowboy gets in Texas."

"What! Those damn wetbacks!"

Fred Moriarty said, "There's a side development to this cutting down on the army, Mr. President."

Everybody looked at him. He said, unhappily. "The veterans. They're forming organizations. One is demanding free tickets on the airlines. First class tickets, with meals, to march on Greater Washington so they can demand a bonus."

A feisty, bearded type from across the table snapped, "There is one matter I think must come to your attention, Mr. President. When we raised tariffs so that foreign commodities wouldn't flood our remaining domestic markets, we put Common Europe and the rest of the world into a tizzy. They raised tariffs right back at us, and our exports have fallen to the vanishing point."

"Well, then at least it balances off even," the President grumbled.

"Not exactly, Mr. President. You see, our economy depends upon the import of copper from Chile, oil and iron ore from Venezuela, tin from Bolivia, and so forth. As a result, we've been spending money abroad consistently, but not making any by exports. Our gold is flowing away from Fort Knox as though there were a leak in the vaults." The feisty one ventured a sour laugh.

Nobody joined him.

Fred Moriarty said, "Mr. President, I think, while we're on the subject of Common Europe and other foreign countries, I ought to bring your attention to another aspect of the withdrawing of our troops from abroad. It seems that it's caused a full scale depression, not only in Common Europe but Japan, Siam—all the countries where we used to have bases. Hundreds of thousands of pimps, whores, bartenders, B-Girls, strip-teasers, hostesses —not to speak of pickpockets, touts, black-marketeers, and types specializing in such endeavor as rolling drunks—have been thrown out of work. All these people were big spenders. When their incomes dried up, business collapsed abroad."

The President looked over his shoulder at Weigand Patrick and muttered, "So this is a brain trust."

Weigand Patrick shrugged apologetically.

Horace Adams again faced the assembly. "Well, where do we go from here, gentlemen? The first time we met, everybody had a pet scheme."

One military-looking type, though dressed now in mufti, cleared his throat.

Patrick leaned forward and murmured, "Major General Oscar Fallout, Retired. The brain trust's military advisor. Before this job, he worked as an advisor for the Napalm, Bazooka and Thumbscrews Manufacturing Company and before that in procurement in the Octagon."

The President said, "Well, general?"

"Yes, sir. I have had passed on to me from a special committee representing the munitions industry, a suggestion that seems fraught with interesting possibilities."

"Well, go on, go on . . ."

"Mr. President, in the past, possible depressions were headed off by military expenditures. Korea came along just in time to give a spurt to lagging heavy industry.

When that scrap unfortunately came to an end, we had the Asian War."

One of the economists snapped, "If you are suggesting another war, general, we might point out to you that they aren't exactly practical any more."

"No, no, not that. I realize, as do all senior military men, that with nuclear weapons, wars can no longer be called upon to solve economic problems, desirable as they used to be. In the past, generals were able to sit comfortably twenty or more miles to the rear and order the lads to take such and such a hill, fort, or whatever, at all costs. But now, when the bombs drop, even generals get killed." The last came out with a certain degree of indignation.

"So," the President said, intrigued, "what is it that this special committee of the munitions industry has come up with?"

"Well, Mr. President, the committee is of the opinion that present laws pertaining to homicide are too, ah, stringent."

Horace Adams blinked. "Stringent?"

General Fallout was shaking his head. "Much too stringent. The committee suggests that each citizen be allowed two homicides. The solving of the population explosion would be a side effect, but most beneficial. But the boom in pistols, rifles, submachine guns, armored vests, ammunition, and so forth, would put the country's industry back into high gear." The general's eyes were flashing inspiration.

Weigand Patrick said gently, "General Fallout, I am afraid you are a dreamer before your time."

But the President was looking thoughtfully at his right-hand man. "I don't know, son. Let's not be too hasty about this." He tapped the side of his nose with a forefinger.

Weigand dropped his voice to a murmur, "Chief, if every citizen of the United States of the Americas was allowed two homicides, or even one, do you think you'd live the week out?"

The President coughed then said, "I am afraid your scheme is impractical, general. Does anyone else have anything to offer?"

A finger rose to request attention.

Patrick murmured, "Dr. Warren Dempsey Witherson, of Moppett, Hastings and Witherson. Public relations. Handled your last campaign."

"Of course, of course." The President beamed down the table at Witherson. "Yes, Doctor?"

Warren Dempsey Witherson came to his feet, his pince-nez glasses in his right hand, an aura of dignity about him.

He said, "Mr. President, I suggest a think tank of businessmen."

"Think tank?" the President said blankly.

Weigand leaned forward, "Chief, Roosevelt had his Brain Trust, Kennedy had his Irish Mafia, Truman had his whiz-kids, and Johnson had his think tanks. Groups of ultra intelligent scientists, philosophers and so forth who'd sit around together and think problems out to a conclusion. Interaction of ideas, that sort of thing."

The President looked over at Fred Moriarty indignantly. "Why doesn't anybody ever tell me anything around here?" He turned back to Warren Dempsey Witherson and his Tri-Di personality was on him again. In fact, he beamed.

"A think tank of businessmen to come up with some way of getting us out of the depression. Tell me more, Doctor. . . ."

Chapter Six

Warren Dempsey Witherson's copter-cab flitted in to the landing ramp of the Doolittle Building and came to a gentle halt.

Witherson peered about, holding his pince-nez glasses to the upper bridge of his nose with the forefinger of his left hand. There was no one else on the ramp for the moment. He cleared his throat and tried the door of the auto-taxi. It, as usual though not always, Witherson had long since found, didn't budge.

He looked at the auto-meter and the sign beneath it which read, *The Slot Will Take Bills or Coins of Any Denomination and Return Your Correct Change.*

Warren Dempsey Witherson peered nervously to right and left again, dipped his thumb and first two fingers into a vest pocket and came forth with a dollar-sized iron slug. He dropped it into the auto-meter slot and waited for his twenty cents change before opening the door and stepping out.

He set his conservatively cut coat, jiggled his malacca cane in preliminary to getting under way, and headed for the building's entrance.

The Doolittle Building was ostentatiously swank and boasted a live receptionist.

Warren Dempsey Witherson bent a kindly eye upon her and fished about in his pockets absently until he came up with a business card. He pushed his glasses back and blinked at the card as though wondering where he had seen the like before. However, he handed it over.

Miss Evans was crisp, after inspecting it. "Yes, Doctor Witherson. Whom was it you wished to see?"

"Eh? Of course, my dear. Professor Doolittle."

Only the slightest flicker indicated she was taken aback. "You have an appointment, Doctor? Perhaps one of his secretaries . . ."

"Appointment? An appointment? Certainly not, my dear." Doctor Witherson beamed at her forgivingly.

Miss Evans placed the card on a scanner and said something softly into an efficient-looking gadget which sat, small and inconspicuous, to her right.

There was a slight flicker again just before she said, "Professor Doolittle will see you immediately, Doctor. He is sending one of his secretaries down."

"Of course, my dear."

The secretary hurried from the lift and came trotting forward. "Doctor Witherson? So sorry to have kept you waiting. Professor Doolittle sent me. I'm Walthers, Doctor."

"Fine, my boy," Witherson beamed at him.

The lift, unlike the others serving the building, was unlettered and Walthers used a key to open its door. It bore them to the highest reaches of the edifice in the shortest of order.

Professor Doolittle came to his feet immediately and marched forward, a heavy paw outstretched, when the two entered his office, which involved the better part of a quarter acre of floor space.

"That will be all, Walthers," he said. "And be sure I am undisturbed, no matter the circumstance." Professor Doolittle puffed out apple red cheeks to the point of resembling Santa Claus.

"Yes, sir." Walthers was gone.

The two men stood back from each other and grinned inanely.

"The Funked-Out Kid!"

"The Professor!"

"By George, it's been a long time, Kid."

"Since . . . let's see, Tangier. Last mark we copped a score from was that winchell in Tangier."

"The last I heard of you, Kid, somebody told me you failed to properly cool off a mark you had just taken on a Big Con down in Miami." The Professor turned and headed for an impressive, volume-heavy bookcase, which turned out to be an imperial-size bar upon the flicking of a hand over an eye-button.

The Funked-Out Kid followed him. "The fix had curdled and for a while I was warm, but I wasn't sneezed."

The Professor chuckled, "What will it be, Kid? You used to drink rye."

The drinks in hand, they found chairs and grinned at each other some more.

Both were in their sixties, but there resemblance ended. Mutt and Jeff came to mind, or perhaps the comedians of yesteryear, Abbott and Costello. The Funked-Out Kid was thin and nervous, The Professor, short, bulky and jovial.

The Professor looked down at the Funked-Out Kid's business card which the receptionist had sent up to him via Walthers. He cackled amusement. "You know, Kid, I almost had them send you packing. Then the name came back to me. Warren Dempsey Witherson. That is an imposing moniker for a grifter." He read from the card. "Ph.D., D.D., LL.D., Litt. D. That is rather laying it on thick, by George."

The Kid adjusted his pince-nez in dignity. "They're all the McCoy, Professor. I bought those doctorates from some of the top diploma mills in Tennessee."

The Professor, chuckling still, made them fresh drinks, returned to his chair, shot a quick glance at his watch. "Well, Kid, it is a real pleasure to see you again. If you are in town for awhile, we ought to get together some night for some reminiscences. Phone up a couple of curves, get a bit intoxicated, that sort of thing. Meanwhile, ah, how is the taw, Kid?"

The Funked-Out Kit scowled at him, then of a sudden broke into a whinny of humor which grew in volume.

It was the Professor's turn to scowl. "Confound it, what is the matter, Kid?"

The Kid let it run down and pushed his glasses back to the high bridge of his nose with his left forefinger. He shook his head. "That's a laugh," he said. "How's the taw? Professor, did you think I came up here to shake you down for a score?"

"I would not put it that way, Kid. We're old timers, By George. Comrades in arms. If your taw is in bad shape . . ." His attitude touched on the pompous.

The Kid grinned at him. "I'm here on business, Professor. What'd you think I've been doing these past fifteen years?"

"I would not know. But once a grifter, always a grifter, Kid."

Warren Dempsey Witherson let his eyes go about the overly swank office. "That doesn't seem to apply to you, Professor."

"Like Hades it doesn't, By George. Kid, I am at the top of the heap in the biggest con since some prehistoric grifter dreamed up religion and put ninety-five percent of the human race on the sucker list. Motivational Research the double-domes call it. Why, Kid, there is not a perfume house in New York that would okay the pornography of their latest ad campaign without checking it out with my lads."

"I know," the Kid said, crossing thin legs. "That's why I'm here, Professor."

The Professor looked at him. "By George," he said. "You do look prosperous at that, Kid. Like you used to in the old days, just after copping a sizeable score. What is your line now, the wire, the rag, the pay-off? Do you use a Big Store?"

The Funked-Out Kid was whinnying again. "We call it public relations, Professor."

"Public relations! Kid, I just cannot see you, particularly in that Ph.D. get-up you are affecting, running around trying to get columnists to plug some Tri-Di starlet just because you have gotten her to wear one of those bottomless swim suits."

"Professor, I'm not getting through to you. Haven't you ever heard of Moppett, Hastings and Witherson, the top PR outfit on the coast? No conning columnists for this grifter. I deal only with top strategy, over-all policy on the highest levels."

"That means, one assumes, you get somebody else to do the work."

"Of course. I tell you, in this field you couldn't knock the marks if you tried."

The Professor brought the bottle of ancient Maryland rye from the bar and set it on the coffee table between them.

"Kid, I fail to see where motivational research, interviews in depth, the applying of psychoanalytical techniques to market investigation and the various other jazz we deal with, could tie in with public relations."

Warren Dempsey Witherson leaned forward to launch his pitch. "It's a big operation, Professor. My PR outfit and your motivational research agency are just two elements. Also involved are a Tri-Di studio, a couple of ad agencies, a couple of toy manufacturers, a TV network and a few more of the boys."

The Professor looked at him. "Big operation is correct."

"To make it brief, Professor, we're going to manufacture a fad. Remember, back when we were youngsters, the Davy Crockett fad? Started off as a movie. Before it was through there were being sold more than 300 Davy Crockett products."

"I remember, By George. Coonskin hats, buckskin shirts, flintlock rifles, Davy Crockett records."

"Right," the Funked-Out Kid beamed in satisfaction. "In all, it was estimated that a third of a billion dollars was spent on that fad."

The Professor hissed through his dentures.

"And they were amateurs," the Kid said. "They exploited it hit and miss. Fell into some of the best scores by pure accident. This time, Professor, we're going to milk our fad like pros." He took off his pince-nez glasses and shook them at the other.

"We got a new angle, Professor. Most of these fads are aimed at kids. Davy Crockett, the hula hoop, the Space Man fad. But kids don't have money to spend. Not the way grown up marks do. So this fad is going to be for adults."

"Go on," the Professor said. "Confound it, you've got me interested."

"That's all," Warren Dempsey Witherson beamed. "We're all set to go. We're going to settle on an adult hero, make a movie, write some songs, manufacture a fad like never before, and we're going to milk it all ways from Tuesday. The winchells won't know what hit them. And best of all, it's all legit."

"You mean the fix is in? By George, Kid, an operation of this magnitude would be nationwide. How could you possible manage it?"

Witherson continued to beam. "Professor, the fix goes all the way to the White House. As a matter of fact, I am part of President Adams' brain trust. As such, I suggested a think tank of businessmen, which intrigued him.

It has been formed. The Opedipus Group, we call ourselves."

"Oedipus Group?"

"It's Greek. Very impressive."

"You don't mean *Eidos*, do you Kid?"

"What does that mean?" Witherson scowled.

"Eidos, from the Greek *eidos*, something seen, form,
akin to. Actually, the formal contents of a culture, en-
compassing its system of ideas, criteria for interpreting
experience, and so forth."

Warren Dempsey Witherson was shaking his head in
admiration. "I can see, Professor we've got to have you
in the think tank."

The Professor leaned back. "By George, the whole
thing is rather inspiring the way you propose it, Kid.
Just who have you decided upon to feature as this adult
hero?"

"We don't know."

The Professor looked at him.

"That's where you come in, Professor," the Funked-
Out Kid said reasonably.

Chapter Seven

The knock at the door came in the middle of the night,
as Frol Krasnaya had always thought it would. He had
been but four years of age when the knock had come
that first time and the three large men had given his
father a matter of only minutes to dress and accompany
them. He could barely remember his father.

The days of the police state were over, in the Soviet

Complex, so they told you. The cult of personality was a thing of the past. The long series of five-year plans and seven-year plans were over and all goals had been achieved. The new constitution guaranteed personal liberties. No longer were you subject to police brutality at the merest whim. So they told you.

But fears die hard, particularly when they are largely of the subconscious. And he had always, deep within, expected the knock. However, not here in Greater Washington, even in the grounds of the spacious Soviet Complex Embassy where Frol Krasnaya, in common with all other Soviet personnel, were quartered.

Frol Krasnaya allowed himself but one chill of apprehension, then rolled from his bed, squared slightly stooped shoulders, and made his way to the door. He flicked on the light and opened up, even as the burly, empty-faced zombi there was preparing to pound again.

The first of the zombi twins said expressionlessly, "Comrade Frol Krasnaya?"

If tremor there was in his voice, it was negligible. He said, "That is correct. Uh . . . to what do I owe this intrusion upon my privacy?" The last in the way of bravado.

The other ignored the question. "Get dressed and come with us, Comrade."

At least, they still called him comrade, that was something.

The zombis stood watching him emptily as he dressed.

They marched him down to the mansion lawn where a mini-jet helicopter awaited them. At this time of night, the grounds were deserted. They swooped into the air, and in ten minutes were at the Johnson Memorial International Jet Port.

When they disembarked from the small craft, the two goons assumed positions to each side of him, and they began to march toward a long, low Tupolev rocket-jet. He considered only briefly shouting and running for it. Defecting to the West. The trouble was, the West wasn't particularly interested in defectors from the Soviet Complex any more. There had been so many of them, over the years, that they were a drug on the market. And with all the unemployment these days, jobs for Soviet citizens on the lam were hard to come by.

Inside the craft, he was moderately surprised. He, and his two zombis, were evidently the sole passengers, and it was outfitted in luxury, greater luxury than he had ever run into in an aircraft before. In fact, he was dubious that even Ambassador Nicolas Stanislov would have ordinarily so traveled.

There was no mystery as to their destination. The jets whooshed them into the upper reaches, and then the rockets took over. They were landing at the Vnokovo airport within two hours, a two hours that had been spent without communication with the two police goons. A monstrously large Zim hover limousine was awaiting them to speed them into Moscow.

They by-passed Red Square and skirted the Alexandrovski Sad park along the west side of the Kremlin. They entered at the Borovitskij Gate, went up the cobblestoned incline there without loss of pace and drew up before the Bolshoi Kremlevski Dvorets, the Great Kremlin Palace.

Two sentries snapped to attention as they entered. Evidently Frol's guards needed no passes. A sixteen-step ornate staircase led them up from the ground floor to a gigantic vestibule the vault of which was supported by four monolithic granite columns. They turned left and entered an anteroom. More guards who snapped to attention.

One of Frol Krasnaya's escort approached a heavy door

59

and knocked discreetly. Someone came, opened it slightly, evidently said something to someone else back in the room and then opened it widely enough for Krasnaya and his goons.

Inside, at a desk, sat a lean, competent and assured type who jittered over a heavy sheaf of papers with an electro-marking computer pen. He was nattily and immaculately dressed and smoked his cigarette in one of the small pipelike holders once made *de rigueur* through the Balkans by Marshall Tito.

The three of them came to a halt before his desk and, at long last, expression came to the faces of the zombis. Respect, with possibly an edge of perturbation, Here, obviously, was authority.

He at the desk finished a paper, tore it from the sheaf, pushed it into the maw of the desk chute. Then, to Frol Krasnaya's astonishment, the other came to his feet, quickly, smoothly and with a grin on his face. Frol hadn't considered the possibility of being grinned at in the Ministry of Internal Affairs.

"Aleksander Kardelj," the other said in self-introduction, sticking out a lean hand to be shaken. "You're Krasnaya, eh? We've been waiting for you."

Frol shook, bewildered. He looked at the zombi next to him, uncomprehendingly.

He who had introduced himself darted a look of comprehension from Frol to the two. He said, disgustedly but with mild humor oddly mixed, "What's the matter, did these hoodlums frighten you?"

Frol fingered his chin nervously. "Of course not."

One of the zombis shifted his feet. "We did nothing but obey orders."

Kardelj grimaced in sour amusement. "I can imagine," he grunted. "Milka, you see too many of these imported Tri-Di shows from the West. I suspect you see yourself

as a present-day Soviet Complex G-Man, or possibly
James Bond, the Third."

"Yes, Comrade," Milka said, and then shook his head.

"Oh hush up and get out," Kardelj said. He flicked
the cigarette butt from its holder with a thumb and took
up a fresh one from a desk humidor and wedged it into
the small bowl. He looked at Frol again and grinned.

"You can't imagine how pleased I am to meet you, at
last," he said, "I've been looking for you for months."

Frol Krasnaya ogled him. The name had come through
at last. Aleksander Kardelj was seldom in the news, practically never photographed and then in the background
in a group of Party functionaries, usually with a wry smile
on his face. But he was known throughout the wide
boundaries of the Soviet Complex, if not internationally.
Aleksander Kardelj, a Hungarian, was Number Two.
Right-hand man of Andrei Zorin himself, second in command of the Party and rumored to be the brains behind
the throne.

The Zombis had gone hurriedly.

"Looking for me?" Frol said blankly. "I haven't been
in hiding. You've made some mistake. All I am is the
junior *Pravda* reporter assigned to Greater Washington.
I——"

"Of course, of course," Kardelj said, humorously im-
patient. He took up a folder from his desk and shook it
absently in Frol's general direction. "I've studied your
dossier thoroughly." He flicked his eyes up at a wall
clock. "Come along. Comrade Zorin is expecting us."

In a daze, Frol Krasnaya followed him.

Comrade Zorin. Number One. Andrei Zorin, Secretary
General of the Party, Chairman of the Presidium of the
Central Committee. The heir of Lenin, Stalin, Khrush-
chev, Kosygin, and the other dictators of the Soviet
Complex.

Frol could hardly remember so far back that Zorin wasn't head of the party, when his face, or sculptured bust, wasn't to be seen in every store, on the walls of banks, railroad stations, or bars. Never a newsreel but that part of it wasn't devoted to Comrade Zorin, never a Tri-Di newscast but that Number One was brought to the attention of the viewers.

Frol Krasnaya followed Kardelj in a daze through a door to the rear of the desk, and into a somewhat bigger room, largely barren of furniture save for a massive table with a dozen chairs about it. At the table, looking some ten years older than in any photo Frol had ever seen, sat Andrei Zorin.

He looked ten years older and his face bore a heavy weariness, a grayness, that never came through in his publicity shots. He looked up from a report and grunted a welcome to him.

Kardelj said in pleasurable enthusiasm, "Here his is, Andrei. The average young man of the whole Soviet Complex."

Number One grunted again and took in the less than imposing figure of Frol Krasnaya. Frol felt an urge to nibble at his fingernails and repressed it.

Andrei Zorin growled an invitation for them to be seated and Kardelj adjusted his trousers to preserve the crease, threw one leg up along the heavy conference table and rested on one buttock, looking at ease but as though ready to take off instantly.

Frol fumbled himself into one of the sturdy oaken chairs, staring back and forth at the two most powerful men of his native land. Thus far, no one had said anything that made any sense whatsoever to him since he had been hauled from his bed, two hours and more ago, in the Soviet Embassy of Greater Washington.

Zorin rasped, "I have gone through your dossier, Comrade. I note that you are the son of Hero of the People's Democratic Dictatorship, Alex Krasnaya."

"Yes, Comrade Zorin," Frol got out.

Number One grunted. "I knew Alex well. You must realize that his arrest was before my time. It was, of course, after my election that he was exonerated and his name restored to the list of those who have gloriously served the State."

It wasn't exactly the way Frol knew the story, but he simply nodded. He said, unhappily, "Comrades, I have no idea . . ."

Kardelj was chuckling, as though highly pleased with some development. He held up a hand to cut Frol short and turned to his superior. "You see, Andrei. A most average, laudable young man. Born under our regime, raised under the People's Democratic Dictatorship of the Soviet Complex. Exactly our man."

Zorin seemed not to hear the other. He was studying Frol heavily, all but gloomily.

A beefy paw went out and banged a button inset in the table and which Frol had not seen before. Almost instantly a door in the rear opened and a white jacketed servant entered pushing a wheeled combination bar and hors d'oeuvres cart before him. He brought the lavishly laden wagon to within reach of the heavyset Party head, then made himself scarce.

Number One's heavy lips moved in and out as his eyes went over the display.

Kardelj said easily, "Let me, Andrei." He arose and brought a towel-wrapped bottle from a refrigerated bucket set into the wagon and deftly took up a delicate three-ounce glass which he filled and placed before his superior.

"Have one yourself," Zorin grunted.

Kardelj smiled in self-deprecation. "Not for me, Andrei.

Too weak a stomach for this strong stuff. For me, occasionally a glass of Georgian wine, or perhaps one of kvas from Uzbec."

Zorin grunted, "You don't know kvas from your elbow, Aleksander. I was raised on the stuff." His eyes piggish, he took up a heavy slice of dark bread and ladled a full quarter pound of caviar upon it, grunted and stuffed the open sandwich into his mouth.

He looked at Frol. "Comrade, I am not surprised at your confusion. We will get to the point. Actually, you must consider yourself a very fortunate young man." He belched, took another bite, and went on, "Have you ever heard the term expediter?"

"I . . . I don't think so, Comrade Zorin."

The Party head poured himself some more spirits. "Comrade Kardelj first came upon the germ of this idea of ours through reading of American industrial successes during the Second World War. They were attempting to quadruple their production of war materials in months. Obviously, a thousand bottlenecks appeared, so they resorted to expediters. Competent efficiency engineers whose sole purpose was to seek out such bottlenecks and eliminate them. A hundred aircraft might be kept from completion by the lack of a single part. The expediters found them though they be as far away as England, and flew them by chartered plane to California. I need give no further examples. Their powers were sweeping. Their expense accounts unlimited. Their successes unbelievable." Number One's eyes went back to the piles of food, as though he had grown tired of so much talk.

Frol figited, still uncomprehending.

While the Party leader built himself another huge sandwich, Aleksander Kardelj put in an enthusiastic word. "We're adapting the ideas to our own needs, Comrade. You have been selected to be our first expediter."

"Expediter? To . . . to expedite *what?*"

"That is for you to decide," Kardelj said blithely. "You are our average citizen. You feel as the man on the street feels. You're our, what the Yankees call, Common Man."

Frol said plaintively, "But I don't know what you mean, Comrade. What is this about me being, uh, the average man? There's nothing special about me."

"Exactly," Kardelj said triumphantly. "There's nothing special about you. You're the average man of all the Soviet Complex. We have gone to a great deal of difficulty to seek you out."

Number One belched and took over heavily. "Comrade, we have made extensive tests in this effort to find our average man. You are the result. You are of average age, of average weight, height, of education and of intelligence quotient. Your tastes, your ambitions, your . . . dreams, Comrade Krasnaya, are either known to be, or assumed to be, those of the average citizen." He took up a rich baklava dessert, saturated with honey, and devoured it.

Andrei Zorin took up a paper. "I have here a report from a journalist of the West who but recently returned from a tour of the Soviet Complex. She reports, with some indignation, that the only available eyebrow pencils were to be found on the black market, were of French import, and cost twenty rubles apiece. She contends that Soviet women are indignant at paying such prices."

The Party head looked hopelessly at first Frol and then Kardelj. "What is an eyebrow pencil?"

Frol took courage. He flustered. "They use it to darken their eyebrows—women, I mean. It comes and goes in popularity."

Karadelj said triumphantly, "See what I mean, Andrei? He's priceless."

Zorin looked at his right-hand man. "Why, if our women desire this . . . this eyebrow pencil nonsense, is it not supplied them? Is there some ingredient we don't produce? If so, why cannot it be imported?" He picked at his uneven teeth with a thumbnail.

Kardelj held his lean hands up, as though in humorous supplication. "Because, Comrade, to this point we have not had expediters to find out such desires."

Number One grunted and took up another report. "Here we have some comments upon service in our restaurants. This Western writer contends that the fact we have no tipping leads our waiters to be surly and inefficient. The tourist trade is important." He glowered across at Frol. "Typical of the weaknesses you must ferret out, Comrade."

He put the reports down with a grunt. "But these are comparatively minor. Last week a truck driver attached to a meat-packing house in Kiev was instructed to deliver a load. When he arrived it was to find they had no refrigeration facilities. So he unloaded the frozen meat on a warehouse platform and returned to Kiev. At this time of the year, obviously, in four hours the meat was spoiled." He glowered at Kardelj and then at Frol. "Why do things like this continually happen? How can we think we have overtaken the West when on all levels our workers are afraid to take initiative? He delivered the meat. He washed his hands of what happened afterwards. Why, Comrades? Why did he not have the enterprise to preserve his valuable load, even, if necessary, make the decision to return with it to Kiev?"

He grunted heavily and settled back as though through, finished with the whole question.

Aleksander Karedlj became brisk. "This is your job. You are to travel about the country, finding bottlenecks, finding shortages, ferreting out mistakes and bringing them to the attention of those in position to rectify them."

Frol said, "But suppose . . . suppose they ignore my findings?"

Number One snorted, but said nothing.

Kardelj said jovially, "Tomorrow the announcements will go out to every man, woman and child in the People's Democratic Dictatorship. Your word is law. You are answerable only to Comrade Zorin and myself. No restrictions whatsoever apply to you. No laws. No regulations. We will give you identication which all will recognize, and the bearer of which can do no wrong."

Frol was flabbergasted. "But . . . suppose I come up against some, well, someone high in the Party, or, well, some general, or admiral?"

Kardelj said jocularly, "You answer only to us. Your power is limitless. Comrade Zorin did not exaggerate. Frankly, were cold statistics enough, the Soviet Complex has already overtaken the West in per capita production, particularly in view of the depression now hitting them. Steel, agriculture, coal mined, petroleum pumped. All these supposed indications of prosperity. Why, our porpoise program is far and beyond theirs. We've not only taught *our* porpoises, based in the Sea of Okhotsk, to speak Russian, but to read in the Cyrillic alphabet. Beginning next week there will be a special edition of *Pravda* printed for them on plastic." He flung up his hands again, in his semi-humorous gesture of despair. "But all these things do not mesh. We cannot find such a simple matter as . . . as eyebrow pencils in our stores, nor can we be served acceptably in our restaurants and hotels. Each man passes the buck, as the Yankees say. No man wants responsibility."

"But . . . but me . . . only me. What could you expect a single person to do?"

"Don't misunderstand. You are but an experiment. If it works out, we will seek others who are also deemed potential expediters, to do similar work."

Frol said carefully, "From what you say, I . . . I can override anyone in the Soviet Complex, except yourselves. But what if I antagonize one of you? You know, with something I think I find wrong?"

The second in command of the Party chuckled, even as he fitted a fresh cigarette into his curved holder. "We've provided even for that, Comrade. Fifty thousand Common Europe francs have been deposited to your account in Switzerland. At any time you feel your revelations might endanger yourself, you are free to leave the country and achieve sanctuary abroad." He chuckled whimsically again. "Given the position you will occupy, a man above all law, with the whole of the nation's resources at his disposal, I cannot imagine you wishing to leave. The Swiss deposit is merely to give you complete confidence, complete security."

Chapter Eight

Weigand Patrick, standing at the side of the bed, looked down in open admiration. He said, "Now that's what I call table stuff. Turn over."

"No," Scotty said into the large pillow where she had burrowed her head.

"Why not?"

"I'm embarrassed."

"Embarrassed! After the type clothes you wear around all day? Or, rather, don't wear."

Scotty said, her voice muffled, "I've never been in a man's bed before."

He sat on the edge of it and reached out a hand.

"Hey," she said. "Cut that out! What do you think I am, a sailor?"

He said, "This is what's known as preliminary sex play. It's in all the instruction manuals. You gotta have sex play."

"Oh yeah. Well, play somewhere else."

"Here?"

She drew in her breath. "That's . . . different."

"You mean better?"

"I said, different."

"Turn over."

"Turn out the lights."

"Why? I want to see you. I'm hung up on redheads. It runs in the family, my old man's life-long ambition was to go to bed with a redheaded woman in black underwear. But he never did."

"Why not?" her voice was intrigued.

"My mother wouldn't let him. Turn over."

She said into the pillow, "Have you got your clothes off?"

"Yes."

She dug her head further into the pillow.

"I'm wearing pajamas," he said.

She half turned, indignantly. "How come you insist I be stark naked and you wear pajamas?" Then her eyes widened, accusingly. "You're only wearing the *tops*."

"That's all I ever wear," he said, reaching for her. "Now about this preliminary sex play. First, we start here . . ."

Her eyes rolled up and her mouth went slack.

The phone screen buzzed.

"Holy smokes!" he protested.

"What's that?" she muttered.

"My private line to the White House."

"Well . . . stop doing that . . . for a minute. You . . . you'd better answer it'"

"No. Damn it."

"Stop doing that, WeeWee Patrick. Take your head away. That's not what you're supposed to do anyway . . . I'm sure. You'd better answer it. It's probably some emergency."

"Of course it's an emergency. It's always an emergency. Let somebody else worry about it."

She sat up abruptly. "You'll *have* to answer it. I couldn't concentrate, anyway. Knowing some emergency was on."

"Not even if I did this?"

Her eyes rolled up again. "You cut that out, you queer, and go answer the phone. Tell them you're sick, or something. Refer them to Fred Moriarty."

"Ha," he grumbled. "That bastard's trying to get my job." He sat erect on the bed's edge and glowered at the still buzzing phone screen.

"Well, you don't want the job, anyway."

"I don't know," he said lowly, still glaring at the device which was attempting to summon him. "There's an awful lot of unemployment in this country, and presidential assistants aren't that much in demand."

"I thought you were a newspaperman."

"Newspaperman, for God's sake? Do you know how many newspapermen are still working? The publishers have finally gone the whole hog. *The New York Times* has amalgamated with *The Los Angeles Times*. They met in Kansas City and assimilated the *Star* while they were at it."

He came to his feet, in disgust, and moved toward the phone screen.

"Hey," Scotty said. "Don't turn that thing on, until I get out of the way."

Weigand leered at her over his shoulder. "Why not? I'd like the word to get around, the high quality stuff I get into my bed. A reputation like that and all the broads start wondering just what it is you have. Your reputation gets big enough and you can't fight them off. Look at Don Juan, look at Casanova, look at Rubirosa. They didn't know what hit 'em. Look at that old timer Tommy Manville."

"Yeah, Tommy Manville," she sneered. "He inherited Ponce DeLeon's pants."

"Ponce DeLeon's pants?"

"The old jerk who explored Florida looking for the Fountain of Youth. He was just about to bathe in it, when the Indians raided. His pants fell in. He fished them out. Then had to beat a retreat."

He scowled at her, looked over at the screen, looked back. "What the hell are you talking about, at a time like this?"

"Ponce DeLeon's pants. So long as you wore them, you were hot for everybody. But then . . ."

He got it. "When you took them off . . ." He shook his head. "That's the kind of girl I fall for. What a mind. I bet you made that up on the spur of the moment."

He turned the instrument so that the screen faced a different corner of the room, and sat down before it. He flicked the switch.

It was Fred Moriarty.

Fred said, "Where were you? I was about to try somewhere else."

"I'm here," Weigand said disgustedly. "What the hell is it? I'm busy. Or, at least, want to be."

The Presidential Appointment Secretary said, "Weigand, you'd better get over here soonest. I've got something I'm not sure I know how to handle."

"Sounds like this new strain of clap. What?"

"An inventor that's been trying to get in to see the Chief for the past couple of weeks."

"Well, why didn't you let him? God knows, the Sachem'll see just about anybody these days, hoping something'll come up."

"I thought he was a crackpot."

"All right, then send him over to the Office of Science and Technology, Crackpot Division, or whatever they call that department that investigates new inventions."

Fred Moriarty's face was harried. "I was going to, but he wouldn't take the brush-off. He didn't want to show his damn invention to anybody but the President, but finally, kind of in despair, he showed it to me."

Weigand Patrick was beginning to become intrigued.

From the bed, Scotty, in an urgent whisper, said, "Look, either perform or get off the pot. Are you coming back, or not?"

"Shhh," he said, over his shoulder. "Just a minute."

He turned back to the phone screen and his colleague. "Well, what is the big invention?"

"I can't tell you over the phone."

Weigand Patrick looked at him. "This is a special line."

"I don't care. Lines have been tapped before."

"Well, give me a hint."

"I can't."

"Well, where is this crackpot inventor?"

"I've got two of the Secret Service boys guarding him."

"Holy smokes," Weigand said. "You really have got maiden aunts in your pants. Can't you give me any idea of what the invention will do?"

Fred Moriarty said very slowly, "If I'm any judge, it

72

will boom the Chief's popularity poll rating to 95 percent, overnight."

"Ninety-five percent! Do you know what it is now?"

"There isn't any now."

"Ninety-five percent!"

Fred Moriarty said very slowly, "It is estimated that the agnostics and athiests in this country number five percent of the population. We'll get everybody else."

"Holy smokes."

"You're telling me."

"I'll be right over!" He slammed off the switch of the phone screen, got up and hurried in the direction of his clothes.

Scotty looking at him from the bed, blinked and said, "Where did it go?"

"What?" he said absently, struggling into his shirt.

"That . . . that thing."

He said hurriedly, "Look, honey, I've got to make a bee-line over to the White House."

"What for?"

"I don't know."

She stared at him in indignation. "You mean to tell me, you bring me here and then before you even get started you have to dash off on some silly errand for Old Chucklehead?" She said suspiciously, "That was Fred Moriarty. What's going on?"

"Evidently, something so secret that he was afraid to tell me on the phone," Weigand said, struggling into his pants.

She said, "I didn't know they went away like that."

"What went away?"

"You know."

"Honey, there's a lot of things you obviously don't know. It will be my greatest privilege to teach you,

73

later." He added, as an inducement, "They only go away temporarily." He added, indignantly, "Besides, it didn't go away, it just shrunk, kind of."

"Are you coming back later? Should I wait?"

He rolled his eyes upward and groaned in pure misery. "I guess not. I have a sneaking suspicion that this particular emergency is going to string on for awhile."

In the outer office to the presidential study, Fred Moriarty was waiting for him.

"Well," Weigand Patrick snapped, "where is he?"

"I've got him in your office, with Steve and Wes guarding him."

"Is he that tough? What was he trying to get at the Sachem for? What the hell is this invention, anyway?" Weigand Patrick looked sardonic. "Or do you think this office might be bugged too?"

A flicker of apprehension passed over the appointment secretary's face, but then he shook his head. "You'll have to see on your own."

Weigand turned, "Well, let's go, then."

"Not me."

Weigand turned back and stared, "What'd'ya mean, not you?"

"I've seen it, and it gives me the shakes."

"By God, this place is turning into a nut factory. I wish the hell I'd become a Baptist missionary like my dear old mother wanted." He turned back to the door again.

Fred Moriarty said urgently, "Don't let Steve and Wes be there when he demonstrates it."

Weigand Patrick was staring again. "Why not?"

"It's the toppest secret there's ever been. This secret makes the Manhattan Project look like a Women's Sunday Afternoon Bridge and Gossip Society."

"Jesus H. Christ," Weigand said. He turned and left Fred Moriarty's office and headed for his own in the White House west wing.

Steve Hammond was standing outside Patrick's office door, his right hand under his jacket lapel.

Weigand snapped at him, "What the hell's going on?"

"Yes, sir, Mr. Patrick. Mr. Moriarty's instructions. The subject is inside. Wes is on guard in there."

"Does this guy look as dangerous as all that?"

"Well, no sir. From what Mr. Moriarty says, *he's* not dangerous. Mr. Moriarty says just to be sure that nobody gets to him—except you, of course, Mr. Patrick."

"Thanks," Weigand said. He pushed open the door of his office and entered.

The office of Weigand Patrick, press secretary, special assistant, right-hand man, and operational brains of the President of the United States of the Americas, had been decorated to its occupant's tastes. There was a very large desk, fouled high with everything that a desk could conceivably accumulate. There was a small bar in the corner. There were book shelves, filled with an assortment less orthodox than might be expected in a bureaucrat of his ranking. There were half a dozen very comfortable chairs, and what Weigand called his casting couch.

In one of the very comfortable chairs sat an unknown. He was about five-foot four, would go perhaps a hundred and fifteen pounds, carrying a suitcase and after being caught out in the rain, and wore a lost pup expression. His scrawny beard gave the impression that moths not only made a custom of bedding down in it, but carousing there.

Weigand Patrick looked first at him, then at the Secret Service man who had scrambled to his feet at

Weigand's slamming entrance. He had been seated in the ultra-comfortable upholstered swivel chair which was the press secretary's pride and often joy.

"Wes," Weigand smiled benignly at the bodyguard, "if I ever catch you in my chair again, I'll have you shot at dawn on the Octagon paradeground, after having had utilized on you some of the Nazi war surplus they have over in the museum there." He added, gently, "Do you doubt I could have that done, Wes?"

"Well, no sir," the other blurted. "But I don't think the President would like that, Mr. Patrick."

"To the contrary, the way he's feeling these days, I think he'd be over to watch when they got around to those testicle squeezers. Get the hell out of here."

"Yes, sir. I'll be at the door, Mr. Patrick." He got.

Weigand Patrick looked at the other occupant of the office. He said, "I'm Weigand Patrick. It's been said that I pinch hit for Horace Adams, under certain circumstances."

"Newton Brown," the other said, bobbing his adam's apple, and blinking at the door through which the Secret Service man had just exited. "My friends call me Newt."

"I'll bet they do." Weigand went over to the bar. "Would you like a drink?"

"Well . . . do you know how to mix a John Brown's Body?"

"A John Brown's Body? What are its essentials, and what do they do to you?"

The little man nodded. "That's a good question," he said. "Too many people don't ask. Frankly, in the morning you feel like you're moldering in your grave. I named the concoction after an ancestor. The ingredients are an egg, rum, absinthe, metaxa and pulque."

"Pulque?"

"Pulque. I have to have mine shipped up specially

from Mexico. You can substitute dark beer, but it's not the same."

"Dark beer we have," Weigand said, miffed. He prided himself on his bar. He made a mental note to order some pulque.

He mixed, taking the other's instructions as he went. Eventually, they wound up, tall glasses in hand, facing each other, Weigand behind his desk.

Weigand Patrick sipped his and said, "Holy Smokes."

"Good, aren't they?" the other beamed.

Weigand peered down into his glass. "What happened to the eggshell? I never heard of dropping an eggshell into a drink before."

"Gives calcium to your system," Newton Brown said. "It's usually dissolved by this time."

Weigand Patrick coughed. "Okay," he said. "So much for the amenities. I understand you're an inventor."

"That is correct, sir." The other sighed. "I might almost say, the last of the traditional inventors. The posterity of the inventor of yesteryear, a descendent of the alchemist of old, if you will, who worked in his own garret; of the talented tinkerer of old, who had his laboratory in cellar, or, later, garage. Today . . ." the little man sighed ". . . inventions are made in assembly-line laboratories where a scientist might not even know the nature of the final product upon which he is expanding his cerebral labors."

Weigand ignored the fruity language. "Newton Brown, Newton Brown," he said. "The name escapes me. I don't believe I have ever heard of any of your own particular, ah, breakthroughs."

Newton Brown finished off his drink, without a flinch, and handed his glass over to his host, rather than putting it down.

He sighed. "No, I suppose not. Most of my work has been suppressed, one way or the other."

"Suppressed?"

"That is correct." He brought a wallet from his clothes, fished around in it and handed Weigand Patrick a slip of yellow paper.

Weigand, scowling, the empty glass still held in his right hand, looked at it. "Fifty thousand dollars. Holy Smokes!" It was a check from the Associated Towel Manufacturers of the United Americas.

"It's always like that," the little man was complaining. "Something always happens to my work, it never reaches the public. I can't afford not to take this check, and obviously now they'll suppress it."

"Who'll suppress what?" Weigand Patrick said, staring at the pleasant sum.

"The Associated Towel Mnaufacturers," Newt Brown sighed. "They're just bought up my dry water discovery."

Weigand looked at him.

"Dry water, dry water," Brown repeated. "Endless possibilities, obviously. Absolutely revolutionize irrigation. Carry it around in burlap bags. Also, veterinarians expressed an interest, for washing animals such as cats who don't like to get wet. I stumbled upon it while experimenting with *light* water. I'm very much a basic research scientist, you know. Pure research. Science for science's sake. All that sort of thing." He added, sadly, "Quite a genius."

Weigand got to his feet and went over and concocted the concoction again. He brought the two drinks back and handed one of them to the other.

He said, cautiously, "What did you figure *light* water would do?"

The other sipped his drink appreciatively and leaned

forward as though confidential. "You've heard of *heavy* water, obviously? Well, I concluded that if I could devise a *light* water it would revolutionize reducing and end obesity overnight." For a moment the little man seemed inspired in his dream. His eyes brightened.

"I . . . I don't believe I get you," Weigand said.

"Obvious," Newt Brown said. "You must know that at least ninety percent of the human body is composed of water. Well, if I could substitute *light* water for regular H_2O in a person's chemical make-up, he'd weigh considerably less. Simple, isn't it?"

For a brief moment, Weigand Patrick let his mind consider some of the ramifications. Then he shook his head for clarity, and looked down into his drink again, accusation there.

"Not exactly," he said. "But what happened to your light water experiments?"

"Oh, you government people suppressed them. Some bureau or other, I forget which one."

"The government?" Weigand scowled. He had almost certainly never heard of Newton Brown before.

The little man nodded earnestly. "As you undoubtedly know, heavy water is extremely important in nuclear fission. Well . . . it's obvious, isn't it? One experiment leads to another and I was beginning to dabble in reverse nuclear fission with my light water, when they clamped down on me."

"Reverse nuc . . ."

But Brown held up a restraining hand. "Sorry, but I have given my word not to discuss it. Undoubtedly, you are in a position to be cleared for this information. But until you are, and until I have received permission to . . ."

"All right, all right. You seem to be in quite a rut,"

79

Weigand said. He was beginning to feel the drink—if you could call it a drink. "First it's dry water, then it's light water."

The other retrieved his check and put it back in his wallet with a sigh. "The compound has always fascinated me. There should be *some* sensible use for it—obviously it's a flop as a beverage."

Weigand Patrick said sarcastically, "Have you given any thought to black water?"

"Black water? It's possible advantageousness seems to elude me."

"Maybe for people who don't care if they're dirty or not, to wash with."

Newton Brown blinked at him. "I fear you jest."

"Yeah, maybe," Weigand Patrick said in resignation. "Look, let's get to the point. The president's appointment secretary seems to think you have some, well, rather far-out invention. He tells me you have been trying to get to the President with it."

"Ah, well yes."

"Okay. What is it?"

Newton Brown pursed his lips. "Perhaps I could best illustrate by stating that I am spiritually opposed, morally opposed, to the present stance of President Horace Adams' in containing Finland and conducting the police action in the Antarctic."

Actually, Weigand felt the same way; however, it wasn't his branch of responsibility. He said blandly, "However, Mr. Brown, I am afraid your opinions are not those of the most farsighted, the most highly informed and the most spiritually oriented . . ."

Weigand Patrick broke off in mid-sentence and his eyes bugged as they had never bugged in the thirty-odd years of the existence of Weigand Patrick.

For above the head of Newton Brown, frustrated inventor extraordinary, there floated what would only be described by the most negatively prejudiced as a halo.

It was a halo as painted by the most delicate masters of the Renaissance, a vertible soft rainbow of a halo. There were mother-of-pearl aspects, too. It was possibly the single most beautiful thing that Weigand Patrick had ever seen in his life. It was faint, it was delicate; but there were no two ways about it. Newton Brown had a halo over his head.

Weigand said shakily, "Excuse me." Taking his glass over to the small sink that was part of the bar, he poured the rest of his drink down.

On second thought, he took up a bottle of twelve-year-old Irish, poured a triple slug, and knocked it back.

His grandparents had been religious but not since them had the family given much thought to the here-after and related subjects. He came back and sat down again and looked at his guest. The halo was gone. However, Weigand Patrick was still shaken.

He said, "Look. I respect your . . . ah, spiritual opinions."

Newton Brown said nothing.

Weigand Patrick said carefully. "However, uh . . . well, the President's position on his international stands are . . . well . . . of the highest moral . . ."

"I think they're unholy . . ."

The halo faded in again, above Newton Brown's head.

Weigand Patrick had come back to his swivel chair. He got up again and went back to the bar and poured himself another double Irish in a daze. He knocked it back. He returned to his desk.

He said, "Uh, I am not very well . . . That is, I am not very spiritually, uh, oriented." Happily, the halo was gone.

The other's drink was gone. He said, "I beg your pardon?" holding his glass out in the obvious need for a refill.

Weigand said, "I . . . well, I suppose I've neglected my religious obligations. Only this evening I . . . well, that's not important. The thing is, I've never thought in terms before . . . that is, not until now . . . of, of well, taking holy orders . . ."

Newton Brown said interestedly, "You know, that was the first response of your colleague, this Frederick Moriarty."

"I'll bet it was," Weigand muttered. "Look, I'm not feeling exactly . . . I think I better get in touch with the staff psychiatrist and . . ."

"Oh, that won't be necessary."

"What do you know about it?" Weigand all but snarled. "I know when I'm not feeling well. Besides, I think I've been drinking too much . . . or something."

"I'll show you how it works," the other said reasonably. Weigand Patrick looked at him. "How what works?"

Newton Brown brought an object from his pocket. It looked like a rather elaborate cigarette case with a button on the side. "I call it the Aurora Borealis," he said. "Makes it easier for the layman to comprehend."

"You call *what* the Aurora Borealis? Listen, you'll never believe this, but you know that I thought I saw a . . ."

Newt Brown interrupted by ostentatiously pushing the button on the seeming cigarette case. The halo was there, above his head. He let the button off, the halo was gone.

Weigand Patrick bug-eyed again.

The little inventor handed him the cigarette case. "It's not at all as complicated as you might think. The fact is, scientists have known for some time that every human being—every animal for that matter—has a magnetic-electric aura about them. Invisible, of course. Something

like the electric fields which surround the Earth and are
especially prevalent at the North and South poles. Dis-
charges of ions through this aura are what causes the so
beautiful Aurora Borealis, the so-called Northern Lights.
Now, what I've done——"

"Wait a minute now, you've lost me. What I want to
know is . . . this damn thing . . . it'll work on anybody?"

"Of course. Try it."

Weigand swallowed and pressed the button. Nothing
seemed to happen.

Newt Brown said in satisfaction, "Of course. Anybody
at all. Looks very good on you. Rather dashing."

Weigand Patrick stumbled to his feet and made his
way to the small bathroom connected with his office. He
stared into the mirror above the lavatory.

He said, "I'm a saint," and pushed the button.

The halo was there.

Newt Brown was correct. On him, it looked rather
dashing. As though he was some medieval warrior-saint,
somebody like Sir Galahad.

Weigand Patrick stared at his image and muttered,
meaninglessly, "His strength was as the strength of ten,
because his heart was pure."

He returned to his desk and sat the cigarette case
down very carefully. He looked at Newt Brown, who
was wearing a smirk, and said, "You mean this thing will
work for anybody at all?"

"Like I said, even animals have the invisible magnetic-
electric aura. All my device does is power it."

"You mean," Weigand demanded, "even a jackass, if
he pressed this button, would have a halo around his
head?"

"Well, I don't know how a jackass could press a button, is all."

"Well, I do," Weigand muttered. "Just a minute. Let

me think, damn it." He ran a hand over his chin nervously. "I've got to think about this."

He turned suddenly to his phone screen, flicked it on and snapped, "Mr. Moriarty's office."

When Fred Moriarty faded in on the screen, Weigand snapped, without preliminaries, "Listen, the Tri-Di speech the Sachem is going to make. That revival of President Roosevelt's Fireside Chat . . ."

"I know," Fred said. "I'm way ahead of you."

"Every time he makes one of those cornball platitudes the speechwriting boys have been digging up, like: *All we have to fear, is fear itself,* and *a chicken in every pot——*"

"I'm way ahead of you," Fred Moriarty repeated.

Weigand Patrick said despeartely, "Listen, have you mentioned this to anybody at all? *Anybody . . . ?*"

"No. Nobody but you . . ."

"Hang on," Weigand said. "Don't leave your office." He flicked off the phone screen and spun on Newton Brown. He leveled a finger at the inventor, who was beginning to show nervous symptoms. "How many people know about this device? How many have you demonstrated it to?"

Newt Brown swallowed. "I work alone. Veritable hermit . . . so to speak. Tradition of the alchemists and all that——"

"Answer me, dammit!"

"Nobody," Newt Brown protested. "Nobody but you and Mr. Frederick Moriarty."

Weigand came to his feet, went to the office door, opened it and called, "Steve, Wes, in here on the double."

The two efficient looking Secret Service men came darting through the door.

Weigand Dennis pointed at Newton Brown. "That man

84

is the biggest potential threat to the President's security in the country. Guard him with your lives!"

With a squeal, Newt Brown was out of his chair and scurrying for the door, zig-zagging between the three larger men.

He almost made it. Steve Hammond flicked a blackjack from a hip pocket and took a swing at him as he passed, and missed. Wes, now in a gunfighter's crouch, blurred into motion and magically there was a .357 Caliber Magnum in his hand.

"Clear out of the way," Wes yelled. "I'll nail him."

However, Weigand Patrick had stuck a foot out, tripping up the desperate little man, so that he smashed, face first, into the rug.

While the two burly Secret Service men grabbed him up by both arms, Weigand Patrick glared at them. "Holy Smokes, I said *guard*, not kill him." But then he twisted his face in thought. "Although, come to think of it, maybe that'd be the easiest thing."

"Help," Newt Brown squealed. "Police!"

"Shut up!" Weigand said. "I've got to think." He went back to his bar and took down another slug of the Irish. It didn't seem to have any effect.

He turned finally to the two Secret Service men. "Take him over to Blair House and stick him in the south suite. You're not to leave him, night or day. And nobody else is to get near him. Above all, don't let him talk to anybody. If anybody trys to talk to him, shoot them."

Steve Hammond said briskly, "Nobody talks to him but us, eh?"

A new thought came to Weigand Patrick and he glared. "Listen," he said. "The same thing applies to you two. You don't talk to him, either. Steve, if Wes talks to this man, shoot Wes; Wes, if Steve talks to him, shoot Steve."

The little man said pathetically, "Suppose I have to go to the bathroom, or something?"

"Use sign language," Weigand snapped. "All right, get out of here."

When they were gone, he stared down at his desk for awhile. Finally, he reached out and switched on the phone screen. It took a time to get the person he wanted.

When the other had faded in, he said, "Look, Edgar, what ever happened to that prison down on Dry Tortugas?"

"What prison?"

Weigand Patrick said impatiently, "Following the Civil War, and Lincoln's assassination, there was a lot of hushing up about the trial and the people involved with Booth. The doctor who had treated Booth was shipped down to that prison and spent the rest of his life there, the strictest orders being that he not be allowed to talk to anybody. Sort of a Man-In-the-Iron-Mask sort of thing."

The one on the screen said blankly, "What about it?"

Weigand Patrick said, "I have four men I want sent to that prison and kept there under the same circumstances. Absolutely no conversation with anybody at all, even prison guards."

The other could see it was obviously a matter of the highest security. In his day he had been a man of quick reactions, quick decisions.

"Very well," he snapped, his somewhat aged voice not quite cracking. "Who are the four?"

"Two of the President's Secret Service guards, Steve Hammond and Wes Fielding, and the man they're guarding, an inventor named Newton Brown."

"Got it, Weigand. And who is the fourth man we take down to Dry Tortugas?"

"Fred Moriarty."

86

Chapter Nine

The two were seated at the heavy mahogany table when the Professor bustled in, followed at a trot by his secretary, Walthers.

They had been killing time discussing the latest developments of Project Porpoise.

Les Frankle said, "That's what they get for teaching overgrown fish to talk."

Jimmy Leath said, "Porpoises aren't fish. They're mammals, like we are; and have as big a brain capacity. It's just that they live in the ocean, instead of on land. What's wrong with teaching them to talk?"

"First they wanted pay to keep track of the herds of meat whales, so the President sent them a committee of long-winded negotiaters, and gave them a long song and dance about the Wagner Act, or something. At any rate, now they've formed a union."

"Lads, lads," the Professor said jovially. "Let us be about business."

The two came to their feet until the roly-poly older man took a chair at the table's end.

At first glance, possibly owing to the similarity of their dress, they might have been taken for being from the same mold, but not at second. The thinnest was wry and bitter of face; the youngest, unsure and unhappy.

The Professor had an informal word for each of his youthful staff. "Well, James how is the ulcer? Are we still on milk?"

Jimmy Leath was still on milk.

The Professor turned to the other. "Lester, has Irene

convinced you as yet that you should resign from Doolittle Research and take a position a bit more, ah, worthy
of your scholarly abilities?"

Les Frankle flushed. "Well, no sir, not yet."

The Professor smiled at him in fatherly condescen-
sion. "I can not quite see her point, lad. Where would
your efforts gain greater remuneration than here? Especially in these days of unemployment."

Les squirmed. "Well, it's not that, Professor Doolittle.
Irene's a do-gooder . . . well, in the best sense of the
word. She thinks the fact that the best brains in the
country are going into such fields as advertising, sales
promotion, motivational research to learn how best to
con the consumer . . ."

The Professor's shaggy white eyebrows went up.
"Con?"

Les said apologetically, "A but of slang Irene used,
sir. It's derived from confidence man."

"*Indeed.* So our crusader, Irene, lacks sympathy for
our free enterprise society, eh? By George, where would
you lads be, fresh out of the university, if there were not
such organizations as Doolittle Research, ah, to take you
in, and give you the opportunity to exercise your fledg-
ling abilities?"

Les Frankle lacked the ability to dissimulate. He said
earnestly, "Well, that's her point, sir. She says that such
organizations as this take the country's best brains, use
them while they're still fresh and trained in the latest
techniques, then in a few years discard them for somebody younger and fresher. And by that time the individual is either disillusioned . . ." he looked at Jimmy
". . . or has ulcers, or is an alcoholic, or some such."

"A discouraging picture, By George," the Professor
chuckled. "However, I suppose we should get to business lads."

He turned to Jimmy Leath. "So what have our depth interviews revealed in the way of an adult hero around whom we could build a fad to end all fads?" He added unctuously, "Thus helping to end the depression."

The emaciated psychologist bunched his right hand into a fist and rubbed it across his stomach. "On the first level of conscious, rational thought they think in terms of the president, or some top business figure, especially one who's worked his own way up. If you take in the past they'll come up with Lincoln, Washington, possibly Jesus."

Les grunted. "That's on the rational level," he muttered. "What happens when we get down to the preconscious, the subconscious?"

Jimmy looked at him and nodded. "Now, that's another thing. They'll run everywhere from some Tri-Di star, especially one who's hung on for a long time and always played sympathetic, masculine roles, to some military hero, ranging from Alexander to Custer."

The Professor was frowning, albeit benignly. "And when we get to the deepest levels of consciousness?"

Jimmy rubbed his stomach again and grimaced. "Billy the Kid, Wild Bill Hickok, Nero, the Marquis de Sade, Hitler——"

"Hitler!" Les Frankle ejaculated.

Jimmy nodded. "You'd be surprised how many can identify with someone who exercised absolute power."

The Professor said jovially, "Lads, lads, we are departing from reality. A gunman or a great sadist of the past, I hardly think would do."

Jimmy twisted in his chair and said, "What about Wyatt Earp? He was a gun thrower but usually on the side of the law."

"Usually, but not always," Les nodded. "I thought about him. A good muckraker would soon have our hero

89

all dirtied up. Besides, he's old hat. He was on TV for years back before the depression."

"How about Daniel Boone?" Jimmy said.

"Too nearly like Davy Crockett. That Wild West that Was bit has been done too thoroughly," Les said. "At long last it's on it's way out."

"Amen," Jimmy murmured.

The Professor looked at him a bit testily. "Possibly you are correct James. But we have been weeks upon this, confound it. What is an alternative?"

Les said unhappily, "I thought of J.E.B. Stuart, the cavalry commander."

Jimmy said, "The military is always good. Half of the heroes our probes dug up were military. Lots of blood and guts."

The Professor said, "Lads, remember the requirements I gave you. This fad is for adults, By George, not children. I submit that if we made a Confederate general our hero we could sell toy sabers to children, Confederate grey uniforms and slouch hats. But that would be about it. Lads, let us start thinking *big*."

They sat in long silence.

The Professor looked at Les Frankle indulgently. "Well, Lester, where are these super-brains your good wife, Irene, complains that Doolittle Research is milking?"

Les colored and said unhappily, "Well, Irene had an idea."

"Irene! My dear Lester, I informed you of the high security nature of this project. By George, what would happen if the think tank's campaign were to be revealed before we even got underway? The public must think this fad spontaneous, By George, or it will never take!"

Les said, "I discuss all my work with Irene, sir. You've got to remember that she's a psychologist too. One of the best."

90

Jimmy said, soothing stomach pains with massage, "What'd she suggest? I still say some military figure."

"Her idea comes under that category—in a way," Les said. "Jeanne d'Arc."

"John Dark?" the Professor said, "Confound it, Lester, I've never even heard of the gentleman."

The two looked at him. Les smiled as though trying to be appreciative of a humorous sally. Jimmy closed his eyes, as though his ulcer was on campaign.

"Joan of Arc," Les said. He looked at Jimmy. "That gives you your military."

"A woman," Jimmy grumbled. "Not even a woman, a girl. I thought we were looking for a hero."

The Professor pursed plump lips. "Women spent some eighty percent of the average family income. Tell us more, Lester."

Les said, "Well, Irene thinks that Joan has just about everything." He looked at Jimmy again. "The muckrakers wouldn't be able to dig up much about her. She was only nineteen and a virgin when they burned her and there's a lot of sentimental pull in a martyr." He looked back at Professor Doolittle. "Irene says you could use her sword as a symbol."

"A symbol?"

"Irene says all big fads—or movements—have to have a symbol. Davy Crockett had the coonskin hat, the Nazis had their swastika. For that matter, the Mohammedans had their crescent and the Christians their cross."

The Professor said, "By George."

Jimmy growled, "What could you sell in the name of Joan of Arc?"

Warren Dempsey Witherson hacked his throat clear and said, "What could we sell, in the name of Joan of Arc?"

The Professor refreshed both their glasses. "Kid, you are not up on your history. She is a natural. She hasn't been done for decades in the movies. We shall have to do a super-spectacular, in the Tri-Di medium, this time. Some old playwright, Bernard Shaw, did a play on her. We shall revive it on Broadway and sent out three or four road shows to boot. Mark Twain wrote a biography of her, in fictional form. It is on the public domain. We shall issue it in a special deluxe limited edition, in regular hardcovers and finally in paperbacks. We shall line up a top dressing house in Paris and start off a Joan of Arc style revival. It is about time women got something brand new in the way of fashion. They can't think of anything else to reveal."

"There isn't anything else left to reveal," Warren Dempsey Witherson told him. "They've revealed everything."

"We'll hide it again," the Professor explained. "The Demure Look. Pageboy hair-do. Heather perfume. *Fleur-de-lis* designs on everything from textiles to earrings."

"Flour de lee?" Witherson said.

"It is kind of a design the old French kings used, according to one of my lads. That is just the beginning. Wait until we unleash all the boys. We shall start a Joan of Arc comic strip, of course. And Joan of Arc dolls for the tots. Then we will have to concoct some items for the Dauphin."

"The dolphin?" Witherson said blankly. "Dolphins are porpoises, aren't they? You mean we're even going to sell this fad to those talking fish they've been training to herd whales?"

"Dauphin, Dauphin, not dolphin. Jimmy Leath, one of my double-domed lads suggests we change history about a bit and make the French prince her boyfriend. Then we shall be able to cop a few scores from the men, too."

"Can we do that?" the aged grifter said nervously.

"Don't be a winchell, Kid. They made a hero out of Davy Crockett, did they not? Did you ever read a biography of that character? We can make a lover out of Charles, or whatever his name was."

Warren Dempsey Witherson looked at his long-time friend in admiration. "Where'd you get all this poop, Professor?"

Professor Doolittle was modest. "I have a secretary do up a brief from the Encyclopedia," he said. "I shall have it sent around to you."

"I guess I'll buy it, Professor," Witherson said finally. "I'll take the shuttle down to Greater Washington tomorrow. The President's having another brain trust meeting. The depression's getting worse by the minute. Then, given his approval, I'll lob over to Frisco and get the Oedipus Group, the businessman's think tank, to work. Anything special you can think of?"

"One thing. Have them line up every manufacturer in the country that is set to turn out swords."

. Witherson blinked.

"Little decorative swords, scabbards and belts. A sword about two feet long. In every price range, from a few bucks up to bejeweled deals to go with evening wear— assume there are a few broads still in the country that can afford evening wear. It is our symbol, the sword. Kind of a crusader-like cross for a hilt and guard. You will have some boys in the ad outfits who will get the idea. We want to have the manufacturers all sewed up before the wisenheimers begin to jump on our bandwagon."

Chapter Ten

Old Sam, sprawled out on a park bench with several of his cronies, was saying, "You fellers expect too much from the govermint. It don't stand to experience to expect too much from the govermint. You never could."

One of the others said, "Why, I dunno, Sam. Seems to me the govermint does pretty good. When I was a youngster back into the first depression, if somebody doled out a bowl of watered down soup, all the newspapers yelled it was creeping socialism. Now maybe nine folks out of ten is on relief. What can you call that but progress?"

Sam said, "That ain't what I meant. Though I ain't saying this is a *better* depression than the last one. One thing, we didn't have inflation back them days. In fact, it was kinda the other way around. Things got cheaper. Everybody was going around shining shoes. There was three shoeshine men for every pair of shoes that was up to taking a shining. But what did they get? Five cents to shine a pair of shoes."

He motioned, with a sweeping gesture, at the several hundred shoeshine men who lined the edges of the park, none of them busy. "But then the govermint found out you didn't need any gold in Fort Knox to back up the money. All you needed was an automated printing press. Now we got inflation. Shoe shines, a dollar a throw. Sure, I admit, that's progress, it's a cry and shame to ask a growed man to shine shoes for five cents."

"Well, what did you mean?" one of the others yawned.

Sam said, "I mean you can't expect these govermint fellers to be smart. Too busy, for one thing. You take into the Second War. When we first got into it, some big wheel in Washington, he figgered people wasn't war conscious enough, like they was over to England and France and all. So what did he figger out? He passed a rule against sliced bread. So everybody went out and had to buy bread knives so they could slice their own bread. And then about six months later, the govermint decided it was okay to slice bread again. The big emergency was over. So those bakeries that still had their old bread slicers, they oiled them up again and started slicing the bread. And the bakeries that didn't, they hadta buy new ones."

One of the others said, "I knowa better un than that. I was living out to California. In those days they was rationing gasoline like crazy. You hadta have coupons and all. Anyway, out in the oil country we was producing high octane gas for the war planes, and a by-product, like, of aviation gas, is white gas. They had white gas all over the place, and finally no place to store it all. So, do you think they give it out to the people? Shucks no, that ain't the govermint's style. They poured it out on the ground."

One of the oldsters squirmed in his seat in memory. "I was in England during the war. It wasn't so bad in England. Those Limeys are a caution. Talk about govermint fellers not being so smart. Those there Limeys were. They used to charge us Americans rent for the airfields we was flying from to protect London from the Messerschmidts and all."

Old Sam said, "That's where I was for a spell. England. Got good draft brew in England. The best is Bass Ale. I figure I musta drank three, four hogsheads of Bass Ale whilst I was to England."

The air force veteran was indignant. "You don't know Bass from a hole in the ground," he grumbled. "The best beer into England is dark Stout. I must drunk half the country dry of its Stout."

One of the others said, "Them Limeys wasn't so smart. Remember when they was up against it, like, with all Hitler's submarines and all? Well sir, Roosevelt he gave them fifty destroyers to help out, and you know what they did with them? They put 'em in drydock for six months or so changing 'em around so that officer's quarters would be larger and the enlisted men's quarters would be smaller. That's the British for you."

"That's the military mind for you," Old Sam said.

"What's a military mind?"

"The kind where the owner can take off his shirt without unbuttoning the collar."

"Heh, heh, that's pretty good Sam."

Chapter Eleven

Number One was radiating fury as he stalked heavily down the corridors of the Ministry of Internal Affairs. On the surface, his face displayed nothing—which meant nothing. There was simply a raging aura of trouble.

Veljko Gosnjak, posted with one other before the office of Aleksander Kardelj, winced when he saw the Party head approaching. He muttered from the side of his mouth, "Watch out. He's on a rampage. In this mood, he'd as well set you to filling salt shakers in the Siberian mines as . . ."

But Andrei Zorin was now near enough that he might hear, and Veljko Gosnjak cut himself off abruptly and came to even stiffer attention.

Number One ignored them both and pushed on through the door.

Even as his right-hand man looked up from his work, Zorin was growling ominously. "Zeit! Kardelj, I am beginning to suspect that, American Hollywood saying is correct. If you have a Hungarian for a friend, you don't need any enemies. Do you know the latest from that brain-wave experiment of yours?"

Kardelj was close enough to the other personally to at least pretend lack of awe. He grinned and said, "You mean young Frol? Sit down, Andrei. A drink?"

The Number Two Party man swiveled slightly and punched out a code on a series of buttons. Almost immediately, an area of approximately one square foot sank down from the upper right-hand corner of his desk to rise again bearing two chilled glasses.

Zorin snorted his anger but took up one of the glasses. "These everlasting gadgets from the West," he growled. "One of these days, this confounded desk of yours will give you an electric shock that will set me to looking for a new assistant." He threw the contents of the glass back over his palate. "If I don't start looking before that time," he said ominously.

Kardelj said, "But what is it that young Frol has done?"

His superior's face resumed its dark expression. He growled, "You know Velimir Crvenkovski, of course."

Kardelj raised scanty eyebrows. "Of course, vice chairman of the Secretariat of Agriculture."

Andrei Zorin had lowered his clumsy bulk into a chair. Now he said heavily, his voice dangerous, "Velimir and I were partisans together. It was I who converted him to the Party, introduced him to the works of Lenin while we squatted in foxholes."

"Of course," the other repeated. "I know the story very well. A good Party man, Comrade Crvenkovski, never failing to vote with you in meetings of the Executive Committee."

"Yes," Zorin growled ominously. "And your precious Frol Krasnaya, your expediter, has removed him from his position as Supreme Commissar of Agriculture in Bosnatia."

Aleksander Kardelj cleared his throat. "I have just been reading the account. It would seem that agricultural production has fallen off considerably in the past five years. Ah . . . Comrade Crvenkovski evidently had brought to his attention that wild life in the countryside, particularly birds, accounted for the loss of hundreds of thousands of tons of cereals annually."

"A well-known fact," Zorin rasped. He finished what remained of his drink, and reached forward to punch out the order for a fresh one. "What has that got to do with this pipsqueak using the confounded powers you invested him with to dismiss one of the best Party men in the Soviet Complex?"

His right-hand man had not failed to note that he was now being given full credit for the expediter idea. He said, still cheerfully, however, "It would seem that Comrade Crvenkovski issued top priority orders to kill off, by whatever means possible, all birds. Shotguns, poison, nets were issued by the tens of thousands to the peasants."

"*Well?*" his superior said ominously. "Obviously, Velimir was clear minded enough to see the saving in gross production."

"Um-m-m," Kardelj said placatingly. "However, it seems as though the balance of nature calls for the presence of wildlife, and particularly birds. The increase in destructive insects has more than counter-balanced the amount of cereals the birds once consumed. Ah, Zorin," he said with a wry smile, "I sould suggest we find another position for Comrade Crvenkovski."

The secretary-receptionist looked up at long last at the very average-looking young man before him. "Yes?" he said impatiently.

The stranger said, "I would like to see Comrade Broz."

"Surely you must realize that the Commissar is one of the busiest men in Transbalkania, Comrade." There was mocking sneer in the tone. "His time is not at the disposal of every citizen."

The newcomer looked at the petty authority thoughtfully. "Do you so address everyone that enters this office?" he asked mildly.

The other stared at him, flabbergasted. He suddenly banged upon a button on the desk.

When the security guard responded to the summons, he gestured curtly with his head at the newcomer. "Throw this fool out, Petar," he rapped.

Frol Krasnaya shook his head, almost sadly. "No," he said. "Throw *this* man out." He pointed at the secretary-receptionist.

The guard called Petar blinked at each of them in turn.

Frol brought forth his wallet, fidgeted a moment with the contents, then flashed his credentials. "State expediter," he said nervously. "Under direct authority of Comrade Zorin." He looked at the suddenly terrified receptionist. "I don't know what alternative work we can find to fit your talents. However, if I ever again hear of you holding down a position in which you meet the public, I will . . . will . . . see you imprisoned."

The other scurried from the room before Frol thought of more to say.

Frol Krasnaya then looked at the guard for a long moment. He said finally, unhappy still, "What are you needed for around here?"

"Comrade, I am the security guard."

99

"You didn't answer my question." Frol's hands were jittering so he jammed them into his pockets.

Petar was no brain, at best. Finally, however, he came up triumphantly with "Yes, Comrade. I guard Comrade Broz and the others from assassins. I am armed." He proudly displayed the Mikoyan Noiseless which he had holstered under his left shoulder.

Frol said, "Go back to your superior and inform him that I say you are superfluous. No longer are commissars automatically to be guarded. If . . . well, if our people dislike individual commissars sufficiently to wish to assassinate them, maybe they need assassination."

Petar stared at him.

"Oh, get out," Frol said, with attempted sharpness. But then, "What door leads to Comrade Broz's office?"

Petar pointed, then got out. At least he knew how to obey orders, Frol decided. What was there about the police mentality? Were they like that before they became police, and the job sought them out? Or did the job make them all that way?

He pushed his way through the indicated door. The office beyond held but one inhabitant who stood, hands clasped behind his back, while he stared in obvious satisfaction at a wall of charts, maps and graphs.

The average young man looked at some of the lettering on the charts and shook his head. He said, his voice hesitant, "Commissar Broz?"

The other turned, frowning, not recognizing his caller and surprised to find him here without announcement. He said, "Yes, young man?"

Frol presented his credentials again.

Broz had heard of him. He hurried forth a chair, became expansive in manner. A cigar? A drink? A great pleasure to meet the Comrade Expediter. He had heard a great deal about the new experiment initiated by Comrade Zorin and ably assisted by Aleksander Kardelj. Happily, an expediter was not needed in the Transbalkian Steel Complex. It was expanding in such wise as to be the astonishment of the world, both East and West.

"Yes," Frol began glumly, "but——"

Broz was back on his feet and to his wall of charts and graphs. "See here," he beamed expansively. "This curve is steel production. See how it zooms? A veritable Sputnik, eh? Our statistics show that we are rapidly surpassing even the foremost of the Western powers."

Frol Krasnaya said, almost apologetically in veiw of the other's enthusiasm, "That's what I came to discuss with you, Comrade. You see, I've been sitting around, ah, in the local wineshops, talking it over with the younger engineers and the men on the job."

The other frowned at him. "Talking what over?"

"This new policy of yours." Frol's voice was diffident.

"You mean overtaking the steel production of the West, by utilizing *all* methods of production?" The commissar's voice dropped. "I warn you Comrade, the germ of this idea originated with Zorin himself. We are old comrades."

"I'm sure you are," Frol said pessimistically, and suppressing an urge to bite at the skin of his thumb. "However . . . well, I'm not so sure Number One will admit your program originated with him. At least, it hasn't worked out that way in the recent past when something soured."

The other bug-eyed. He whispered, "That approaches cynical treason, Comrade."

The former *Pravda* reporter half nodded, said discouragedly, "You forget. By Comrade Zorin's own orders I . . . I can do no wrong. But so much for that. Now, well, this steel program. I'm afraid it's going to have to be scrapped."

"Scrapped!" the Commissar of the Transbalkanian

Steel Complex stared at his visitor as though the other was rabid. "You fool! Our steel progress is the astonishment of the world! Why, not only are our ultramodern plants, built largely with foreign assistance, working on a twenty-four hour a day basis, but we also have thousands of secondary smelters. Some are so small as to be operated by a handful of comrade citizens; some in backyard establishments by schoolchildren, working smelters of but a few tons monthly capacity."

The newly created State Expediter held up a hand dispiritedly. "I know. I know. Thousands of these backyard smelters exist . . . uh . . . especially in parts of the country where there is neither ore nor fuel available."

The commissar looked at him.

The younger man said, his voice seemingly deprecating his words. "The schoolchildren, taking time off from their studies, of course, bring scrap iron to be smelted. And they bring whatever fuel they can find, often pilfered from railway yards. And the more scrap and fuel they bring, the more praise they get. Unfortunately, the so-called scrap often turns out to be kitchen utensils, farm tools, even, on at least one occasion, some railroad tracks, from a narrow gauge line running up to a lumbering project, not in use that time of the year. Sooner or later, Comrade Broz, the nation is going to have to replace those kitchen utensils and farm tools and all the rest of the scrap that isn't really quite scrap."

The commissar began to protest heatedly, but Fro Krasnaya shook his head and tried to firm his less than dominating voice. "But even that's not the worst of it. Taking citizens away from their real occupations, or studies, and putting them to smelting steel where no ore exists. The worst of it is, so many young engineer friends tell me, that while the steel thus produced might have been a marvel back in the days of the Hittites, it hardly reaches specifications today. Perhaps it might be used ultimately to make simple farm tools such as hoes and rakes; if so, it would make quite an endless circle, because that is largely the source of the so-called steel to begin with—tools, utensils and such. But it hardly seems usable in modern industry."

The commissar had gone pale with anger by now. He put his two fists on his desk and leaned upon them, staring down at his seated visitor. "Comrade," he bit out, "I warn you. Comrade Zorin is enthusiastic about my successes. Beyond that, not only is he an old comrade but my brother-in-law as well."

Frol Krasnaya nodded, unenthusiastically, and his voice continued to quiver. "So the trained engineers under you, have already warned me. However, Comrade Broz, you are . . . well, no longer Commissar of the Steel Complex. My report has already gone in to Comrades Zorin and Kardelj."

Chapter Twelve

Weigand Patrick, a sheaf of papers held in hand, came happily into the office of the President's personal secretary. He opened his mouth to say something, snapped it shut again.

"Holy smokes!" he blurted. "Who did it!"

"Did what?" Scotty MacDonald said.

"Your blouse. Who tore it?"

"Oh, don't be silly. This is the latest thing. The Cretan Revival."

"Cretan Revival! Wasn't that Agnes Sorel Revival bad

enough? Now both of them are sticking out." He added, suspiciously, "And you've put lipstick or something on the tips."

"I have not."

"You have so. You're a shameless hussy. Which reminds me. When are we going to finally cosummate this seduction?"

Scotty snorted. "The way you operate, I'm thinking of getting somebody else to do the job."

He looked at her incredulously. "You can't do that."

"Why not?"

"Because I owe it to you to be first. I'm the most incomparable lover in the world."

"Ha!"

He leaned over her desk earnestly. "But I am. I'm half German, half Irish, and half French and everybody knows that makes the most competent lover possible."

"That makes three halves," she muttered sarcastically, "and that's not even counting half-assed."

"What?"

"Nothing," she yawned. "What makes you such an incomparable lover? What do you do that anybody else doesn't?"

He looked around the room, as though checking that no one else might hear, then bent nearer and whispered, "I kiss a woman's navel."

She stared at him, "Kiss a woman's navel? What's so wonderful about that?"

"Yes, but, *from inside?*"

"Oh, shut up, you fool. How's it going?"

"So far, so good. We had to move the whole shebang into the Green Room, so we could crowd all the news boys in."

She looked at him suspiciously. "Something's going on here I don't know about. What's the point in having the press present at a Fireside Chat? It's live. They could get it on their Tri-Di sets."

Weigand Patrick grinned slyly. "I want them present. Real eye witnesses. So nobody can say later it was a Tri-Di rigged optical illusion. I wonder what happened to that kid from *Pravda,* Frol Krasnaya. I especially wanted *Pravda* to be there."

"Another thing. What happened to Fred Moriarty? He hasn't been around for a week."

Weigand put his forefinger to the side of his nose in a burlesque of the presidential gesture of slyness and winked at her. "He's all right. He'll probably be back after the elections are over. He's taken a trip south."

"Something's going on here, WeeWee Patrick, that I don't think I like. What's Old Chucklehead all done up in that conservative suit for? He looks like a preacher. Usually, he tends toward Hawaiian shirts and slacks a juvenile delinquent would consider far out."

"Don't call him that!" Weigand said. "And stop calling me WeeWee. You'll see. After this broadcast, this Administration will have a prestige that'll carry it on for the next half dozen campaigns. I'm thinking of running him at least four times, like Roosevelt."

"That can't be done, any more."

"That's what you think, honey. After tonight, we're going to have Congress sitting in our hand."

"Well, watch out what they do in your palm," Scotty snorted.

Weigand looked at his watch. "I'll have to get on in there. The Sachem is scheduled on in ten minutes. I want to make some preliminary remarks, especially to that bastard Harrison from *Newsweek* who's been writing those Anti-Adams columns."

He looked down at her severely, "How about tonight. Let's have a definite answer. What do you say?"

Scotty said sarcastically, "As Benjamin Franklin put it, Masturbation is its own reward."

He glared at her for a moment then said, "Listen, that reminds me of something. That song and dance you were giving me the other night about Ponce DeLeon's pants. How they fell in the Fountain of Youth. What finally happened?"

"What do you think happened? He became the biggest foul-up in the history of seduction. Finally, the Indians killed him."

"Hmmm. The Indian *men* or the Indian *women?*"

She snorted at him. "Guess."

Weigand Patrick staggered back into Scotty's room, his face ashen.

Scotty MacDonald, who was still staring in fascination at the Tri-Di box, in the corner of her office, turned to him.

"Holy smokes," he muttered.

"What in the world happened, there?"

"Holy smokes," he protested.

She said, "There was something funny in the transmission. It was like a comedy effect. Some kind of static."

He groaned and sank into a chair, and put his head in his hands.

"The halo," he said. "The damned halo was on wrong."

"Halo?" Scotty said. "You mean that thing like a ferris wheel, or a fireworks pinwheel, or whatever it looked like?"

"It was supposed to be horizontal," he moaned loudly. "*Horizontal* not vertical."

"Old Chucklehead sure looked funny," Scotty said sympathetically.

Polly Adams wandered in from the presidential study, her expression vaguely troubled.

She said, "Weigand, I think Horace was looking for you."

He groaned aloud.

The First Lady said vacantly, "I'm going to have to tell William to stop putting so little vermouth in the Martinis—or something." She brightened slightly. "Perhaps I should see my oculist."

Weigand moaned.

Polly Adams said, "Perhaps I'll just tell him to put *less* vermouth in." She wandered out again.

Scotty looked after her thoughtfully. She said, "I'm going to have to suggest to Hilda that Polly be sent back to that beauty-and-health diet spot in Colorado, to get dried out again."

Weigand groaned and said, "Scotty, get me Edgar, will you?"

"Edgar?"

"On the phone screen. Fred Moriarty's coming back sooner than I thought."

Chapter Thirteen

The conference table was crowded, the room thick with cigar smoke, Walthers was trotting back and forth to the bar, refreshing glasses.

A large tweedy type, a huge bent-stem pipe in the side of his mouth, was saying, "We'll have to issue these on various price levels. Make it a status symbol, the amount you've blown on your Pilgrimage of Jeanne d'Arc game."

Somebody interrupted. "I don't like using them fancy foreign names. What's the matter with using her right name, Joan of Arc?"

Les Frankle, sitting to one side, said unhappily, "The only record we have of her signature, she signed her name *Jeanette*." He hadn't pitched his voice high enough to be heard.

A fat man in the gaudy clothing of the Coast, puffed cheeks and rumbled in agreement. "Ed's right. Using, like, French words and all that'd just antagonize folks back in the boondocks. Make her sound too high falutin. Let's call her Joan of Arc."

The tweedy type closed his eyes momentarily, in mute protest but said, "Why don't we do this? On the game sets peddling for only ten dollars, we'll call it the Joan of Arc Pilgrimage. But on the sets retailing for twenty-five and up, we'll use the Jeanne d'Arc name. The people with boodle enough left to invest that amount in a game will get an added status symbol in the French."

The Professor, at table's end, had been beaming benignly at the discussion. Now he put in, "Gentlemen, we must remember in concocting this game to strike the correct intellectual level. We do not wish something as double-domed as *Scrabble*, that would eliminate too many potential customers. Nor anything as simple as *Parchesi*, that is for children and this is an adult fad."

Jimmy Leath, as silent thus far as Les Frankle, grumbled, "And nothing as crass as *Monopoly*. Remember, Joan is a saint. Very high moral tone, that sort of thing."

The tweedy type took his pipe from his mouth and said, "We have all that in mind. However, the Pilgrimage is strictly for adults, but Joan is taking on with the kids too."

"Sure is," someone else muttered. We flubbed on the mother and daughter Joan of Arc clothes sets. Way behind on orders."

"I suggest we bring out a simplified form of the game for children," the tweedy type said.

"For children and our simpler adults," Les Frankle said unhappily.

"Very well, By George," the Professor said. "So it is with the Pilgrimage game. The Maid is really catching on."

"What's this *the Maid* stuff?" the fat man from California said. "You're talking about Joan, aren't you?"

Les Frankle spoke up, loud enough to be heard this time. "Well, women belonging to the Jeanne d'Arc Clubs have taken to calling her The Maid of Orleans. Irene says it's an instinctive reaction toward the virgin principle which dominates——"

"Who's the hell's Irene?" the tweedy type wanted to know.

Les Frankle looked at him. "Irene's my wife," he said. "Doctor Irene Frankle." He shifted uncomfortably. "She's also national president of the Jeanne d'Arc Clubs."

"*She is?*" the Professor blurted. "No wonder we were not able to get a percentage of the dues from those clubs."

Somebody else said, "We worked that out two weeks ago. It'd be too obvious if our syndicate tried to get in on spontaneously organized clubs. Too bad, though, they've swept the nation."

The Professor looked at Les accusingly. "You failed to inform me of Irene's membership, not to speak of her presidency, By George."

"Well," Les said doggedly, "you know how Irene is, sir. She's got a regular phobia about joining all these women's do-gooder outfits and all. She believes that organizations like this syndicate . . ." he flushed and nodded around unhappily to the table as a whole ". . . are, well, destroying the nation."

The tweedy type blurted, "Just what do you mean by that, young man!"

Les looked at him unhappily. "Well, that's what Irene says, sir. Such organizations as Doolittle Research, the other MR outfits and the ad agencies manipulate human motivations and desires and develop a need for products with which the public has previously been unfamiliar, perhaps even undesirous of purchasing. She thinks that's ultimately turning the country into a nation of idiots, besides wasting natural resources."

The fat man was on his feet. "See here! I didn't come to this conference to be insulted." He glared at Professor Doolittle. "Who is this young ass, Professor?"

Doolittle came to his own feet, and lifted his chubby paws placatingly. "Gentlemen, gentlemen, please." He smiled benignly at Les Frankle, then returned to his confreres seated at the table.

"You members of the Oedipus Group think tank are, ah, pragmatic businessmen. My lad, Les, here, is a high trained double—that is, psychologist from one of the nation's very top universities. His field is mass behavior, gentlemen, and, By George, he knows it. In discussing mass behavior, gentlemen, you draw on Durkheim in sociology, Korzbski in semantics, Whitehead in symbolic logic—I could go on. How many of you are acquainted with the works of these, ah, to use the idiom, crystal gazers? Gentlemen, if the past couple of decades has taught the businessman anything, it is that we need more whiskers—ah, that is, professors—not fewer. My lads here, Lester and James, are top men in their fields, as you are in yours. We need them." He chuckled. "And they need the money we pay them."

He said indulgently, "And now shall we have a report from our publisher? Undoubtedly, you gentlemen are already aware that our biography of Joan is still at the top of the non-fiction best sellers, and two of our novels or

her are pushing second and fourth places. But now, this
series of children's books. . . ."

Chapter Fourteen

The knock came at the door in the middle of the night,
as Aleksander Kardelj had always thought it would.

From those early days of his party career, when his
ambitions had sent him climbing, pushing, tripping up
others, on his way to the top, he had expected it eventually.

Oh, his had been a different approach, on the surface,
an easygoing, gentler approach than one usually connected with members of the Secretariat of the Executive
Committee of the Party, but it made very little difference
in the very long view. When one fell from the heights,
he fell just as hard, whether or not he was noted for
his sympathetic easy humor.

The fact was, Aleksander Kardelj was not asleep when
the fist pounded at his door shortly after midnight. He
had but recently turned off, with a shaking hand, the
phone screen, after a less than pleasant conversation
with Andrei Zorin.

For the past ten years, Kardelj had been able to placate Zorin, even though Number One be at the peak of
a surly rage, rages which seemed to be coming with in-
creasing frequency of late. As the socio-economic system
of the People's Democratic Dictatorship became increasingly complicated, as industrialization with its modern
automation mushroomed in a geometric progression, the
comparative simplicity of governing was strictly of yes-

teryear. Industrialization calls for a highly educated element of scientists and technicians, nor does it stop there. One of sub-mentality can operate a shovel in a field, or even do a simple operation on an endless assembly line in a factory, but practically all workers must be highly skilled workers in the age of automation, and there is little room for the illiterate. The populace of the People's Dictatorship was no longer a dumb, driven herd, and their problems were no longer simple ones.

Yes, Number One was increasingly subject to his rages these days. It was Aleksander Kardelj's belief that Zorin was finding himself out of his depth. And he who is confused, be he ditchdigger or dictator, is a man emotionally upset.

Andrei Zorin's face had come onto the phone screen already enraged. He had snapped to his right-hand man, "Kardelj! Do you realize what the . . . that idiot of yours has been up to now?"

Inwardly, Kardelj had winced. His superior had been mountingly difficult of late, and particularly these past few days. He said now, cajolingly, "Andrei, I——"

"Don't call me Andrei, Kardelj! And please preserve me from your sickening attempts to fawn, in view of your treacherous recommendations of recent months."

Kardelj had never seen him this furious. He said placatingly, "Comrade Zorin, I had already come to the conclusion that I should consult you on the desirability of revoking this young troublemaker's credentials and removing him from the——"

"I am not interested in what you were *going* to do, Kardelj. I am already in the process of ending this traitor's activities. I should have known, when you revealed he was the son of Alex Krasnaya, that he was an enemy of the State, deep within."

Kardelj had enough courage left to say, "Comrade, it

112

would seem to me that young Krasnaya is a tanglefoot, but not a conscious traitor. I——"

"Don't call me comrade, Kardelj!" Number One roared. "I know your inner motivation. The reason you brought this Trotskyite wrecker to his position of ridiculous power. The two of your are in conspiracy to undermine my authority. I've heard about you Hungarians. The only people in the world that can go into a revolving door behind you and come out first! This will be brought before the Secretariat of the Executive Committee, Kardelj. You've gone too far, this time!"

Aleksander Kardelj had his shortcomings but he was no coward. He said, wryly, "Very well, sir. But would you tell me what Frol has done now? My office has had no report on him for some time."

"What has he done! You fool, you traitorous fool, have you kept no record at all? He has been in the Kirghiz area where my virgin lands program has been in full swing."

Kardelj cleared his throat at this point.

Zorin continued roaring. "The past three years, admittedly, the weather has been such, the confounded rains failing to arrive on schedule, that we have had our troubles. But this fool! This blundering traitorous idiot!"

"What has he done?" Kardelj asked, intrigued in spite of his position of danger.

"For all practical purposes he's ordered the whole program reversed. Something about a sandbowl developing, whatever that is supposed to mean. Something about introducing contour plowing, whatever nonsense that is. And even reforestating some areas. Some nonsense about watersheds. He evidently has blinded and misled the very men I had in charge. They are supporting him, openly."

Zorin, Kardelj knew, had been a miner as a youth,

with no experience whatsoever on the soil. However, the virgin lands project had been his pet. He envisioned hundreds upon thousands of square miles of maize, corn, as the Americans called it. This in turn would feed vast herds of cattle and swine so that ultimately the Soviet Complex would have the highest meat consumption in the world.

Number One was raging on. Something about a conspiracy on the part of those who surrounded him. A conspiracy to overthrow him, Andrei Zorin, and betray the revolution to the Western powers, but he, Andrei Zorin, had been through this sort of plot before. He, Andrei Zorin, knew the answers to such situations.

Aleksander Kardelj grinned wryly, and reached to flick off the screen. He twisted a cigarette into the small pipelike holder, lit it and waited for the inevitable.

It was shortly after that the knock came on his door.

Chapter Fifteen

Marv and Phoebe Sellers sat at the kitchen table of their house at 4011 Camino de Palmas, Tucson, Arizona.

Marv looked around at their packed belongings bitterly.

"Dave oughta be here with his truck, pretty soon," he said. "You sure your folks don't mind us moving in with them?"

Phoebe shrugged. "I suppose they mind, Marv. But what can they do? It's happening all around town; people move in with each other to save rent. How long do you think it'll take to sell the house?"

"I don't know, Phoebe. Houses ain't moving any too good

114

these days. Practically nothing's moving that I can see except maybe these crazy Joan of Arc fad things. You'd think folks would have more on their mind than running around wearing little swords during times like these."

"Keeps their minds offen their troubles, I guess," Phoebe said placidly. "Can't begrudge them that." She looked at him. "What do you think we'll get for the house, Marv?"

"Not very much, we ain't got much equity into it. Where's Old Sam?"

"He's in the next room, messing around in some of that old junk he had stored away in a trunk in the garage. What're we gonna do, Marv?"

He shrugged his depression. "I don't know, Phebe. Just go on relief like everybody else, I guess. What else?"

"I heard tell the city was cutting back on relief. They run out of money. They ain't even paying the teachers and the garbage men any more. It's getting to be a chore, burying the garbage out in the yard though precious little garbage we got these days, anyways. We eat it."

Old Sam came in chortling.

"What've you got there, fer crissake, Gramps?" Marv said disinterestedly.

"You'll see," the oldster chuckled. He had a big piece of cardboard in one hand, a box of crayons in the other. He laid the cardboard out on the table, selected a crayon and began to color in a big black zero.

Marv, frowning, got up and looked over his shoulder. He read, slowly, *Unemployed. Please Buy an Apple. 50¢.*

Old Sam chortled again. "You young people never listen to me when I tell you about the old days. You'll see. I'll make us some pocket money."

Marv said accusingly, "That sign used to read 5¢. How come you've upped it to 50¢?"

"Inflation," Old Sam said cryptically. "Found this here sign in the bottom of my trunk. Kind of forgot about it. You stand out on the street corner with a box of apples and this sign. Mint money."

"I'll bet, Gramps," Marv muttered.

Chapter Sixteen

The President was slumped in his chair at his brain trust round table, after still another disastrous conference. The only ones left were Fred Moriarty, and Weigand Patrick.

"Double-domes," Horace Adams said in complaint. "Craminently. First one wants to cut back government expenditures by firing half the bureaucracy. That puts near ten more million people on unemployment. Another one wants to bring up prices, like Roosevelt did, by plowing under cotton, that sort of thing. But they want to go him one better. This depression is *really* big. This time, they want to pour petroleum back into the wells, and shovel coal back into the mines."

Weigand Patrick and Fred Moriarty held their peace.

The President mumbled, "But that one from Princeton's right. We've got to save money some way. Fort Knox is practically empty."

His face brightened. "There's one thing, Weigand, get in touch with the National Aeronautics and Space Council to discontinue the Space program. Can't afford to be shooting all that crap up into the sky. If they won't allow me to liberate Mozambique and contain Finland, I don't see how we can afford to colonize the moon."

Weigand blinked. "Yes, Mr. President," he said. "The

116

moon base. How about the men we already have up there?"

"How many of them are there?"

"Eight altogether," Moriarty supplied.

"How much will it cost to bring them back?"

Moriarty looked vague. He had a wonderful tan these days, from his recent subjection to the Floridian sun; however, from time to time, his glances at Weigand Patrick were less than comradely.

Weigand clicked his pipe stem against his teeth unhappily. "I'd estimate about a billion dollars, Chief."

The President scratched himself. "This heavy underwear Polly has me in sure itches. You'd think that cutting down on the burning of oil would be something unnecessary in the White House."

Weigand lit his pipe. "Sets an example, sir," he said. "Johnson used to turn out the lights."

Horace Adams looked at him balefully. "Whatever you're smoking in that thing, smells like what I put on my strawberries."

"Strawberries?" Moriarty said blankly. "I put sugar and cream on mine."

The President snorted, "In the garden, not in the plate."

Weigand sighed and put his corncob back in his pocket.

The President thought about the space colonists on the moon for a long moment, sighed at another of his projects going down the drain and grunted. "Leave them there. They're expendable. Raise a big monument to them. It'll be cheaper. I'll speak at its dedication. Very sentimental."

Weigand winced but held his peace.

Horace Adams snorted, "What do you think about this reopening relationships with Cuba?"

117

"Well, it has its points, sir," Moriarty said. "Keep the unemployed a bit more tranquil. Back when times were booming, everybody was in a hurry and smoked cigarettes. Now that everybody's sitting around, watching Tri-Di, they've got time for a long smoke. Some people are pretty serious about that new slogan: What this country needs is a good dollar cigar—what with inflation."

The President grunted. "Talking about slogans, what do you think about the one proposed by Professor Markham to keep up morale? Prosperity Is Just Around the Corner."

Weigand said thoughtfully, "I think I've heard that somewhere before. My instinct is to believe it won't be well received by the older generations."

The President glared at him. "Confound it, Weigand, why don't *you* come up with something? You're supposed to be my whizz-bang advisor."

Weigand Patrick stirred in his chair, automatically he reached for his corncob, remembered and put it back. He said slowly, "To tell the truth, Mr. President, I think I have the germ of an idea."

"Well, in the name of Moses, what is it? I've been listening to drivel for the past four hours, a little more can't hurt."

Patrick nodded and absently reached for pipe and tobacco pouch still once again.

"Sir, remember when I was telling you how a depression got started? The slow start, and then the snowball effect? Just like boom begets boom, bust begets bust?"

"How could I forget, damn it? It was the first time I ever heard of a depression."

"Yes, sir. Well, it occurred to me that *somewhere* this depression had to start. Some single place in the country. Some single action." He paused for effect.

118

The President was staring at him, as was Fred Moriarty. a glimmering of hope far behind their eyes.

"So?" Horace Adams rasped.

Weigand shrugged his lazy shrug, and lit the corncob. "So, suppose we trace it down. Suppose we get to this root of the evil. This starting point."

The President still stared. His voice was slightly hoarse.

"Then what do we do?"

Weigand Patrick replaced the tobacco pouch in his right pocket, the matches in his left. He blew smoke from his nostrils.

"We play it by ear," he said.

Later, on his way back to his own office in the Right Wing, Weigand Patrick passed through Scotty's room.

She said, "Well, what did Old Chucklehead come up with this time? Another big plan to dam up the Missouri River and have it flow backward over the Rocky Mountains?"

"Nothing special," Weigand told her.

She made a face. "Listen, do you think we ought to shoot him?"

"Shoot him!" he blurted. "Holy smokes!"

She said, "Well? Here the country's in the biggest emergency in its history, and we've got the biggest chucklehead in the executive mansion, ever, and that's saying a lot when you consider some of the past ones. Talk about the bland leading the bland, ha!"

He said reasonably, "It doesn't do any good. It's been tried and you always wind up with somebody worse than the one you shot."

Scotty said worriedly, "We've got to do something. Did you catch that Tri-Di speech from the Senate, that old queen Smogborne?"

"What'd he have to say?"

"Legalization of homosexuality between consenting males. Like the British. He claims that the number of homos that would shack up together would start a boom in housing, and house furniture."

Weigand thought about it. "You know, come to think of it, in Hollywood alone. . . ." He shook his head in marvel. "I'd like a blow by blow description of the first night in that town if they legalized homosexuality."

Scotty snorted. "I wonder if he includes Lesbians. The way my sex life is going, I might consider——"

"Hey! None of that now. Listen, as soon as I get this new project under way——"

"Ha!" Scotty snorted. "My juices are already beginning to dry up, waiting for you. I'm an old maid and don't know it. Look, I hate to bring this up again, but why don't you marry me?"

"Marry you?" Weigand said plaintively. "I keep telling you, I'm a great lover, but I'd be a lousy husband. I'm so improvident, I can go into a cold shower and come out three dollars poorer."

Chapter Seventeen

"Doublets and hose?" Warren Dempsey Witherson said blankly. "Pseudo-mail? What in the hell is pseudo-mail?" He pushed his pince-nez glasses back onto the bridge of his nose with his left forefinger and stared at Jimmy Leath.

"Pseudo-mail is a new type of sweater we've brought out for men. It's practically the only thing selling now in sweaters. The industry is in a tizzy."

Witherson was still blank. "But what is it?"

"Pseudo-mail is a form of weave that makes the sweater look like mail." Neither of the two older men had yet reacted, so he grunted and added, "Mail was the predominant type of armor used in the days of Jeanne d'Arc."

"Oh," Warren Dempsey Witherson beamed. "And we're to publicize it, eh? My boy, from what you say, it doesn't need much publicizing."

"No sir. It seems to have swept the country, whether men want it or not. Our research shows that women, ultimately, buy, or influence to the decisive point, the buying of approximately eighty-five percent of male clothing."

"Well, how about these tin shirts the women are wearing?"

Jimmy ran a hand back through his hair in irritation. "Well, that's another thing. We didn't start that. It was spontaneous and other manufacturers got in on it before we could dominate the field."

"What's this, By George?" the Professor interjected, indignantly. He had been sitting quietly until now.

"Corselets," Jimmy Leath growled. "They're making them largely out of aluminum, but sometimes the lighter steel alloys. God knows, you've seen enough of the Joan of Arc illustrations we've put on the calendars and such. The popular idea is that in combat she wore a corselet. It's body armor, the breast plate and the back piece together."

Witherson was staring at him. "You mean, some grifter not on our team has managed to con the marks into wearing——"

The Professor interrupted indulgently. "What the good doctor is saying, James, is that it seems unlikely that a modern, style-conscious woman would be seen in public in such a contraption."

"I don't know, sir," Jimmy said. "The way they've done them up, they look cute. Besides, it wasn't until just lately they wore them in public, especially for evening wear. At first, it was just at their club meetings. You know, something like the Shriners in their Arab outfits, or the American Legion, or the Boy Scouts."

"Club meetings, eh?" the Professor said thoughtfully. He flicked his hand over an eye-button on his desk and said into empty air, "Walthers, send in Mr. Frankle."

While they waited, he said to Jimmy. "What's this about doublets and hose?"

Jimmy snorted. "That's another one that Les seemed to underestimate in his depth research. He figured there'd be a small market for 15th Century costume for masquerades. What we didn't figure on is the pressure these women seem to be able to put to bear once they get on the Joan of Arc kick. That and the fact that men haven't had any really basic change in their clothes since the Civil War. We're still wearing the same basic coats, vests and long trousered pants Lincoln did."

Witherson hacked thoughtfully a few times and then said, "I'll put the boys to work on it. Maybe we can get President Adams to give his next press conference in this new outfit. Doublet and hose, eh? I'll bring it up at the next brain trust meeting."

Jimmy shuddered but said, "It's no use our trying to pick it up now. Every men's clothing manufacturer in the country is switching. In a week or so, you'll be out of style wearing a suit."

Les Frankle, worried of expression, came in and said, "Yes, sir."

Doolittle picked up a report from his desk. "You wouldn't know anything about this complaint from the

French vintner concern that handles the Jeanne d'Arc Lorraine wines, the Saint Joan Rheims champagne and Joan of Arc Three Star Cognac?"

"Well, no sir," Les said. "Not much. I've been looking into this gold and diamond charm bracelet project with the designers from Tiff——"

The Professor interrupted easily. "Before I forget, you had better drop that charm with Joan being burnt at the stake. The one with the chip rubies for fire. A bit on the bad taste side, lad. By George, this fad must be kept on the highest moral level. Is that not so, Doctor?"

Doctor Witherson cleared his throat. "Our only motivation," he beamed. "That and aiding our great President to combat the depression."

"Now, these riots in Kansas by the members of the Jeanne d'Arc Clubs. This dashing into bars and liquor stores, breaking up bottles with those swords of theirs. Really, By George, what is up?"

"Well, sir, from what Irene says, the newspapers have the wrong idea. It's not a Carrie Nation sort of thing at all."

"Irene!" the Professor blurted.

"Who's Carrie Nation?" Jimmy Leath said.

Les said, "A feminist back in the Victorian period. She was a temperance leader. Used to go into saloons with a hatchet and break up the place."

"You mean," the Professor demanded, "That these Kansas riots aren't of a temperance nature?"

Les said uncomfortably, "Well, no sir. Not according to Irene. She says they're a spontaneous rebellion against those French wine companies using the Jeanne d'Arc name. It seems as though United Consumers reported on the Jeanne d'Arc wines and cognacs and found them unacceptable buys. Uh . . . I believe dishwater was the descriptive term."

"United Consumers!" the Professor blurted. "That consortium of subversives."

"Well, yes sir," Les said, flushing. "It seems as though the clubs have a ruling that all members have to subscribe to the montly United Consumers reports. Uh . . . Irene kind of rammed that requirement through."

Witherson was indignant. "This should be actionable. How could those Frog . . . ah, that is, French vintners possibly turn out a first grade product when you consider the score we rake off before——"

"Ah, Doctor," the Professor said placatingly. "We'll consider the matter in executive council, later."

Les said, "I think we're going to have trouble on that sports car deal too. That air cushion model that looks vaguely like an armored horse, and has the head of the Maid on . . ."

"Trouble?" Witherson bleated. "Why, the take we were to get on that——"

"Doctor, Doctor," the Professor said. He turned a pompous eye on Les Frankle. "I suppose you have further inside information from Irene?"

"Well, in a way. She mentioned, kind of in passing, at dinner last night, that the clubs were going to boycott the car. Too big and heavy for average use, too expensive to run, and most likely the style will be obsolete within a year. Besides that, she says half the cost went into its silly decorations. According to Irene, it's time for the women of the country to put their feet down in regard to the kind of cars we're buying."

The Professor's eyes went to Jimmy Leath. "Well, James, my lad, do you have any ideas? Both the French wine deal and the line-up with the Saint Joan sports car were sizeable amounts."

Jimmy grunted sourly. He said, "We're putting out three different Jeanne d'Arc magazines now, one for the upper lowers, one for the lower middles and one for the quality market. We might suggest to the concerns involved that they step up their advertising and at the same time we'll do some free articles pushing their products."

The Professor pursed plump lips, "Now, James, we begin to get somewhere."

Les was shaking his head, unhappily. "Club members have been infiltrating the magazine staffs, according to Irene. It seems that it can't be helped because nobody else is in a position to know what the readers want. Nobody else is up enough on the Maid and her principles."

"Her what?" Witherson said blankly, pushing his glasses back.

"Her beliefs," Les said earnestly. "What she really stood for. Anyway, club members are largely editing the three magazines the syndicate launched and beginning next week they're not going to take any ads that aren't absolutely accurate in describing the product advertised. If Jeann d'Arc wine tastes like dishwater, they just won't accept the ad." He added, lamely, "At least, that's what Irene said."

"Lester," the Professor said, his voice lacking its usual beneficient quality. "Irene seems to have taken an inordinate interest in the affairs of the Oedipus Group."

"Oh, no, sir," Les Frankle said hurriedly. "It's not that. You see, Professor Doolittle, Irene has had this interest in Joan, the Maid of Orleans, ever since she was a child. It's a regular phobia with her."

It was a full Oedipus Group conference again. The room smoke filled again. Walthers trotting about with drinks again. Professor Doolittle presiding again, his youthful staff to one side, Doctor Warren Dempsey Witherson to the other.

The Professor kept his own report until the last, beaming benevolently at his colleagues as they reported on Tri-Di movies and television, on radio programs and song records and tapes, on games for both adults and children, on textile sales, on swords, armor and the new medieval revival styles, on tours to France and publishing house sales of biographies, novels and comic books.

The Professor beamed through it all. Save for minor upsets, and intrusions of Johnnies-come-lately who were continually climbing aboard the Joan of Arc bandwagon, the reports were upbeat in nature.

When at last he came to his own feet, the hush was pronounced. It was not like the Professor to have kept himself from the limelight for so long.

The Professor dry washed his hands, jovially.

"Well, gentlemen, we now come to the jackpot, By George. Until now, all has been peanuts, as idiom would have it."

"Five million net from our Jeanne d'Arc Pilgrimage game isn't exactly peanuts," the tweedy type muttered. He was in Donegals today, a curved Peterson shell briar in his mouth.

"Peanuts," the Professor cackled indulgently. "Gentlemen, what is the biggest single industry in this great and glorious nation of ours?"

"Automobiles," somebody growled. "We already got into that flop of a sports air-cushion car up in Detroit."

"A.T. and T." the fat man from California said. Of them all, he looked the most ridiculous in doublet and hose. "The biggest single company is Telephone."

The Professor waggled a happy finger at him. "The biggest company, perhaps, but not the biggest industry, By George. Gentlemen, the biggest industry in this great nation of ours is government. It hires more people, it

126

spends more money, than any other six groups of industries combined."

Witherson blinked at him. "You mean we're going to take over the government, Professor?" He hacked his throat clear, pushed his pince-nez glasses back on the bridge of his nose, nervously.

The Professor eyed him benignly. "Only in a manner of speaking, my dear Doctor."

He turned his eyes back to the others. "Gentlemen, I have been approached by representatives of both political parties. Both realize the position we occupy. Gentlemen, the way matters are shaping up, the elections this fall could be the nearest thing to a tie our glorious country has seen for many a decade. Yes, By George," he beamed, "if we should stand idly by and not, ah, perform our duty, the election could well be a tie."

Warren Dempsey Witherson cleared his throat again. "Our duty?"

The Professor's voice was gentle. "The only term, my dear Doctor. To arrive at a decision on just whom to support, and then, ah, throw the full resources of the Joan of Arc movement into the blanace."

The tweedy type said, "What decision? Who offered the most?"

"We are still dickering," the Professor told him.

Jimmy Leath growled, "Sir, are we going to be able to deliver the vote of the Joan of Arc fans? That's the question."

The Professor turned on him, kindly. "James, my lad, that is where our think tank comes in. In putting over this fad of ours, and enriching ourselves in the process, we have also built up the strongest team in the fields of motivational research, advertising, psychology applied to sales research, mass behaviorism and related subjects that this great nation has ever seen. By George, it is most inspiring."

He waxed eloquent, flourishing a fat, freckled paw in emphasis. "Gentlemen, some fifty percent of the women voters of America are presently influenced by the Joan of Arc fad. Of these, at least thirty millions are deeply involved. We have the next election in the palm of our collective hand. We could even re-elect Horace Adams, which ordinarily would seem an impossibility."

The fat man from California was beginning to get the message. "Why, why . . . it's the biggest thing since . . . since. . . ."

"Since Didius bought the Roman Empire," Jimmy Leath murmured, massaging his stomach.

They broke into excited jabbering.

The tweedy type was saying thoughtfully. "We'll have to line up the star of our original Tri-Di movie. Lots of the Joan fans identify her face with the original Joan. Then we'll have to line up the actors on TV and radio who portray Joan. Then we'll have to swing our magazines, even the comic books, over to our candidate."

"Who's that?" somebody said stupidly.

"Who knows, so far?" Witherson said reasonably. "You heard the Professor, the dickering is still going on."

"We'll really have to probe this in depth," Jimmy was muttering, intrigued. "Cover the country like smog. Find out what all these dizzy dames want our candidate to consider the issues of the day, besides the depression, of course. Control the widest blanket of polls, do the greatest number of depth interviews, ever seen. Given the Joan fans to begin with, as a lever, we can take this country like Grant. . . ."

The Professor was beaming still. "Gentlemen," he said. "I can assure you, By George, that we are not about to sell our services for small return. When all the smoke has cleared, we here in this room will be in the catbird seat."

Les Frankle said unhappily, "Irene isn't going to like this."

Chapter Eighteen

Weigand Patrick took in the long rows of computers, the clacking sorters and tabulators, the collators and key punches.

He shook his head and said, "Let's get out of this noise."

The other led him to an office. The door that closed behind them was soundproofed.

"Holy Smokes," Weigand said, "how do you do any thinking in that?"

"We don't have to do any thinking," Rod Watson told him. "The machines do the thinking."

Weigand Patrick looked at him, even while fumbling in his doublet pocket for his pipe. "Damn these fancy clothes," he muttered.

Watson said, "And after they've done their thinking, we bring the results into offices like this and think about what they thought about."

"Very funny," Weigand said. "I'll tell the President how this department produces jollies."

Rod Watson blanched.

Weigand said, "Okay, okay, I won't really. He's on a retrenchment binge these days. Bring down expenses. Let go some of the millions of governmental employees that've been pyramiding ever since Hoover. He put the whole Navy in mothballs. Economy is economy, I suppose, but if you ask me firing the Air Force is kind of gelding the lily."

"Fired the Air Force?" Watson said unbelievingly.

"That's right. He figures, what do you need an Air Force for with all the missiles we've got? At any rate, how far did you get today?"

Rod Watson walked around to the other side of his desk, sat down and selected a report. "Detroit," he said, "According to the computors, the beginning of the big crackup was when Detroit cut back production and laid off about a hundred thousand men. That's when it really started snowballing."

Patrick was lighting his pipe. He shook his head wear-

"No," he said. "You don't understand what I want from you, Watson. That wasn't when it started snowballing. By that time, the avalanche was well under way."

Watson was scowling at him.

Weigand Patrick pointed with his pipe stem at the second button on the other's fancy doublet. "Why did Detroit cut back?"

Watson blinked. "Why? Why, isn't that obvious? The new model cars weren't selling."

"Why? Take it further back."

Rod Watson looked distressed. "See here, Mr. Patrick, the Bureau of Statistics isn't omniscient."

Weigand Patrick puffed gently on his corncob. "Then it better get that way. Don't forget the Air Force, Rod, old man."

Watson closed his eyes in anguish. "Just what is it you want, Mr. Patrick?"

"Go further back," Weigand Patrick waved vaguely in the direction of the machine rooms. "Somewhere in all that accumulated data in there, you can find the *beginning* of it all. The first single grain of sand that started down the mountainside, joggling other grains, then pebbles, then rocks, until finally the avalanche was on us."

Watson groaned.

Chapter Nineteen

Andrei Zorin sat at his desk in the Ministry of Internal Affairs, a heavy military revolver close to his right hand, a half empty liter of vodka and a water tumbler, to his left. Red of eye, he pored over endless reports from his agents, occasionally taking time out to growl a command into his desk mike. As tired as he was, from the long sleepless hours he was putting in, Number One was in his element. As he had told the incompetent, Kardelj, he had been through this thing before. It was no mistake that he was Number One.

He snapped into the mike, "Give me Lazar Jovanovic." And then, when the police head's shaven poll appeared in the screen of the phone screen, "Comrade, I am giving you one last chance. Produce this traitor, Frol Krasnaya, within the next twenty-four hours, or answer to me." He glared at the other, whose face had tightened in fear. "I begin to doubt the sincerity of your efforts in this, Comrade Jovanovic."

He flicked off the instrument, then glowered at it for a full minute. If Jovanovic couldn't locate Krasnaya, he'd find someone who could. It was maddening that the pipsqueak had seemingly disappeared. To this point, seeking him had progressed in secret. There had been too much favorable publicity churned out in the early days of the expediter scheme to reverse matters to the point of having a public hue and cry.

The gentle summons of his phone screen tinkled, and he flicked it on with a rough brush of his hand.

And there was the youthful face of Frol Krasnaya, currently being sought high and low by the full strength of the Internal Affairs Secretariat. Youthful, yes, but even as he stared his astonishment, Andrei Zorin could see that the past months had wrought their changes on the other's face. It was more mature, bore more of strain and weariness.

Before Zorin found his voice, Frol Krasnaya said diffidently, "I . . . I understand you've been, well . . . looking for me, sir."

"Looking for you!" the Party head bleated, his rage ebbing in all but uncontrollably. For a moment he couldn't find words.

Krasnaya said, his voice jittering, "I had some research to do. You see, sir, this . . . this project you and Kardelj started me off on——"

"I had nothing to do with it! It was Kardelj's scheme, confound his idiocy!" Number One all but screamed. "Everything goes wrong at once. His ridiculous scheme to pass the West by teaching our porpoises not only to talk but to read. The fool! The criminal fool. What sort of thing did he have printed on the waterproof plastic paper for them to read? Karl Marx's *Das Kapital!* And now the doubly-damned creatures have organized Soviets and expropriated the herds of whales we had turned over to them for grazing! No! Don't connect me with Kardelj's idiotic schemes!"

"Oh? Well . . . well, I had gathered the opinion that both of you concurred. Anyway, like I say, the project from the first didn't come off quite the way it started. I . . . well . . . we, were thinking in terms of finding out why waiters were surly, why workers and professionals and even officials all tried to, uh, beat the rap, pass the buck, look out for themselves and the devil the hindmost, and all those Americanisms that Kardelj is always using."

Zorin simmered, but let the other go on. Undoubtedly his police chief, Lazar Jovanovic, was even now tracing the call, and this young traitor would soon be under wraps where he could do no more damage to the economy of the Soviet Complex.

"But, well, I found it wasn't just a matter of waiters, and truck drivers and such. It . . . well . . . ran all the way from top to bottom. So, I finally felt as though I was sort of butting my head against a wall. I thought I better start at . . . kind of . . . fundamentals, so I began researching the manner in which the governments of the West handled some of these matters."

"Ah," Zorin said as smoothly as he was able to get out. "Ah. And?" This fool was hanging himself.

The younger man frowned in unhappy puzzlement. "Frankly, I was surprised. I have, of course, read Western propaganda while I worked for *Pravda* in Greater Washington and to the extent I could get hold of it in Moscow, and listened to the Voice of the West on the wireless. I was also, obviously, familiar with our own propaganda. Frankly . . . well . . . I had reserved my opinion in both cases."

This in itself was treason, but Number One managed to get out, almost encouragingly, "What are you driving at, Frol Krasnaya?"

"I found in one Western country that the government was actually paying its peasants, that is, farmers, not to plant crops. The same government subsidized other crops, keeping the prices up to the point where they were hard put to compete on the international markets."

Young Krasnaya frowned, as though in puzzlement. "In other countries, in South America for instance, where the standard of living is possibly the lowest in the West and they need funds desperately to develop themselves, the governments build up large armies, although few of them have had any sort of warfare at all for over a century."

"What is all this about?" Number One growled. Surely, Lazar Jovanovic was on the idiot traitor's trail by now.

Frol took a deep breath and hurried on nervously. "They've got other contradictions that seem unbelievable. For instance, their steel industry will be running at half capacity, in spite of the fact that millions of their citizens have unfulfilled needs, involving steel. Things like cars, refrigerators, stoves. In fact, in their current depression, they'll actually close down perfectly good, modern factories, and throw their people out of employment, at the very time that there are millions of people who need the factory's product."

Frol said reasonably, "Why, sir, I've come to the conclusion that the West has some of the same problems we have. And the main one is politicians."

"What? What do you mean?"

"Just that," Frol said with dogged glumness. "I . . . well, I don't know about the old days. A hundred, even fifty years ago, but as society has become more complicated, more intricate, I simply don't think politicians are capable of directing it. The main problems are those of production and distribution of all the things our science and industry have learned to turn out. And politicians, all over the world, seem to foul it up."

Andrei Zorin growled ominously, "Are you suggesting that I am incompetent to direct the Soviet Complex?"

"Yes, sir," Frol said brightly, as though the other had encouraged him. "That's what I mean. You or any other politician. Industry should be run by trained, competent technicians, scientists, industrialists—and to some extent, maybe, by the consumers—but not by politicians. By

134

definition, politicians know about politics, not industry. But somehow, in the modern world, governments seem to be taking over the running of industry and even agriculture. They aren't doing such a good job, sir."

Zorin finally exploded. "Where are you calling from, Krasnaya?" he demanded. "You're under arrest!"

Frol Krasnaya cleared his throat, apologetically. "No, sir," he said. "Remember? I'm the average Soviet citizen. And it is to be assumed I'd, well . . . react the way any other would. The difference is, I had the opportunity. I'm in Switzerland."

"Switzerland!" Number One roared. "You've defected. I knew you were a traitor, Krasnaya. Like father, like son! A true Soviet would remain in his country and help it along the road to the future."

The younger man looked worried. "Well, yes, sir," he said. "I thought about that. But I think I've done about as much as I could accomplish. You see, these last few months, protected by those 'can do no wrong' credentials, I've been spreading this message around among all the engineers, technicians, professionals, all the more trained, competent people in the Soviet Complex. You'd be surprised how they took to it. I think it's kind of . . . well, snowballing. I mean the idea that politicians aren't capable of running industry. That if the Soviet Republics are to ever get anywhere, some changes are going to have to be made."

Number One could no more than glare.

Frol Krasnaya rubbed his nose nervously, and said, in the way of uneasy farewell, "I just thought it was only fair for me to call you and give a final report. After all, I didn't start all this. It wasn't me who originated the situation. It was you and Kardelj who gave me my chance. I just . . . well . . . expedited things." His face faded from the screen, still apologetic of expression.

Andrei Zorin sat there for a long time, staring at the now dark instrument.

It was in the middle of the night, when the knock came at the door. But then, Andrei Zorin had always thought it would . . . finally.

Chapter Twenty

Weigand Patrick was seeking a moment of refuge in his west wing office. Slumped in his swivel chair, a half-consumed highball in his hand, he eyed the Tri-Di set emptily.

Senator Dethwish was being interviewed by a newsman:

". . . now Senator, this new proposal that the Congress consider giving the country back to what remains of the Indian tribes. I understand it's one of your pet projects."

The senator was obviously indignant. "Well, what about it?"

"I understand the Indians are proving cagey. As that spokesman of theirs, Chief Chicken Little, put it, after what the white man has done to the country——"

"See here," the Senator broke in heatedly, "If the Indians don't like this country they can go back to where. . . ."

"Yes?" the reporter urged.

"No, come to think of it, they can't."

Weigand groaned, and flicked the set off, just as a knock came at the door.

Steve Hammond stuck his head in Weigand Patrick's office door warily. "Mr. Patrick, you know that inventor, the one you sent us with down to Dry Tortugas?"

"How could I forget him?" Weigand Patrick growled.

"Well, he's here again."

"Here again! Well, throw him out!"

"Yes, sir." The head disappeared.

"Hey, wait a minute," Weigand yelled. He finished his drink and put the glass down.

The head came back.

Weigand thought about it. He sighed.

"What does he want?"

Steve Hammond looked blank. "I don't know."

"All right, damn it. Send him in. But listen . . ."

"Yes, sir."

"You stand right outside that door, just in case."

"Yes, sir." Steve Hammond's head disappeared again.

The scrawny beard still looked as though it could use a dosage of mothballs, and the facial expression was still that of a lost pup. But Weigand Patrick was not thrown off guard, this time.

He said, "Sit down Mr. Brown."

The other perched on the edge of a straight chair, and bobbed his Adam's apple. "My friends call me Newt."

Patrick glared at him. "Name one."

Newt Brown considered that for a moment and changed the subject. "I came to you first," he said. When there was no immediate response he went on. "My latest research. I've finally found a use for water."

"Oh, great. What's that got to do with me?"

"It'll solve all the problems that beset the world, Mr. Patrick."

"What are you going to do," Weigand said sarcastically "blow it up?"

"Oh no. Not at all. Just the opposite."

Weigand Patrick said cautiously, "What's the opposite of blowing up the world?"

Newton Brown was obviously launching into his pitch

now. "Mr. Patrick, what this world needs is love. Every great thinker in the history of the world has advocated love. Love thy neighbor as thyself was taught long, long before Jesus."

"All right, all right," Weigand said. "Every religious teacher, every philosopher down through the centuries has advocated that we love one another. Man seems to accept the teaching in principle, but when he gets around to dealing with his fellow man, he usually winds up clobbering him, instead."

Newt Brown beamed, as though at a receptive student. "Right," he said.

Weigand Patrick looked at him. "So what are you going to do with water to change all that?"

"Oh, it's not primarily the water. That's just my method of distribution.

"Of what."

"L.A."

Weigand looked at the other for a long moment, wondering if he really wanted to continue this conversation.

Finally, he said, "Los Angeles is already distributed all over hell's half acre. It stretches from San Francisco to San Diego."

"Not Los Angeles—L.A. My new hallucinogen, Love Acid." He hurried on. "We'll dump it in the reservoirs."

"Wait a minute. A new hallucinogen. What's wrong with LSD? Didn't we have enough trouble with the old ones?"

Newt Brown made a scoffing gesture. "LSD, mescaline, psilocybin. Old hat."

"What was that last one?"

"I mean they're antiquated. Nothing. Love Acid is the ultimate hallucinogen. It will solve *all* of the world's problems. No more wars, No more depressions. Everybody will love everybody."

138

In spite of his caution, Weigand Patrick was becoming intrigued.

"How would it end the depression?"

"What causes depressions? The flow of industry ends. When the owner of an industry cannot make a profit, he closes it down, not caring that there might be thousands of consumers who need the product he manufactures. He doesn't care, though. All he's interested in is making a profit. Now if he *loved* everybody, he wouldn't give a hoot about profit. He'd just want to supply his product to those who needed it."

Weigand Patrick left off consideration of some of the socio-economic ramifications of that, for the time being.

He said, "Now if I get this right, what you want to do is dump this new hallucinogen of yours in the drinking water of the whole country."

"Correct."

"And then everybody would love everybody else?"

"That is correct," Newt Brown beamed.

"Holy smokes."

"Obviously."

"Then, I suppose, after you've dosed everybody in the United States of the Americas, you'll turn it over to Common Europe, the Soviet Complex, and. . . ."

Newt Brown nodded emphatically. "Absolutely. If they refuse the gift, we'll lob it over into their reservoirs by rocket missile. Use up the whole stock pile. We won't want nuclear missiles by that time anyway, we'll *love* everybody, not want to kill them."

"Holy smokes." Weigand Patrick shook his head, momentarily overwhelmed. Something came to him and he narrowed his eyes at the other. "How do I know it works?"

"Oh, it works all right, all right. I've tried it out on all sorts that supposedly hate each other, on cats and dogs, on cobras and mongooses, on ferrets and rats. Oh, it works all right."

"You mean it works on *animals* too?"

"I told you. It's universal. It works on everything."

"You mean, I could give a dallop of this stuff to my worst enemy and then he'd love me?"

Newt Brown was uncomfortable. "Well, admittedly, that's the one shortcoming."

Weigand Patrick looked at him.

Newt Brown squirmed in his chair unhappily. He said, "I assume your worst enemy is a man?"

That didn't quite come through. "Of course."

Newt Brown said grudgingly, "Then, yes. I'm afraid so."

"You're afraid what?"

"He'd want to love you."

A suspicion was beginning to dawn in Weigand Patrick. "Look here," he growled. "When you say that everybody would love everybody, after taking this L.A. of yours, how do you mean——"

"Love, love," Newt Brown said impatiently. "You know what love is."

"There is love and love," Patrick said dangerously. "I love the President's private secretary. I also love my country, and chocolate cake with vanilla ice cream. I also love a parade, but I've never wanted to go to bed with one."

Newt Brown bobbed his adam's apple. "This is the kind of love you undoubtedly feel for the President's secretary."

Weigand stared at him. "You mean this L.A. of yours that you want to slip into the nation's drinking water is a universal aphrodisiac?"

"You might put it that way. I prefer to think——"

"And this Mickey Finn to end all Mickey Finns would give everybody——"

"Everything, not just everybody," Newt Brown injected.

". . . hot pants?"

The self-proclaimed inventor summoned his dignity. "That is not the way I would explain it."

Weigand Patrick yelled, "Hammond!"

Steve Hammond burst into the office, .38 Magnum revolver at the ready.

Newt Brown winced.

"Yes, sir," the Secret Service bodyguard snapped.

"Do they still have chains?"

Steve Hammond looked at him blankly. "Chains, Mr. Patrick?"

"In the old days, the king, or whoever, would yell, *thrown him in chains*."

Squealing terror, Newt Brown tried to scurry toward the door, but Steve Hammond had him in an arm lock.

Holding the still mewling inventor, with one hand, he turned back to Weigand Patrick. "Well, no sir, I don't think so. All we've got now is handcuffs and leg irons."

"Okay. Get him into handcuffs and leg irons, and into some top security cell."

"Yes sir," Steve Hammond thought about it for a moment. "What's the charge?"

"Charge?"

The bodyguard was apologetic. "Well, yes sir. There ought to be some charge." He added, "Don't you think?"

"Get him into handcuffs and leg irons. I'll put the Department of Justice on it. They ought to be able to figure out something."

When Newton Brown and his escort were gone, Weigand Patrick snapped on his phone screen, growling, "Love thy neighbor, yet."

The girl on the White House switchboard said, "I beg your pardon, Mr. Patrick?"

"Get me Rod Watson, over at the Bureau of Statistics. Holy smokes, we've got to find out where this damn depression started, and why."

"Yes sir, that's what I thought you said."

Chapter Twenty-One

Warren Dempsey Witherson's copter-cab floated gently onto the Doolittle Building's landing ramp and bumped to an easy halt.

Automatically, his eyes flicked right and left, while he fiddled in his doublet pocket for a slug. He found it, slipped it into the auto-meter slot, secured his change and opened the cab door.

There were half a dozen pickets, women in shiny corselets, their short swords buckled to their sides. Doctor Witherson ignored the placards they bore and scurried for the lobby, his pince-nez held in hand.

He had a key to the private elevator now and didn't bother to check with the receptionist.

On the top floor, devoted solely to the offices and private quarters of Professor Doolittle himself, he hurried toward the *sanctum* of the motivational research head.

Walthers did no more than look up from his desk and say, "Good morning, Doctor. The Professor is expecting you."

Doctor Witherson mumbled something that wound up with my boy and was past.

The Professor, his calm for once vanished with the

142

snows of yesteryear, was bellowing at his two-man brain trust.

"The police," he was yelling. "How about the police? A mob can't just storm a Tri-Di station and demolish it!"

Jimmy Leath, who sat at the Professor's desk, a phone held to one ear, said, "Professor, it's a difficult situation. For one thing, this mob isn't a bunch of juvenile delinquents from Harlem or Brooklyn. Some of it's composed of the biggest names in the Blue Book. Besides that, they're all armed with their swords." His eyes went ceilingwards. "I thought those swords were supposed to be decorative, that they weren't meant to take a point or an edge. They seem to be able to chop up doors and furniture with them like they were machetes."

"They *were* only decorative to begin with!" the Professor roared.

Les Frankle said unhappily, "Well, Irene didn't think that was practical so——"

"Irene!" the Professor roared. "Don't ever mention that woman again, Frankle!"

"Yes, sir."

Doctor Witherson, his eyes popping, blatted at Jimmy Leath, "What's happened? I mighta known it. We haven't been cooling off these marks the way we shoulda!"

"Shut up, Kid," the Professor roared. "Confound it, you never were any good in the clutch."

Les said mildly, "Irene says. . . ."

The Professor scowled blood and destruction at him.

Les flushed and went on, "That is, what's really happening is that it's been a long time since women have got up on their high horse about something. It's been almost a century since the temperance movement. And women's suffrage, of course, all came about, so there's been no more suffragettes for as long as anybody can remember."

Jimmy was frowning. "Those that had a cause complex could always go into regular politics."

Les said, "Well, yes, but according to Ire . . . that is, women have never got very far in ordinary politics. They, uh, haven't been able to understand them very well—at least, up until now."

Jimmy Leath, still at the phone, growled, "Neither have men."

The Professor glared at him. "This is no time for levity, James." He spun back to Les. "Go on, confound it. What's happened? You're supposed to be our mass behavior expert."

Les said doggedly, "Well, sir, it was something women could understand. Something they could get riled up about. Being beaten over the head with sales propaganda that had them scrapping their last year's refrigerator because it was white instead of pink. Or changing their perfectly acceptable brand of soap for something twice as expensive, because it was a status symbol, to use a new brand containing super-lanolin. When you hit a woman in the pocketbook, you hit her where it counts."

"SO!" the Professor bellowed.

"Well, sir, all they needed was a banner under which to unite. Something to bring them together in this depression."

"You mean the Joan of Arc fad, you confounded ass!"

"Well, yes sir. You see, the origianl Joan was a reformer. Well, more than that. An actual rebel, according to . . . Well, anyway, she was a non-conformist and revolted against society as she found it. Well, sir, your think tank syndicate, the Oedipus Group, made her the country's ideal. And once the women really got involved in her image they wanted to . . . uh . . . emulate her. So they had to look around for something to rebel against, sir."

Doctor Warren Dempsey Witherson, who had been

taking in only about half of this, spending most of his time and attention at the window, whined, "What's that big crowd gathering down there?"

"Shut up, Kid," the Professor growled. "I got to think."

Jimmy Leath said reasonably, "All the thinking has been done, Professor Doolittle. All the cards are down."

The Professor, his rage ebbing up again pointed a shaking finger at him, then spun and leveled it at Les. "You two. You sold us out. You could have figured this, eight months ago. You're fired, understand!"

"Well, yes sir," Les nodded unhappily. "We kind of figured we would be."

Witherson whined, "Professor, there's a whole mob of marks getting together down there. We better take it on the heel and toe."

The Professor's rage broke. His hands came up, palms upward. "Lads," he said, "How could you do it? You were my team."

Jimmy ran his hand through his hair, uncomfortably. "Not exactly, sir. Like you've said, over and over, you just hired our brains. There wasn't anything ever said about loyalty. When Les first brought up the suggestion about using Joan of Arc as our heroine, we could have given it a whirl, given it a trial run, compiled some sample depth interviews, put it on the computer. In fact, either of us probably could have pretty well guessed what was going to happen—like Les Frankle's wife, Irene, evidently did."

"Then *why*, why, lads, didn't you warn me!"

Les said, as unhappy as his colleague. "Well, it was rather fascinating, the whole thing. You see, you kept talking about the money you paid us and how you were buying our brains, but the fact was we were more interested in observing the working mechanics of your organization than anything else. Fascinating, sir. Absolutely.

I'm no engineer, but I continually get a picture of an enormous machine slipping its clutch, or belt, or however they say it, and going wild."

Witherson whimpered, "Professor, they're beginning to stream into the building. They're waving them swords!"

Les walked over to the window beside him and peered down, "There's Irene," he said, shaking his head. "Out in front."

Witherson whirled and caught the Professor's doublet sleeve. "Listen, we gotta get out of here. We're warm! You must have some back way, if I know you, Professor. It's your building, you had it built."

The Professor shook him off.

He said to his ex-brain trust, pleadingly, "Listen, lads, By George. There must be some angle. Some way of rescuing this situation."

Les was shaking his head earnestly. "Well, I don't think so, sir. Jimmy and I put it on the computors last night."

The Professor, now beginning to allow the Funked Out Kid to pull him toward the door, demanded, "Well, how did they ever get rid of that original Saint Joan of. . . ." Then he stopped and his eyes narrowed. "They burnt her at the stake, didn't they?"

Les nodded, and spoke above the roar that suddenly was coming from the outer offices. "Yes, sir. They had to do that to shut her up, sir. And sir, well, I don't think it'll be so easy to burn Irene."

The Professor and the Funked Out Kid had made it down the secret elevator, out the back, and into a copter-cab.

Even as the Professor dialed a destination, with a shaking hand the Kid was whining. "On the lam again. Warm again, after all these years."

146

"Don't be silly, Kid," The Professor said, with shaky joviality. "We've got enough of a taw stashed away to live happily ever after off in Spain or Switzerland. I've had it all planned for years. A hideout apartment here in town where we can disguise ourselves. A vehicle to take us to the Canadian border. Lots of funds in a safe deposit box to grease our way. We're as safe as in our mother's arms, Kid. Remember, the fuzz isn't after us, just a bunch of hysterical dames. It was all legit, as far as John Law's concerned. You were even in the President's brain trust."

They pulled up before an imposing edifice.

"What's this?" the Kid whined apprehensively.

"Bank. My safe deposit box. We've got practically all the money left in the country. Let's hurry, Kid." The beam had returned to his eye, the pomposity to his manner.

The Funked Out Kid fumbled for a coin, stuck it into the copter-cab's slot and reached for the door handle.

It was then that the cab's lights began flicking red, a siren began to ululate from its hood.

The Funked Out Kid wrenched at the door, which held tight.

And a voice from the cab speaker said, "You are under arrest for utilizing other than legal tender, and face a five year imprisonment for counterfeiting. This is a police decoy cab of the Bureau of Transportation. You will remain seated until an officer of the law has arrived."

The Professor turned a beady eye on the Funked Out Kid who shrank back into the upholstery.

"By *George*," the Professor said.

Chapter Twenty-two

Weigand Patrick, flanked by the two cold-eyed Secret Service men, came up to the cement walk, taking in from the side of his eyes the unkempt condition of the old house's lawn. It wasn't just the lawn. The place could have used a coat of paint—or two. One of the shutters was hanging from a single hinge. There was newspaper stuffed in a broken window.

Patrick grunted. "Place looks better than most, these days."

The others said nothing.

He mounted the wooden steps, which creaked forbiddingly, and knocked on the front door, assuming, without trying, that the bell would be out of order.

An elderly woman peered out at them. She looked like every other elderly woman he had ever seen, all combined. She would have no trouble getting an extra's job as an old lady, in any Tri-Di production Hollywood made—if Hollywood had been making any Tri-Di shows these days. Who could afford to advertise on Tri-Di anymore?

Weigand Patrick said politely, "Is this where Marvin Sellers lives?"

She said immediately, "If you're bill collectors——"

"We know, we know. Mr. Sellers couldn't pay if we were, but we're not."

"You can't get blood out of a turnip," she said.

"A very apt phrase you've coined," he bowed gently.

She turned and yelled over her shoulder, "Marv! Marv!" and then disappeared.

Marv came to the door and looked at them in suspicion. "Yeah?"

148

Weigand Patrick looked at the other for a long moment.

"So you're the one who started all this," he murmured.

"What?" Marv said suspiciously.

Weigand Patrick said, "Can I talk to you privately?"

"Well, I don't know. Why? I guess so. Come on in." He held the broken-screened door open. "In here's the parlor."

Weigand Patrick and the two Secret Service men followed the bricklayer into the Victorian period living room.

Marv Sellers said, "Sit down, gents. What's all this about?"

Weigand Patrick said tightly, "Boys, this talk has to be absolutely private."

Guns flowed into the hands of the two ultra-trained operatives. One stationed himself to the side of the window, staring out, empty of eye. The other stood at the door, open the mildest of cracks so that he could see into the hall beyond.

"Hey, what the hell's going on?" Marv Sellers protested.

The two Secret Service men ignored him.

"Sit down, Mr. Sellers," Patrick said soothingly, as he reached for his pipe. "I'm a special representative from the President." He brought forth credentials, handed them to the other, and then fumbled for his tobacco pouch.

"Special representative from the President? You mean of the United States?"

"That is correct, Mr. Sellers." Patrick got his pipe going, then brought forth another sheaf of papers. He checked through them, found what he wanted.

"Mr. Sellers, two years ago, on Saturday, May 12th at ten p.m., you phoned the Wilkins Appliances Shop and told them to come get a new deep freeze you had bought shortly before. Mr. Sellers, that action on your part precipitated the current economic slump."

Marv Sellers bug-eyed him. "Who, me?"

"That is correct." Patrick held up a hand. "Yes, yes, I know what you are thinking. That many people send back appliances, cars, every other commodity. And usually this is simply a part of the workings of the economy, part of the give and take of the everyday business scene. However, private enterprise, as a socio-economic system, is a sensitive mechanism. Evidently, ours had been running at a delicate balance. It was your individual unpremeditated act that unleashed tiny forces that became larger forces and still larger, finally leading to the utter collapse of our economy."

"Jesus," Marv Sellers said. "Me?" He thought about it, round eyed. "Wow. I'm surprised the President didn't send the F.B.I. after me."

Patrick said soothingly, "He couldn't have even had he wanted to, Mr. Sellers. He let the F.B.I go last week as part of the government retrenchment. All except Edgar, of course. There were no longer any bankrobbers, there's nothing left in the banks to rob, and the Communists are no longer desirous of taking over the country."

Marv spread his hands. "Well, all I can say is, I'm sorry. There's nothing I can do about it. Here I am, living with my wife's people. No job. Flat broke."

Weigand Patrick was nodding. "It's a top secret, last ditch try. Back in Washington, we've dubbed it Project Sellers. We're up against the wall, Mr. Sellers."

"Project Sellers?" Marv blurted.

"Correct." Weigand Patrick turned his eyes to the Secret Service man at the window. "Steve, let me have that envelope."

"Yes, sir." Steve Hammond brought a long envelope from his inner doublet pocket, brought it over to Patrick and then returned to the window and his guard duties.

Patrick said, "Remember, this is topmost security. Highest priority. Everything would immediately be ruined if it got out. It all must be spontaneous. Not even your wife must know, Mr. Sellers." He handed over the envelope.

"Phoebe? I can't even tell Phoebe?"

"Absolutely no one."

Marv Sellers hesitated, but then, as though hypnotized by a snake, slowly opened the envelope.

And brought forth a thick sheaf of spanking new banknotes.

"What's this?" he said.

"Obviously, money."

Sellers chuckled bitterly. "U.S. Government money?"

Patrick said, "I know, I know. However, there are still sixteen pounds of gold in Fort Knox. This money has been issued based on that."

Sellers was round eyeing him again.

Patrick said hurriedly, "And there'll be more when you've spent that. The President is arranging for a loan from Monaco. It seems that the present Prince of that country has a soft spot for America. His mother was an American, or something."

"All right," Sellers said. "I'm as patriotic as the next one. What do I do?"

Chapter Twenty-three

Phoebe and Marv Sellers and Old Sam moved back into the house on Camino de Palmas the following day. It had never sold, anyway.

Marv was admirably stubborn. He had a government job. He'd tell Phoebe and Old Sam nothing more than that.

The same day, he phoned Barry Benington.

"Mr. Benington," he said. "I've had a change of mind."

"Change in mind? What's that, what's that?" the old man wheezed.

"That car I sold you. You know, I liked that car. I'd like to buy it back."

The old man turned sly. "Why, I don't know about that, Mr. Sellers. I've rather taken to it myself."

Marv said, "I'd be willing to pay you five hundred more than you gave me for the old wreck."

"Five hundred? Well, I don't know. I've had her polished up, you know, spent a lot of money on that beautiful car."

"I'll make it a thousand," Marv said.

"It's a deal!" the oldster wheezed quickly.

That afternoon when Bill Waters came up on his bicycle to deliver some bologna and cheese to old man Benington, the other met him at the kitchen door.

Benington wheezed, "Bill, what's the price of one of them Buick Cayuses?"

Bill Waters looked at him. "I thought you bought yourself a used car, Mr. Benington."

"Yeah, but I'm tired of it. Sold it back. I always did kinda hanker after one of them air-cushion cars. Can you still get me one?"

Bill Waters felt a tremor. He said, trying to keep his voice even, "Well, I sort of closed up my place. But, come to think of it, I guess I've still got the franchise. I could certainly order one from the distributor in Denver."

"Now, you do that for me, Bill. I've got the cash money right here for a down payment."

Some of Bill Waters elan, long submerged, surfaced. He gushed, "Mr. Benington, you'll love these new model cars. I understand they're built so low you have to enter them through a manhole."

Marv Sellers was saying to Jim Wilkins, "Yep, what we need is one of them new deep freezes. Phoebe wants one of them cerise models."

Wilkins was taken aback. "You got the down payment, Mr. Sellers?"

"Thought I'd just pay cash."

"I can sure as hell order you one. We don't have any demonstrators in stock. The shop's closed."

"That's all right. I'll pay you now. And look, Jim. The other day, I was reading about a nuclear Martini stirrer. Has a little atomic pack in it, like. Stir your Martinis for twenty years, before running down. Now a gadget like that——"

Jim Wilkins said quickly, "I know where I can order you one. I'll get several of them. You know, it's about time I opened up that shop of mine again."

"Sure is," Marv said.

When Norman Foxbeater drove past the *Lovee Dovee Hottee Doggee Shoppee* he was mildly surprised to find the place hadn't folded its doors. In fact, it seemed to be having quite a play.

Whatever brought him to enter, he couldn't say. Possibly it was becuse it was so unusual to see even mild business.

He sat in a small booth and allowed the waitress to bring him a dish of very small weiners, a portion of baked beans and some potato salad. The baked beans were fabaulous.

He recognized a few of the faces. Over there was a

bricklayer who had once worked briefly for the Foxbeaters in the building of a backyard barbeque. What was his name? Sellers or something. And over there was Barry Benington, who'd once had an account with Foxbeater and Fodor. And on the other side of the room was Bill Waters and his wife. When times had been better, Bill had belonged to the country club. Foxbeater nodded to him and received a cheerful wave in return.

Hmmm. Things were evidently looking up for Bill Waters.

Mrs. Perriwinkle came sailing by, all smiles, a dish of her tiny hot dogs in hand.

She recognized him and came to a halt.

Foxbeater said, "You seem to be doing quite a business, Mrs. Perriwinkle."

"Oh," she lied airily, "it's always like this. If the truth be known, one of these days I'll be dropping by to put some of my earnings back into Mutual Funds." She swept on.

He looked after her.

An hour later he came into Mortimer Fodor's office.

"Mortimer," he said thoughtfully, "my instinct tells me it's time to pull that money out of Switzerland and invest in American securities."

His senior partner looked at him. "Oh? Well, good. Get this all ironed out and I'll be able to retire. I'll bet I can get a yacht built for a pittance these days."

"Ummmm," Foxbeater nodded. "But don't put it off too long. Get your order in while things are still slow."

They were seated around the kitchen table.

Phoebe said, "Guess what? Mr. Edwards wants me to come back to work. They've got a whole batch of new gadgets they're going to market."

Marv said, "Oh? Such as what?"

"Oh, a whole lot of things. When everybody was out of work a lot of these technicians and inventors and all didn't have anything else to do so they kind of puttered around in their cellar and garage workshops and laboratories and came up with just about everything. Like the electric spoons. There's a little stud on the side. You can switch it all the way over from stirring your coffee to eating soup."

Marv said, "Well, I've got news too. Heard from my old boss. He's going to be constructing a new factory. Place where they'll be manufacturing air-cushion roller skates."

Old Sam groaned. "Back to the rat race," he said. "I knew it wouldn't last. They ain't making them like they used to. In the old days, a depression was good to last for nigh onta ten years."

"Knock it off, Gramps," Marv growled at him.

The old boy came to his feet. "I better put away that apple sign of mine fer future reference. I'll bet the next one will be a doozy."

Chapter Twenty-four

"Yes, sir," Weigand Patrick said, with satisfaction. "It worked."

The President was jubilant.

He rubbed his hands together. He chortled, "Now we can get back to my Far-Out Society. And we can get that police action down in the Antarctic going again. Scotty, get me Admiral Pennington, on the phone. We're going to take him out of mothballs. And instruct the Octagon to discontinue melting down the Fifteenth Fleet."

"Yes, Mr. President," Scotty said.

"And Scotty, take a letter to those Porpoise Union smart alecs. Tell them that their request for human children to experiment with, to teach them the porpoise language, is out of the question. Ah, think of some good excuse. We've got to keep those whales coming, now people will be able to afford meat again. Ah, tell them that human kids have a hard time breathing under water, or something." He tapped the side of his nose slyly.

"Yes, Mr. President," Scotty said.

The President added thoughtfully, "I wonder how those boys up on the moon are doing."

"Well, sir," Weigand said, "That's going to be one of your first problems, now that the depression is over. It seems that at the same time we deserted our moonbase, and raised that monument to the space heroes, the Russkies also were running out of cash, and abandoned theirs. So the two bases evidently got together, merged their resources, the hydroponic tanks they get their food from, and such, and proclaimed the Republic of Luna. They've taken over all the TV and Communications relay stations, and are making some pretty stiff demands about rates before any Earth governments can use the services."

"What!" the Chief Executive yelled. "They can't do that to us, the ingrates! I'll liberate them!"

Chapter Twenty-five

Weigand Patrick flicked on the phone screen and growled, "Yes, what is it?"

It was Scotty. She said, "Listen, I want you to do me a favor."

"I'd climb the highest mountain, I'd swim the deepest river——"

"Great. I'm at my apartment. Look, I left a report on my desk. What's the chances of bringing it over?"

"What do you think I am, a delivery boy?" he wailed. "I'm busy. That Oedipus Group, the think tank outfit, they've fouled up the women's vote something awful. I've got to——"

"Please, the report's very . . . confidential. I wouldn't want anyone else to see it."

"All right, all right. I'll be over."

He flicked the phone screen switch off, muttering, got up and headed in the direction of her office.

He rang the bell, pushed at the door, found it ajar, and entered.

He was scowling, as he closed the door behind him, "Scotty," he called. "Come and get this damn report, I've got to get back to the office."

She came quickly from behind the door, grabbed him in a judo hold.

"Hey!" Weigand Patrick yelled.

He felt himself flying through the air, his arms and legs going every which way.

"Hey!" he yelled, landing flat on his back on the bed, the covers of which had been turned down neatly.

Scotty stood over him, a wicked gleam in her eyes, even as she began to unbutton her dress.

"No, look," he said desperately. "I've got a press conference waiting."

"Let it wait," she growled.

157

URSULA K. LEGUIN

.... 107029 City of Illusion — $1.25

.... 478024 Left Hand of Darkness — $1.50

.... 669531 Planet of Exile — $1.25

.... 732925 Roncannon's World — $1.25

.... 900779 A Wizard of Earthsea — $1.25

Available wherever paperbacks are sold or use this coupon.

🌑 ace books, (Dept. MM) Box 576, Times Square Station
New York, N.Y. 10036

Please send me titles checked above.

I enclose $............... Add 20¢ handling fee per copy.

Name ....

Address ....

City..................... State............. Zip........

33E

DAWNMAN PLANET

Ron Bronston was sworn to protect the United Planets' dream—the pursuit of freedom and progress on all of the 3,000 human-inhabited planets of the galaxy.

As an operative of the secret section of the United Planets' Bureau of Investigation, Bronston was called upon for some very unusual missions. But the present crisis was without precedent.

Man's sovereignty in his galaxy was challenged by a single madman and the super-weapons of the Dawnmen, the mysterious aliens from the unexplored vastness of the galaxy's center. Bronston, alone, had to find a way to stop them.

DAWNMAN
PLANET

by

Mack Reynolds

ace books
A Division of Charter Communications Inc.
1120 Avenue of the Americas
New York, N.Y. 10036

PART ONE

I

Supervisor Sid Jakes was in fine fettle. As his men inspected the papers of the VIPs at the door and finally ushered them into the highly guarded room, he took over and pleasured himself in presenting the exhibit.

The exhibit was in a square box which resembled a combination coffin and deep freeze, which is exactly what it was. The exhibit itself was a small charred creature about the size of a monkey or rabbit. However, signs of clothing or harness could be made out, and what would seem to be side arms.

The routine went almost identically with each visitor. At the door, Ronny Bronston, or one of the other Section G operatives, would finish the identification and call out such as, "Sidi Hassen, Hereditary Democratic-Dictator of the Free-wealth of the Planet Medina."

The ruler of Medina would come forward, invariably blank of face; and with a gesture, as though presenting his most valued possession, Sid Jakes would indicate the exhibit.

The Section G agents had come to expect the same initial reaction each time.

It was: "What is it?"

Sid Jakes would grin happily, but hold his peace.

The VIP, his eyes probably bugging by now, would

5

say, in absolute astonishment: "Why, it's an alien life form!"

The sharper ones would sometimes say, that first time: "It's an *intelligent* alien life form!"

Supervisor Jakes let them remain long enough to realize the full significance of the badly burned, deep-frozen carcass; then, invariably stemming a flow of questions, he would usher the VIP to an opposite door, where other Section G operatives took over.

The secret room cleared, they would begin all over again.

"His All Holiness, Innocency the Sixteenth, Presidor of the Holy Theocracy of the Planet Byzantium."

His All Holiness would step forward and gape in turn at the charred body of the tiny creature. "It's an intelligent alien life form! But there *is* no intelligent life in the galaxy, save Created man!"

There was only one break in the routine.

Ronny Bronston had been standing to one side for the nonce, while his two companions guarding the door processed the latest arrival.

One of them began to say, "The Supreme Matriarch Harriet Dos Passos of the Planet . . ."

Ronny snapped "She's a fake!"

The newcomer darted in the direction of the freezer box which contained the alien carcass, yelling. "I've got a right . . .!"

Ronny put out a foot, cold-bloodedly, and she went down, arms and legs going every which way.

"Sorry, lady," he said. "Admission is by invitation only."

"Get her, boys" Sid Jakes snapped, coming forward quickly himself. Ronny and the other two grabbed for the intruder.

6

But she was made of sterner stuff than they had assumed. She rolled, bounced to her feet and scrambled toward the freezer.

She stared into its interior, eyes bugging as all eyes had bugged that morning. Finally, she turned and faced them, her expression unbelieving, as all expressions had been unbelieving. She turned to face four cold faces, four leveled Model H hand weapons.

Sid Jakes said, "If she makes one move, any move at all, muffle her." He grinned at the intruder. "That was bad luck for you, the fact that you managed to see it, you silly flat. Do you think we'd go to this much security if it wasn't ultra-important? Now, let's have it. You're obviously not Harriet Dos Passos. Who are you, how'd you get here, and who sent you?"

The other snapped, her voice not as yet shaky, "I'm Rita Daniels, from Interplanetary News. That's the corpse of an intelligent alien life form in there. I'm not stupid. There isn't supposed to be other intelligent life in the galaxy. Our viewers have a right to know what's going on here in the Commissariat of Interplanetary Affairs. United Planets is a democratic . . ."

Sid Jakes interrupted, still grinning "You'd be surprised, my stute friend. Now, once again, who sent you?"

"My editor, of course. I demand . . ."

Sid Jakes made a gesture with his head at one of the Section G operatives. "Terry, take her over to Interrogation. Use Scop . . ."

The news-hen bleated protest, which was completely ignored.

". . . to find out the names of every person who might remotely know about this romp of hers. The editor, possibly her husband, if she has one, the editor's wife, secretaries, fellow reporters, absolutely everybody. Then send out men to round up every one of these. In turn, put them on Scop and get the names of everyone they might have mentioned this to."

"How far do we follow it, Sid?" the agent, named Terry asked.

Sid Jakes laughed wryly, as though the question were foolish. "To the ultimate. Even though you wind up with everybody in Interplanetary News in Interrogation. We've got to have everybody who even suspects, or might possibly suspect, the existence of our little friend, here." He made a gesture with a thumb at the alien in its box.

The agent nodded, then asked one last question: "After interrogation, what?"

Sid Jakes said flatly, "Then we'll have to memorywash her. Completely wash out this involved period, no matter how far back you have to go."

The newswoman shrilled. "You can't do that! Under United Planets law, I've got . . ."

Ronny Bronston shook his head at her. "You're not in the hands of United Planets, in the ordinary sense of the word, girl friend. You're in the hands of Section G."

"But you're a section of the Bureau of Investigation, Department of Justice of the Commissariat of Interplanetary Affairs! I have my rights!"

Sid Jakes didn't bother to argue. He said to his other operative, "Get about it, Terry. This is bad. On your way over to Interrogation, if she makes any attempt to break away, muffle her, but tune your gun low. We don't want her out for too long. She probably had no idea of what she was looking for, when she broke in here. Somewhere there was a leak, we've got to find the source of her knowledge that something was coming off. But, above

8

all, we've got to prevent her from spreading what she saw."

Terry said, "Right, Sid. Come along! You heard the Supervisor. One wrong move and you're muffled; and, believe me, it hurts."

Rita Daniel's last protest, as she was marched out the door, was shrilled back over her shoulder. "You . . . can't . . . do . . ."

"Famous last words." Sid Jakes grinned at his two remaining men. "Come on boys, let's finish. There's only a few more to go." He looked at Ronny approvingly. "That was a neat trick. How did you spot her?"

Ronny snorted deprecation. "She was too romantic. She was wearing makeup disguise, trying to resemble the real Matriarch. She'd have been better off altering the Tri-Di identification portrait in the credentials. We have no record of what the real Dos Passos looks like. She just recently came to office."

They processed the remaining VIPs, then sealed the secret room and put it under armed guard.

Sid Jakes and Ronny Bronston, one of his favorite field men, went on to the conference hall, where they had been sending the viewers of the exhibition.

"Where's the Chief?" Ronny asked. He was what could only be described as a very average man. It was one of his prime attributes as a Section G operative. He was of average height and weight. His face was pleasant enough, though hardly handsome—a somewhat colorless young man of about thirty. He was less than natty in dress and his hair had a slightly undisciplined trend. He had dark hair and brown eyes, and he absolutely never stood out in a crowd.

He was also as devoted an agent as was to be found in

Section G, whose personnel was selected on the basis of devotion to the United Planets dream.

Sid Jakes, walking along beside him—bouncing along, might be the better term—couldn't have been more different. Even his clothes breathed a happy-go-lucky air. He had a nervous vitality about him that made all others seem lazy of movement. But his appearance was as belying as that of Ronny Bronston; one does not achieve to the rank of supervisor in Section G without abilities far and beyond usual.

Sid said, grunting amusement, "The old man's in hiding until the time comes for the big revelation. He's not about to get into that hive of big shots and let them yell at him at random. I'll have Irene give him the word when all's ready."

The selected men of importance of United Planets had been gathered in an Octagon ultra-security conference room, which had been adjusted to hold the full two thousand of them. Comfortable seating arrangements and refreshment, both food and drink, had been provided. However, there was absolutely no method by which any, no matter of what importance, could communicate with the outside.

The doors were guarded by empty-faced Section G agents, under most strict orders. Polite they were, when this president or that dictator, this scientific genius, or that head of a fanatic religious system, demanded exit or some manner of communicating with family or staff. Polite they were, but unbending. When a burly bully-boy, from the feudalistic planet Goshen, tried to be physical, a short scuffle was sufficient to demonstrate that Section G training included hand-to-hand combat.

Irene Kasansky was seated, efficient as ever, at a desk near the podium. She was answering questions, briskly issuing commands into her order box, when requests involved preferred refreshment or other minor matters, which didn't interfere with the security of the meeting.

There comes a time, Ronny Bronston thought all over again, *when automation falls flat and man returns to human labor.* In this case, the ultra-efficient office secretary-receptionist. For spinster, Irene Kasansky might be, on the verge of middle age she might be, and unfortunately plain—but she was also by far the best secretary in the Octagon.

Now she snarled from the side of her mouth. "It's about time you got here. I've been through more jetsam, these past few hours, than I've had in the past few years managing Ross Metaxa's office. And I thought that was the ultimate. Where have you been, playing dice?"

Sid grinned down at her. "Don't be bitter, dear. You'll get wrinkles and an acid-looking face, and then everyone will stop propositioning you. All's ready to go. Pry the old man away from that bottle of Denebian tequila and let's let loose the dogs of war."

He turned and bounded to the speaker's stand. Holding up his hands, he called: "Gentlemen, gentlemen, ladies. Can we all be seated? The meeting is about to commence."

He held silence then, until all was quiet, which took some time, considering the fact that the most highly individualistic persons in United Planets were gathered before him.

Sid Jakes grinned finally, as though finding the whole thing amusing, and said, "Undoubtedly, you have been spending the better part of the morning discussing among yourselves the significance of the little creature I displayed to you. But now we shall hear from Commissioner Ross Metaxa."

"Who in the name of the Holy Ultimate is Ross Metaxa?" someone rumbled.

And someone else snapped, indignantly, "You have taken *His* name in vain!" The latter worthy was dressed in colorful and flowing robes.

"Please, gentlemen, please," Sid shouted above again rising voices. "Commissioner Ross Metaxa!" he jumped down from the dais and grinned at Ronny.

"The old man can have this job," he chortled. "Every crackpot genius in this section of the galaxy is out there."

Ross Metaxa came in through an inconspicuous door in the rear of the room, immediately behind the speaker's stand. Eyebrows went up. He was flanked by the Director of the Commissariat of Interplanetary Affairs—as high an officer as United Planets provided; and by the President of United Planets—a largely honorary office chosen by interplanetary vote. Once every ten years, each member planet was entitled to one voice, in selecting the president. Metaxa did not seem to be awed by his companions, but rather was obviously accompanied by peers.

Sid chuckled from the side of his mouth. "The old man's hanging it on heavy."

"He knows what he's doing," Ronny whispered back. "He's going to have hard enough a time as it is, getting this assembly to listen to his opinions."

The Director and the President took chairs off to one side, and Metaxa made his way to the podium. He was a man in his middle years, sour of expression, weighty around the waist, and sloppily clothed to the point where it would seem an affectation.

The voices of the two thousand had begun to rise again, questioning, querulous.

Ross Metaxa glowered out at them for a long moment.

Finally he growled, "All right, damn it, let's cut out all this jetsam and get down to matters."

There was an immediate hush of shocked surprise.

Before an indignant hum could rise again, the Commissioner of Section G announced brusquely: "Ladies and gentlemen, to use an idiomatic term of yesteryear, the human race is in the clutch."

II

Someone in the first row of the audience snorted ridicule and called up, "Because of that little creature in there? Don't be a flat!"

The Commissioner of Section G looked at him bleakly. "It should occur, even to the physically conscious Grand Duke of the Planet Romanoff, that the size of the creature in question has nothing to do with it." He tapped his head significantly. "It is what is in here that brought us up short. You see, the little fellow was picked up by one of our Space Forces scouts well over a century ago."

"A century!" one of his listeners bleated. "And we are only informed today?"

A buzz began again, but Metaxa held up a wary hand. "Please. That is one of the things I am here to explain. Our little alien was found in what could have only been a one-man fighter scout. He was dead, his craft blasted and torn, obviously from some weapon's fire. His own vessel was highly equipped with what could only have been weapons: most so damaged, our engineers have yet to figure them out. To the extent they have been able to reconstruct them, they've been flabbergasted.

"The conclusion is obvious. Our intelligent alien, in there, was killed in an interplanetary conflict. How long he had been drifting in space, our technicians couldn't determine, possibly only for months, but possibly for any number of centuries. But the important thing is that there was at least one other warlike, aggressive life form in the galaxy, besides man. Probably, at least two, since it was interplanetary war, which killed our specimen."

The buzz rose again, and was not to be silenced for a time. Ross Metaxa stood and waited it out. But they were anxious for his revelations and finally silence ruled.

He dropped another bomb.

"But we no longer need fear our friend in the other room. Man is in no danger from him and his species."

That set them off once more, but he held firm in silence until they quit their shouting of questions, their inter-audience squabblings, chattering and debate.

At last he held up a hand, and said, "Let me leave that statement for a time. Let me lay a foundation upon which to base what we must discuss today."

He looked out at them, thoughtfully. "Most of you are going to have some reservations about what I have to say.

"Fellow citizens of United Planets: When man first began to erupt into the stars, but a few centuries ago, his travels assumed a form that few could have foreseen. All but lemming-like, he streamed from the planet of his origin. And the form his colonizing took, soon lost all scheme of planning, all discipline. The fact was that any group that could float the wherewithal to buy or rent a space transport, or convert a freighter, could take off into the stars to found their own version of Utopia.

"And take off they did, without rhyme or reason. No, I recall that statement. Reasons they had aplenty: Racial reasons, religious reasons, political reasons, idealistic reasons, romantic reasons, socio-economic reasons, altruistic reasons and mercenary reasons. In a way, I suppose we duplicated, a hundredfold, the motivations the Europeans found to colonize the New World. The Spanish came with sword and harquebus in search of gold, ready to slaughter all who stood before them. The Pilgrims came to seek a new land, where they could practice a somewhat stilted religion, in a manner denied them at home. Large numbers of criminals came, either as convicts being exiled or fugitives from justice. Adventurers of every type zeroed-in, seeking their fortunes. Later, large numbers of Germans came, fleeing political persecution, and large numbers of Irish, fleeing famine."

Ross Metaxa grunted, and flicked his heavy head. "And so it was in space. And in the early years, in particular, there was comparatively little friction. The galaxy is immense, and thus far, we have but touched a slightest segment of it. We are way out in a sparsely populated spiral arm, but there are still inhabitable planets in vast multitude and room for all. Every spacer-load of idealists or crackpots could safely find their habitable planet and settle down to go to hell in their own way."

There was a mumble of discontent over the manner in which he was expressing himself, but he went on, ignoring the objections.

"However, in time, some of our more aggressive planets began to have growing pains. Planets, settled by such groups as the Amish, began to worry about their neighbors on the Planet Füehrerland. This had been settled by a disgruntled group of followers of a political leader of the 20th Century, who had come to disaster in his own time, but whose tradition came down through the years, somewhat distorted in his favor, as traditions are apt to become. Suffice to say that United Planets, based here on Mother Earth, came into being. Its purpose, of course, was obvious. To assist man in his explosion into the stars. The very basis of the organization was Articles One and Two of the United Planets Charter. Citizeness Kasansky, please."

Irene Kasansky, without looking up, read into her desk mike. "Article One: *The United Planets organization shall take no steps to interfere with the internal political, socio-economic, or religious institutions of its member planets.* Article Two: *No member planet of United Planets shall interfere with the internal political, socio-economic or religious institutions of any other member planet.*"

Ronny Bronston knew, even as she read, that not only Irene, but everyone present in the hall knew the articles by heart. Metaxa was simply using this bit of business to emphasize his fling.

When she was done, Metaxa nodded ponderously. "Over the centuries, most planets, though not all, have joined up. Whatever their stated reasons, usually very highflown ones, the actuality is that each wishes the protection of the Charter. Each planet desperately holds on to its own sovereignty."

There was a buzz again, and again he ignored it.

"Always remember, that within our almost three-thousand member planets are represented just about every political and every socio-economic system ever dreamed up by philosophers and economists since Plato, and every religion since the White Goddess, the Triple Goddess, prevailed throughout the Mediterranean. A planet whose economy is based on chattel slavery doesn't want to have its institutions subverted by adherents of feudalism. And a planet with feudalistic institutions doesn't want some entrepreneur from another planet, flying the flag of free enterprise, to come along with creeping capitalism. An atheistic planet, such as Ingersol, doesn't want a bevy of fanatical missionaries from Byzantium, working away at its youth, which hasn't been exposed to religion for centuries."

17

His All Holiness of the Holy Theocracy of the Planet Bysantium called out in a fine rage. "I protest your levity, Commissioner."

Ross Metaxa ignored him.

"All this is not new to you. But, somewhat over a century ago, matters changed, overnight and drastically. Our Spaces Forces brought in our little alien, there in the next room. Suddenly we had to face it. Man is not alone in the galaxy. Thus far, we had thought to be. Nowhere, in our explorations, though, admittedly, they have been but a pinprick on the chart of the Milky Way, did we find signs of intelligent life. Lower life forms, yes, occasionally. But never intelligent life of, say, even the order of the chimpanzee of Earth. But now we had to face the fact that there is intelligent, aggressive, scientifically and militarily advanced life in our galaxy; and, obviously sooner or later, man, in his expansion into the stars, will come up against it. It was but a matter of time."

Someone called out. "Perhaps this life form is benevolent!"

Ross nodded his shaggy head. "Perhaps it is," he answered simply.

His words brought a deep silence. These were not stupid men and women. Largely, they were the cream of the planets they represented. The inference was obvious.

Ross Metaxa dropped another bomb. "So it was," he went on, "that the nature of United Planets changed. Unbeknownst to the individual member planets, a new purpose for its being evolved."

There was heavy electricity in the air.

"No longer was it practical for man to allow such groups as the naturalists—who colonized the planet, Mother—to settle into their desired Stone Age society,

18

rejecting all of man's scientific advance down through the ages. No longer could we condone the presence among our number of the Planet Kropotkin, based on the anarchist ethic that no man is capable nor has the right to judge another. No longer were planets such as Monet to be borne."

"Monet?" someone shouted in query.

Ross Metaxa said, "Originally colonized by a group of artists, musicians, painters and sculptors, who had visions of starting a new race devoted entirely to the arts. They were so impractical that they crashed their ship, lost communication with the rest of the race, and, when rediscovered, had slipped into a military theocracy something like the Aztecs of Mexico. Their religion was based on that of ancient Phoenecia, including child sacrifice to the god, Moloch. Monet, too, claimed the benefits of Articles One and Two, wishing no interference with their institutions."

The representative from Goshen, the bully-boy, who had had the run in with the Section G guards earlier, lumbered to his feet. His voice was dangerous. "And what was this new policy adopted by United Planets, unbeknown, as you say, to the member planets themselves?"

The Commissioner made a gesture with a heavy paw. "Is it not obvious, Your Excellency? It became the task of United Planets, though but a fraction of us have been privy to the fact, to advance the human race, scientifically, industrially, culturally, socio-economically, as fast as it was possible to do so."

"Even though Articles One and Two, the very basis of the Charter were violated?"

The shaggy head lowered, and Ross Metaxa glowered out at them, in their shocked silence. "No matter what was being violated," he growled.

19

A roar went through the hall and he waited it out.

At long last he was able to say, "Nothing could be allowed to stand in the way of the most rapid advance of which we were capable. Sooner or later, we knew, we would come in contact with the potential enemy. A potential friend, too, of course, but that must remain to be seen. Man must be as strong as possible, when the confrontation takes place."

Sidi Hassen of the Planet Medina was standing. All eyes went to him. Medina was one of the strongest planets in the union, though its government was one of the most repressive.

He said, "Commissioner Metaxa, it is obvious that all this is but a build-up. You have admitted that Mother Earth, home of United Planets, has been secretly subverting the institutions of the member planets. Now tell us why it has been necessary to reveal the fact to us, at this late date." There was a dangerous element in his voice.

Sid Jakes chuckled under his breath and whispered to Ronny Bronston, standing beside him. "Our friend has probably just realized where some of his Underground troubles originated. If the boys have been briefing me correctly, that Hereditary Democratic-Dictatorship of his isn't going to last the week out."

The head of Section G nodded agreement. "Very well," he said. "As I mentioned earlier, the charred body you were all invited to see no longer indicates a threat to us." He paused, wanting the drama.

"*Why not!*" came from a hundred voices.

"Because, a few weeks ago, a small exploration task force, driving out beyond the point thus far ventured to, by even the most adventurous of our race, came upon

20

the three star systems which were the origin of our little dead space traveler."

"You mean," the burly representative from Goshen roared, "that we now know where the sneaky little rats come from and they only dominate three star systems?"

Metaxa nodded. "From all we can find, they had evidently spread over a complex of some twelve planets. Planets similar in nature to those that will support our own life form. Our little aliens were also oxygen breathers." He grunted and flicked his head in his dour, characteristic mannerism. "I see most of you have noted my use of the past tense."

He dropped his last bomb. "Our exploring fleet found that each of their twelve planets were now supporting a methane-hydrogen-ammonia atmosphere. They found also that evidently the switch in atmospheres, from one predominately nitrogen-oxygen, had come so suddenly that the inhabitants had no time to attempt protection. They died. Perhaps some survived for a time, including those that might have been in space, when the atmosphere was switched. If so, it would seem they were destroyed by other means. Perhaps our specimen in the other room was one of these. At any rate, ladies and gentlemen of the human race, this whole life form has been completely destroyed by some other intelligent alien life form beyond it." He looked about the large hall with its some two thousands rulers of the member planets. "That, by the way, should be at least a partial answer to the question of whether or not this life form, still further beyond, can be considered benevolent."

There were a hundred questions being roared at him. He ignored them, largely, trying to answer a few that seemed more pertinent.

Someone called, "Where was this discovery of the three star systems made?"

Metaxa said, "Surprisingly near our member planet of Phrygia, which, of course, is the furtherest from Mother Earth in the direction of the galaxy's center."

Irene Kasansky turned to Sid Jakes and said, "Terry wants to talk to you." She handed him a Section G hand communicator.

Sid spoke into it, his eyes darting around the crowded conference room even as he spoke.

He snapped, "All right, 'I'll be right over." He handed the communicator back to Irene, and said to Ronny Bronston, "Come on, Ronny. They're going to be yelling back and forth in here for hours."

Out in the corridor, Ronny said, "What's up?"

The Supervisor summoned a three wheeler. "Terry's cracked that news-hen Daniels, or whatever her name is. Metaxa doesn't need us for awhile. Let's see what she has to say. Imagine that mopsy's gall, trying to crack Section G security."

They climbed onto the three wheeler, and Sid Jakes dialed Interrogation.

Ronny said mildly, "If you ask me, the woman's pretty stute to have got as far as she did. We ought to recruit her."

"Sure, sure," Sid Jakes laughed. "She'd stay with us for a year or so, until she knew every secret in the Commissariat, then go running back to Interplanetary News again. Once a newshound, always . . . Oops, here we are."

Interrogation had come a long way since the days of the Gestapo of the Third Reich, or even the cellar room

with the bright light and the rubber hoses of the Land of
Liberty.

Rita Daniels was sitting at her ease in a comfortable
chair. Terry Harper was across from her. There was a
low table with refreshments between them. Inconspicuously in the background was a Section G stenographer,
in case human witness were necessary.

Terry got up when his supervisor entered. He was an
old-timer in the bureau, due soon for retirement, which
he didn't look forward to. Section G operatives were
strong on the dream.

He said, "Sid, as far as the girl knows, only her editor
is aware she's here."

While Ronny Bronston sank into the chair, Sid Jakes
perched on the stenographer's desk. He said pleasantly
to the newswoman, "And how did he find out something
was cooking at the Commissariat of Interplanetary Affairs?"

The other's face worked under the pressure of trying
to fight off the influence of the drug. "I don't know," she
said.

Sid looked at Terry. "You sent a man over to the editor
yet?"

"Not yet, Sid. Since, so far as she knows, only the editor
is involved, I thought you might want to play it as stute
as possible. If we don't have to throw weight around,
well and good."

Sid patted him on the arm, happily. "Good man, Terry."
He spun on Ronny. "Get over to Interplanetary News
. ." He looked at Rita Daniels. "What's this editor's
name?"

"Rosen. He's on the Octagon desk."

Sid's eyes darted back to Ronny. "Bring him over, but
in such a way that no ripples are started in his office."

"Oh, great," Ronny said. "No ripples. Just sugar talk him into coming into our lair, eh?"

Sid Jakes grinned at him happily. "Ronny, old boy, if you can't do it ripplelessly, nobody can. You're the most inconspicuous man in the bureau."

"Is that supposed to be a compliment?"

III

The Nadirscraper, which housed Interplanetary News, delved a good two hundred levels beneath the surface of Greater Washington. As was the prevailing trend, the face presented to the world of the open air was Antiquity Revival: in this case, Egyptian. Although Ronny Bronston had never been in the establishment before, he had passed it on many occasions, never failing to wince at the architect's conception of the Temple of Luxor.

Now he made his way up an immense approach, flanked by a score of marble sphinxes, through an entrada of soaring columns, seemingly open to the sky, but undoubtedly roofed with ultra-transparent plasti.

There was no point in being less than direct. He marched up to the reception desk, pressed an activating button before one of the live screens, and said, "Bronston of the Department of Justice, Bureau of Investigation, to see Citizen Rosen of the Octagon Desk. Soonest."

The voice said, "Your identification, please."

Ronny Bronston brought forth a flat wallet and performed an operation, which came down—unbeknownst to him—in all identicalness, from a long past period of law enforcement.

He flashed his buzzer.

It was a simple enough silver badge, which glowed somewhat strangely when his hand came in touch with it. It read, merely, *Ronald Bronston, Section G, Bureau of Investigation, United Planets.*

"Than kue, Citizen Bronston. Please state your reason

25

for desiring an appointment with Citizen Rosen."

Ronny said testily, "Bureau of Investigation matter, of a security nature."

"Than kue . . ." the voice faded away.

Almost immediately, a three wheeler approached, and its voicebox said, "Citizen Bronston. Please be seated."

He mounted the scooter, and noted how quickly the pseudo-Egyptian decor melted away, as soon as they had entered a ramp leading into the depths.

The three wheeler took him, first, to a bank of elevators, plunged him an unknown number of levels, emerged, and then darted into corridor traffic.

Interplanetary News, Ronny considered. An octopus, which had spread over almost all the United Planets, and over many man-occupied worlds not affiliated with the confederation. Few, indeed, were the planets that could refrain from the fabulous news dispensing service. Even those worlds, such as Goshen, which were so tightly dominated by the feudalistic clique which suppressed it (keeping the populous ninety-five percent illiterate and taking all measures to keep even the barest knowledge of what transpired on other planets from its people), subscribed. In that case, only the nobility had access to the information purveyed.

It reminded Ronny, as he thought, that some measures were going to have to be taken by Section G to overthrow that Goshen aristocracy. If the planet was ever going to get anywhere, the people were going to have to be given a shove out of the mire of class-divided society.

He wondered, vaguely: *how many languages, besides Earth Basic, did Interplanetary News have to deal with? A thousand? Probably, if dialects were considered.* It seemed that a considerable number of the colonists, who wandered off into space—seeking their Ultima Thule—

made effort to devise a new tongue, or, at least, to revive a dead one. There must be a score of versions of Esperanto alone, out there in the stars, not to speak of such jerry-rigged artificial tongues as: Ido, Volapük, Lingua Internaciona, Lingvo Kosmopolita, Esperantido, Nov-Esperanto, Latinesce, Nov-Latin, Europan, and what not.

The more closely a world identified with United Planets, of course, the more widespread the use of Earth Basic. But the worlds which attempted to keep aloof, usually for religious or socio-economic reasons, could get so far removed, that United Planets—as well as Interplanetary News—had to deal heavily through interpreters.

There even came to mind that far-out world settled by deaf-mutes. *What was its name? Keller, or something.*

The three wheeler came to a halt before a door.

"Citizen Rosen," its voicebox said.

Ronny dismounted and the vehicle darted off into the corridor traffic.

He stood before the door's screen, and said, "Bronston, to see Citizen Rosen."

The door opened; he stepped through, and into the arms of two well-muscled goons. They held him by his arms, pausing a moment, as though waiting for his reaction.

Ronny mentally shrugged. *It was their ball. Let them bounce it.*

Both, still holding his arms, with one hand, each ran their other hands over him in the classic frisk. He didn't resist.

One leered as he touched under the Section G agent's left arm. "Ah, packing a shooter."

The other said, "Take it, Jed."

Ronny said mildly, "If you take that gun, without my deactivating it first, you're a dead man, friend."

27

The other's hand, which had been darting under his jacket, came to a quick pause.

Jed scowled, "Don't give me that jetsam. What d'ya mean?"

Ronny said reasonably, "It's a Model H, built especially for the Bureau of Investigation. It's tuned to me. Unless I, personally, deactivate it, anyone who takes it from me is crisp within seconds."

The two of them froze.

Ronny said mildly, "If it's as important as all that, suppose I deactivate it for you? And you can return it, when I leave. I'm not here to hurt anybody."

"The boss said . . ."

"The boss is obviously a flat," Ronny said, still with an air of bored reasonableness. "Since when does the Bureau of Investigation send pistoleros around to deal with half-baked newsmen?"

One looked at the other. "The boss said . . ." he let the sentence dribble away.

The other said, his voice gruff, "Okay, give us the gun." Their hands dropped away.

Ronny took the gun from its quickdraw holster, touched a hidden stud and presented it, butt first. "Now, can I see this romantic cloddy, Rosen?"

Jed, at least, flushed; but, one leading, one bringing up the rear, they passed through another door and into a quarter acre of office.

Rosen sat behind a desk much too large for him. He bent a sly eye on the Section G agent.

"So . . . The Department of Dirty Tricks, Section Cloak and Dagger."

Jed put the gun on the desk. "He had this on him," he said; the implication being that they had wrested it away from Ronny in desperate fray.

28

Ronny said, "Look, you characters seem to have been taking in a lot of Tri-Di crime tapes, or some such. Why don't we cut out all this maize and get around to the reason for my coming over here. We could have simply summoned you, you know."

Rosen said nastily, "You could have summoned till Mercury turned to ice cubes. What's going on over there at the Octagon? What happened to . . ." He cut himself short.

"To Rita Daniels?" Ronny provided. "She's okay. My supervisor asked me to come over and bring you around to discuss Rita and her assignment."

"Yeah? And then you'd have both of us, eh? Listen, Bronston, what's going on? Half the most important bigwigs in the system have . . ."

Ronny said quickly, "I don't believe you really want to discuss this in front of the boys, here."

"Why not?"

"That's what my supervisor wants to talk to you about," Ronny said mildly.

The other stared at him. He was a smaller man, even, than the Section G operative, and there was a cast of perpetual disbelief in his eyes.

He said finally to his two goons, "Go over there to the far side of the room, but keep your eye on this fella. And don't let his size throw you off."

They went to the room's far end and leaned against the wall, assuming expressions of bored cynicism in the best of Tri-Di crime show tradition. Ronny wondered vaguely if it had always been thus, down through the centuries. Did the bully boys and criminal toughs of Shakespeare's day pick up their terminology and mannerisms from watching the villains in plays and aping them? He was inwardly amused.

As yet, Rosen hadn't asked him to be seated. However, Ron pulled up a chair across the desk from the other, his back to the two goons. He looked at the newsman.

"My supervisor wants to talk to you."

"Before he releases Rita, eh?"

There was a certain quality about the other's voice. Ronny assumed the room was bugged.

"I didn't say anything like that," he said, ever mildly. "Where did you get the idea we were holding Rita Daniels?"

"She hasn't returned."

Ronny shrugged. "Why couldn't she be out having a guzzle or two?" He brought a pen from an inner pocket. "Let me have a piece of paper, will you?"

Scowling puzzlement, Rosen pushed a pad over. He failed to notice that the agent—never departing from the standard motions a man makes when he is about to jot down an item—had depressed a small stud on the supposed writing instrument's side. He failed to notice the faintest of hisses, nor the almost microscopic-sized dart that issued from the pen and pricked into his hand.

Even as Ronny scribbled a note on the paper, Rosen, still scowling, absently scratched the back of that hand.

Ronny pushed the note over. It said, merely, *Come along with me, Citizen Rosen.*

Rosen read it and flushed anger. "Do you think I'm drivel-happy?" he began. Then his face went infinitesimally lax, his eyes, slightly strange. Deep in their depths, there seemed to be a trapped fear.

Ronny came to his feet. "Let's go," he said. "Citizen Jakes is waiting."

"Yes. Yes, of course," Rosen said emptily. He stood up also.

His guards reacted.

Jed blurted, "You ain't going with this funker, are you, Boss? You said you expected him to pull some kinda quick one."

Ronny picked up his gun from the desk, reactivated it and slid it back into its holster. He picked up the note he had written and slipped it into his side pocket. Without looking again at the musclemen, he headed for the door, followed by the chief of the Interplanetary News Octagon desk.

Back at the offices of Section G, in the Bureau of Investigation branch offices, still leading, Ronny pushed his way through to the office of Sid Jakes. The irrepressible Sid was sitting at his desk, legs elevated, feet messing up a half dozen reports that lay there.

The supervisor waved a hand in greeting. "Who's this fella?" he asked happily.

Ronny growled, "You wanted Rosen. So here's Rosen."

Jakes peered at the small newsman. "What's wrong with him?"

"He's got a Come-Along shot in him."

"Holy Ultimate, Ronny. You know that's illegal. Interplanetary News will have you on a kidnap romp charge."

Ronny grunted. "Remember? You were going to give this cloddy and his girl, Rita, a memorywash. That isn't exactly part and parcel of the United Planets Charter, either. But one will wash out the recall of the other, so what's the difference? What's going on between all the bigwigs?"

Before answering, Sid Jakes flicked on his order box, and said into it, "Irene, send me an antidote syrette for a Come-Along. Our boy, Ronny, has been tearing up the peapatch. Okay, okay, I know you're busy." He leered. "But who else could I trust with Ronny's neck at stake?"

He flicked the box off, and turned back to his field man. "That old mopsy's sugar on you, you know."

"How's the chief doing?"

"The old man's still at them, hot and heavy. He's let them know the fat's in the fire now. That, willy-nilly, they're going to have to get together in an all-out cooperation, through United Planets, to meet the danger of these new aliens. It's a madhouse."

Sid looked at Rosen. "Sit down, fella. You look tired."

The terror was in the depths of the other's eyes. The wild desire to escape.

Ronny said, "He's tuned to me, of course." He said to the newsman. "Sit down, Rosen."

Rosen sat down.

Sid Jakes flicked his order box again. "Send Terry Harper over with a charge of Scop."

Ronny said wryly, "Our friend here is going to look like a pincushion before we're through with him, what with Come-Along and its antidote, Scop, and then the memorywash."

There was fear and hate in the depths of the eyes again.

Later, shots administered, they sat around, Jakes, Bronston and Harper, and stared at the Interplanetary News man, freed of the kidnapping drug now, but loaded with Scop.

Sid Jakes grinned at him, as though forgivingly. "Now, my stute friend, how many others, besides you and this Rita Daniels, knew about her assignment to break in on the UP conference?"

The other was trying to fight and couldn't. He tried to hold back each word, and couldn't.

"Nobody . . . except . . . my informant."

Sid nodded encouragement. "All right. And who told you about the meeting at all?"

"Baron Wyler."

Sid looked at Ronny and Terry. "Who's Wyler?"

Rosen took it as a question directed at him. "Baron Wyler, Supreme Commandant of the Planet Phrygia."

"Phrygia!" Ronny blurted. "That's the planet nearest to the alien threat. The Space Forces expedition that found the three star systems, where the little aliens came from, took off from Phrygia as its final base."

Sid Jakes chuckled. "Now we're getting somewhere." He bent a cheerful eye on his victim. "And why did the good Baron tell you about the meeting?"

"I . . . I'm not . . . sure. I think . . . it's because . . . he gives us . . news beats . . . available to him . . . as result . . . of his high . . . office. We . . support . . . his politics . . . on Phrygia." There were blisters of cold sweat on the little man's forehead and his shirt was soaked, but his efforts were valueless. There was hate rather than fear in his eyes now.

"I see," Jakes drawled. "Which would come under the head of interfering with the internal political system of a member planet of United Planets, eh? Naughty, naughty, Rosen. Violation of Article Two. Interplanetary News could lose its license to operate on an interplanetary basis. My, wouldn't your competitor, All-Planet Press just love that?"

But in spite of the levity of his words, his eyes were bleak and he spun to his order box. "If that yoke, Baron Wyler, would break ultra-security to tip off a newsman, who knows who else he might sound off to?" He flicked a switch, and blatted, "Irene, have the boys pick up Baron Wyler of the planet Phrygia and bring him here. Absolutely soonest. Kid gloves, he's a chief of state."

33

The order box squawked a reply and Sid Jakes winced. "All right. Find out soonest where he's staying and send the boys to get him."

He turned to Bronston and Harper. "It's the most delicate situation that's come up in the history of the UP. We've got almost three thousand member planets, but the leaders of only two thousand were let in on the crisis. If the word gets out to some of these more backward, reactionary or crackpot worlds, that they were ignored and that their internal matters have been messed with, they'll be dropping out of United Planets like dandruff."

"What happened?" Ronny said.

Sid Jakes grumbled deprecation. "The conference has knocked off for the day and the delegates have melted away into their various embassies, to hotels, or to the homes of friends. The Holy Ultimate only knows where the Baron is. It'll be a neat trick finding him, if he doesn't want to be found."

IV

When Ronny Bronston came in, in the morning, Irene Kasansky looked up from her desk, and said, in comparatively good humor, "Where've you been, Ronny? The commissioner's been asking for you."

Ronny said mildly, "I've been getting some sleep. Remember? Even Section G operatives have to do it occasionally."

She snorted, but not with her usual acidity. "Jetsam, jetsam. All I get around here is jetsam. Why I don't go drivel-happy . . ."

Ronny grinned at her, pushed through the door beyond her desk, turned left in the corridor and knocked at another door, which was inconspicuously lettered, *Ross Metaxa, Commissioner, Section G*. Ronald Bronston seldom entered here, without the realization coming over him, all over again, that behind this door was possibly the single most powerful man in United Planets, and that not one person in a million had ever heard of him. Ross Metaxa of Section G, the ultra-secret enforcement arm of the inner-workings of United Planets. Section G, whose unstated principle was that the ends justified the means: any means necessary to achieve the United Planets dream were acceptable. As always, when this thought came to him, Ronny Bronston shook his head. He had been raised in another ethic.

By his appearance, once would have assumed that the commissioner of Section G had not seen his bed the night before. Either that, or he had been on a monumental toot. He was red and slightly moist of eye, his clothes more disheveled than before. He looked up grumpily, when Ronny entered.

Sid Jakes was there, too, sprawled in a chair, his hands in his pockets, his face in its all but perpetual grin. Lee Chang Chu was also present, sitting demurely to one side of Metaxa's desk, her *cheongsam* dress emphasizing her oriental background.

Metaxa grunted. "Ronny. Good. We're just about to get underway. Drink?" He made a motion to the inevitable squat bottle that stood at his right hand.

Ronny shuddered. "That stuff? And this time of day?" He looked at the girl. "Hi, Lee Chang." So far as he knew every unmarried man in Section G was in love with the diminutive Chinese girl, despite the fact that she was possibly the most effective agent of them all, and had reached supervisor status, ranking the great majority.

She smiled her slow smile and nodded her greetings, as though too shy to speak out in this gathering of men.

Metaxa grunted, "Sid, bring Ronny up to date."

Sid chuckled happily. "Everything's going to pot. Whether or not we're going to keep the lid on this, even temporarily, is moot. We though we'd selected the two thousand most responsible chiefs of state of United Planets. Actually, what we've got is a madhouse. Hardly any two of them agree on what's to be done. At least a dozen have dropped out of UP."

Ronny stared at him. "Dropped out! But why? In this emergency . . ."

Metaxa interrupted. "They didn't wait long enough to consider the emergency. As soon as they heard that we had been violating Articles One and Two, they resigned."

Lee Chang Chu spoke for the first time. She said softly,

"Self-interest we shall always have with us. There's a sizable percentage of our species that would rather die, and bring down the whole race with them, than face the threat of having their political or religious institutions changed."

There was no refuting that.

Sid went on. "Goshen and some of the other hairy-chested planets want to declare war on the aliens. Right now." He laughed his pleasure at the idea. "We don't even know where they are located in the galaxy, but Goshen wants to declare war. On their own planet, of course, they've resisted the introduction of gunpowder. Afraid that the serfs they exploit might get uppity if there were weapons available capable of knocking over castle walls. But they want to declare war on some unknown aliens, who evidently have the neat trick of changing a whole world's atmosphere from nitrogen-oxygen, to poison gas, overnight. Oh, great." Sid chortled again.

"Get on with it, you laughing hyena," Metaxa grumbled.

Sid said, "Others want to sue for peace. How we can sue for peace is another mystery. Keeping in mind that even if we knew where they came from, we still have no particular reason to believe we could communicate. Or, if we could, that they'd be interested in doing so. But even that's not the end. A few of the member planets want to send missionaries. Missionaries, yet! If there's anything that'll irritate just anybody at all, it's bothering around with his religious institutions. Besides, who ever heard of missionaries being sent from a weaker to a stronger power. It's the stronger power that always beats weaker neighbors over the head with its missionaries."

Ronny said, thoughtfully, "What is our own stand? Section G has been aware of the problem for over a century. What *should* we do?"

Metaxa stirred in his chair. He growled, "For the most part, what we have been doing. That is, speeding up our own development by every means that we can. Scientifically, industrially, socio-economically. . . ."

Ronny frowned at him.

His chief scowled back. "We've got to push toward the optimum socio-economic system. . . ."

Ronny said mildly, "There are nearly as many ideas on what that is as you've got persons who have considered the question."

Sid chuckled.

Metaxa growled, "Please, no humor at this time of day. So far as we're concerned, the optimum social system is one under which the greatest number can exercise the greatest amount of each individual's ability. As much education as the individual can assimilate, all-out encouragement of unusual gifts, absolutely nothing so silly as industrial production cycles that allow such nonsense as unemployment, not to speak of anything as reactionary as featherbedding."

Lee Chang Chu said softly, "It is an optimum which has been realized on few planets, I am afraid."

The commissioner said, "At this point, we are aware that our potential enemy exists, though we are not in contact. But we haven't any reason to believe that he is aware of *our* existence. It is possible that we have another year, another century, another millennium before our cultures touch. Possible, but not probable. To the extent we can delay that meeting, we can be more happily prepared for it. That's our job. Delay, delay, delay, while man continues to advance." He looked at Ronny again.

"And that's where you come in."

Ronny Bronston was taken aback. "What?"

Sid chuckled his amusement.

Ross Metaxa reached his hand out for his Denebian tequila, while saying to Lee Chang, "You're the only one of us that's been to Phrygia. Brief Ronny on the place. That's why I called you in."

Lee Chang nodded demurely. "Are you acquainted with the derivation of the planet's name, Ronny?"

"I don't believe so."

"It was one of the early Greek states. Myth has a story about one of its kings, a cloddy named Midas who had an abnormal love of gold. He befriended Silenus . . ."

Sid put in, "I know that one. The god of drunks."

Lee Chang looked at him from the side of her eyes and went on. "And as a reward Dionysus gave him one wish. He chose the power to turn everything he touched into gold." She twisted her mouth in gentle mockery. "The ramifications are obvious."

She looked at Ronny again. "The name has a certain validity. Phrygia, I mean. The original colonists were a group which rebelled against the growth of what was then called the Welfare State. They were even more emphatic than usual. Many planets have been colonized by elements strong for, ah, free enterprise, and opposed to any interference at all by the state in the management of business—not to speak of democratic ownership of the means of production, distribution and communications. The colonists of Phrygia didn't even believe in common ownership of such things as the post office and highways, not . . ."

Ronny blinked at her. "How can you conduct a post office or . . ."

Sid chuckled. "Ronny, old man, you don't go far enough into history. Don't you remember the Pony Express and Wells Fargo? In the early days, mail was in the hands of private concerns. And quite a hash they made of it, too. And early toll roads and toll bridges were private, too."

"At any rate," Lee Chang went on, "the settlers of Phrygia were strong individualists and great believers in pragmatism. On Phrygia, it's each man for himself and the devil take the hindmost."

"Also," said Sid, "dog eat dog, never give a sucker an even break, and if I don't take advantage of this situation, somebody else will." He laughed.

Lee Chang said thoughtfully, "The characteristic also manifests itself in their interplanetary relations. The Phrygians are great entrepreneurs, great traders. More than once, less advanced member planets have had to evoke Article Two of the UP Charter to avoid being swallowed up, economically speaking, by the stutes from Phrygia." She allowed herself a slight smile. "I suspect, actually, that they are in considerable revolt against the existence of such a restraint. Given a free rein, Phrygia would be in full control of a considerable section of her part of our growing confederacy, in short order."

When she paused, Ronny looked at his superior. "What's this got to do with me?"

Metaxa had slugged back the drink he had poured. As he wiped the heel of his beefy hand over his mouth, he said, "Sid didn't bring you completely up to date. Yesterday, when we found out it was Baron Wyler, who had tipped off Interplanetary News, we sent out a call to have him picked up. Until we are able to concoct some mutually satisfactory plans to present to United Planets as a whole, we want to keep the existence of the aliens secret in order to minimize confusion. However, the good Baron has flown the coop."

Ronny stared at him. "He's gone? Where?"

"Evidently, back to Phrygia. He came to the conference in his own official yacht. Which is, by the way, at least as fast as any Space Forces cruiser, or public transportation. You won't be able to beat him back to his home planet, no matter how soon you start."

It was clearing up now. Ronny looked from one of them to the other. "You want me to go to Phrygia, eh? What do I do there?"

Ross scowled at him. "If we knew, then we wouldn't have to send as good a man. You play it by ear. Do what has to be done."

Ronny grunted at the left-handed compliment. "How big is our Section G force on Phrygia?"

Metaxa looked at Sid Jakes.

Sid was amused. "Only one man," he said. "And he's incognito. Operates under the guise of a member of the UP Department of Trade. The Phrygians are as stute as they come and evidently suspect the true nature of Section G. They don't want any of our operatives stirring around in their affairs."

Ronny came to his feet. "I suppose I'd better get under way." He hesitated. "What happened to Rita Daniels and Rosen?"

Sid shrugged. "We memorywashed them and sent them back to Interplanetary News. They can't complain. They've been violating Article Two in return for news beats."

Irene Kasansky had made the arrangements for his trip out to Phrygia. When Ronny issued forth from Metaxa's sanctum sanctorium, she had looked up at him from her multiple duties on phone screen and order box, at desk mike and auto-files.

"Got your marching orders, eh? Before they're through in there, there won't be an agent left on Mother Earth." She handed a slip of paper to him. "Your shuttle for Neuve Albuquerque leaves at six. You'll have only one hour stop-over. It's all on the paper there. Take care of yourself, Ronny."

It occurred to him only then, why Metaxa and Jakes had sent but one agent to Phrygia. Section G must be impossibly short of men in this crisis. Metaxa must have a thousand sore spots with which to deal. Metaxa had been right, up there on the podium, man was in the clutch and must soon alter all his most basic institutions, or he would be a sitting duck for the ultra-advanced aliens.

Ronny Bronston packed sparsely. He had no idea how long he might remain on the distant planet, which was his destination. It might be a matter of hours or years; he might spend the rest of his life there. However, if the stay were lengthy, he could augment his possessions on the spot. To date, he had no idea of what Phrygia climate or clothing styles might be. Why overload himself with non-essentials?

The roof of his apartment building was a copter-cab pickup point, and it took him little time to make his way to the Greater Washington shuttleport. Within three hours of his exit from Ross Metaxa's office, he was being lobbed over to the spaceport at Neuve Albuquerque.

Irene had made him reservations on an interplanetary liner, rather than assigning a Space Forces cruiser. More confortable than the military craft, of course, but not so fast. He shrugged. It was a long trip, and one to which he didn't look forward.

When Ronny Bronston had been a younger man, working in Population Statistics in New Copenhagen, had someone suggested that he wouldn't enjoy interplanetary travel, he would have thought the other mad. Getting into space was every earthborn boy's dream, and few there were who realized it. Long since, the authorities had taken measures to keep Earth's population from leaving wholesale. These days, when new planets were colonized, the colonists came from older settled planets, other than Earth. Earth, the source of man, could not spare its people. Its sole "industry" had at long last become the benevolent direction of human affairs, a supergovernment. More than four thousand man-populated worlds looked to it, in one degree or another, even those not members of United Planets.

However, no matter how strong the dream, no matter how wrapped up in interplanetary affairs, Ronny Bronston soon came to realize that the actual time involved in getting from one colonized planet to the next was the sheerest of boredom. All passenger activity in space was manufactured activity. There was little to do, certainly nothing to see, once the ship has gone into underspace.

One sits and reads. One plays battle chess, or other games. One talks with one's fellow passengers. One watches the Tri-Di tapes, if one is mentally of that level.

Thus it was, on the first day out, that Ronny Bronston made his way to the lounge, hoping that at least the craft was stocked with reading material new to him.

He sank into an auto-chair, as far as possible from the Tri-Di stage, and reached his hand for the stud, which would activate the reading tape listing, set into the chair's arm. His eye, however, hit upon the fellow passenger seated a few feet to his right.

He frowned, and said, "Don't we know each . . ."

43

and then broke it off. Of course. It was Rita Daniels, the Interplanetary News reporter. He hadn't recognized her at first, since she had been wearing a heavy makeup disguise—trying to look like the Supreme Matriarch, Harriet Dos Passos—when he had seen her last. Now, in her own guise, he realized that she was considerably younger than he had thought—and considerably more attractive.

She was blonde, a bit too slim, with a pert, slightly freckled face, and ignored current hair style in favor of a rather intricate ponytail arrangement. In spite of her pertness, there was another more elusive quality, a certain vulnerableness about her mouth. She was clad in a businesslike, inconspicuous crimson suit, and she obviously was of the opinion that this somewhat colorless young man was attempting to pick her up.

She said cooly, "I am afraid not"—and turned away.

What in the name of the Holy Ultimate was she doing on this vessel? The implication was obvious.

He snapped his fingers. "Citizeness Daniels. Interplanetary News."

She turned on him, her eyebrows high, in surprise. "I'm sorry. You do seem to know me. But . . . I'm afraid . . ."

It came to him suddenly that to reveal his true identity would put her on guard. However, he had an advantage. He knew she had been memorywashed. There was a period of at least twenty-four hours, probably more, of which she remembered nothing whatsoever, nor did her immediate superior, Rosen. It must be a confusing situation, he realized. But advantage, it was.

He said easily, smiling, "You remember me. Just yesterday."

She blinked, her eyes immediately alert. Without doubt, she was keen to take advantage of an opportunity to replace erased memories. "Oh, yes, of course, Citizen . . ."

He grinned at her, both on the surface and inwardly, in true amusement. "Smythe," he supplied. "Jimmy Smythe. I helped you out of that trouble with the bottle of guzzle and the traffic coordinator. Wow, were you drenched, eh?"

She stared at him blankly.

V

"Where are you bound?" he said, the standard traveler's gambit. He was less apt to be suspect if he asked it.

She hesitated, then smiled. "End of the line, I suppose. All the way to Phrygia."

"Some special news story?"

This time the hesitation was longer, but the question was still the expected one anybody, knowing she was a reporter, would ask. She smiled ruefully, and said, "What else? And you?"

He projected embarrassment. "My job is supposed to be kind of secret. Orders are not to discuss it with anybody."

She laughed, obviously not caring. "I'll have to worm it out of you. Probably make a good newstape."

He grunted self-deprecation. "Hardly. Worst luck. It must be something, being with Interplanetary News. You must meet a lot of interesting people."

She looked at him, as though wondering if he were kidding. However, no matter how much of a yoke, he was probably better than no companionship at all, and it was a long trip. Besides, he knew at least something about what had happened to her during her twenty-four hour blackout.

"Well, yes," she drew out. "I suppose so. There's a lot of fun being on the *inside* of everything." She was wondering how she could get around to asking just what the circumstances were under which he had met her. Perhaps the blunt approach would do it. He didn't seem to be particularly stute, not to say devious. At most, there seemed to be a kind of sad sensitivity about him, as though he felt something in life was passing him by.

"How about a drink?" he suggested, looking down at the wine list in the chair's arm. He winced at the prices, as he knew an ordinary traveling salesman type might do.

"In space? Good heavens."

"I'll put it on the expense account," he said, with an air of gallantry. "Oiling up the press, or whatever they call it."

They settled for John Brown's Bodies, and he told her the one about feeling like you were moldering in your grave, came morning.

Then he said, "How do you mean, on the 'inside' of everything?"

She considered that. "Well, back when I was in school I decided that there were two kinds of people throughout the worlds. Those who were on the inside pertaining to everything that really counts, and those who were on the outside, and didn't have a clue. And I decided, then and there, I wanted to be an insider."

He sipped his drink and looked at her, his eyes guileless. "I'll bet you were in your sophomore year, when you thought that up," he said.

"Why . . . as a matter of fact, I suppose I was," she said. "How did you know?"

"I used to work in statistics," he said meaninglessly. He covered over. "But what is an example of being on the inside?"

She touched the tip of her slightly freckled nose, in a young girl's gesture, slightly incongruous on the part of an experienced news-hen. "Well, let's take one of the early examples. Have you ever heard of a man named Hearst?"

He had, but he said no.

"Well, Hearst was the owner of a newspaper chain back about the turn of the 20th Century. At that time, he supported a group that believed the United States was getting into the colony-grabbing game too late. He beat the drums for intervention in Cuba, where a great deal of American capital was invested, against Spain. The story is that he sent a photographer down to take pictures of the war. The photographer cabled that there wasn't any war. And Hearst cabled back, *You supply the photos, I'll supply the war.* And he continued to beat the drums. Not long after, the American battleship *Maine* was sunk in Havana harbor."

Ronny nodded. "I've often wondered who sank the *Maine*," he said.

She looked at him.

He said reasonably, "Obviously, it had to be one of three groups, the Cubans, the Spanish or the Americans. No one else was involved. Of them all, the Spanish had the least reason to sink it. The sad excuse for a war that followed was ample proof that they wanted to provoke no such scrap." He paused, then added thoughtfully, "I wonder if the ship was well insured."

"Look," she demanded, "who's being cynical here, you or me?"

He laughed, as though embarrassed. "Go on."

"So, pushed by Hearst and other drum beaters, President McKinley got increasingly tougher. Unfortunately, the Spanish didn't cooperate. Their queen ordered Cuban hostilities suspended, in an attempt to placate the Americans. They were doing all they could to keep the war from happening. However, Hearst and the other drum beaters hardly mentioned her efforts. And McKinley ignored the fact that the potential enemy had already offered capitulation, when he addressed Congress asking for war measures. To wind it all up, the Spanish were clobbered. It was like taking candy from babes."

Ronny attempted to portray dismay. "So that's what it's like to be on the inside. You mean the press can actually influence the news."

She laughed at him in scorn. "My dear Citizen Smythe, the press today makes the news. We shape it to fulfill our own needs, to realize our own ideals, to build a better race."

He looked at her, wide-eyed, in complete sympathy. "The way you put it, it's absolutely inspiring."

She had his admiring interest now, and responded. "Take for instance," she explained, "some planet of which we don't approve. Suppose that three news items came out of there one day. The first mentions a new cure for cancer; the second, some startling statistics on industrial progress being made; the third mentions a riot by high school children, who overturn some copter-cabs in the streets and throw stones through some windows. What story do you think we put on the interplanetary broadcasts?"

"You mean the last one? Only the last one?"

"Why should we mention the other two?" she said reasonably.

"Well, doesn't it kind of involve freedom of speech, or of the press, or something?"

She scoffed at him. "It's our press, isn't it? The freedom consists of printing what we wish."

"Well, that isn't the way I should have put it. I mean, the right of the public to know . . . or something."

She scoffed again. "Let's have another of these. What

49

did you call them? This time we'll put it on Interplanetary News' swindle sheet." She dialed the drinks. "It's up to us, we who are on the inside, to decide what the public ought to know. They're a bunch of yokes, not up to making decisions."

Ronny thought about it. "Well, possibly the reason they're yokes, like you say, incapable of making competent decisions, is because they're improperly informed. But, anyway, that's the reason you're going to Phrygia, eh? Something really inside is going on."

She sipped the potent drink and scowled at him. "As a matter of fact, I don't know what's going on. But it's something very big. It involves Baron Wyler himself."

"Who's Baron Wyler?" Ronny said, trying to look as though he were trying to look interested.

She was stung by the fact that she didn't seem to be impressing him. "I can see you're not one of those insiders. The Baron is the most aggressive single man in UP. He's Supreme Commandant of Phrygia and Phrygia is the most aggressive planet in the system."

Ronny snorted. "What good does it do to be aggressive these days? Under United Planets, no member planet is allowed to interfere with any other. Where can your aggressiveness, go, besides inward?"

She opened her mouth to retort, then closed it suddenly. She looked into her drink. "These are strong, aren't they, Jerry?"

"Pretty strong, all right. In the auto-bars, they usually have a sign—only one to a customer."

She cocked her head to one side. "Oh, listen. That song." She wagged her head to it, setting her blonde ponytail aswing. It was coming from the Tri-Di stage at the other end of the lounge. "Do you dance?" she said.

"Well, a little. I'm not very good at this rock'n'swing stuff."

She stood up. "Neither am I. Let's try this, it's an old favorite of mine."

He took her in his arms and they joined half a dozen other couples on the small dance floor.

They had taken only a few steps before she said, tightly, "That's what I thought. You're carrying a shooter, aren't you?"

"I beg your pardon?"

She stopped dancing, turned and returned to her chair. She began to pick up her half-finished drink, but then sat it down again, decisively.

He lowered himself to his own seat, across from her, and looked into her eyes.

She said bitterly, "It's that ineffective air of yours. Who are you from?"

He shook his head.

She asked, "How did you know my name?"

"Like I said, I met you yesterday."

"Yes. You also said your name was Jimmy Smythe, and then managed to forget that, not correcting me, when I called you 'Jerry'."

She had him there. Ronny had to laugh aloud.

She said, bitterly, "You look smarter when you laugh. How did you know my name?"

Ronny shook his head, as though sorry she wouldn't believe him.

She said, "If you met me yesterday, then you probably have something to do with the Commissariat of Interplanetary Affairs."

"Why should that follow?" he asked mildly.

"Because yesterday"—she hesitated, then plunged on—through a tip given us by . . . one of our informants, I went to the Octagon, on an assignment from Dave Rosen. I was memorywashed there, and, now, can't even remember the assignment."

Ronny played it out. "Why not ask this—what was his name? Rosen?—what he sent you for?"

"He was memorywashed, too, as you undoubtedly are aware."

He shrugged. "I thought that was very illegal. Who did it?"

"How could we know? I told you, we were memorywashed."

Ronny scowled puzzlement at her. "Well, why not just check back with your informant and find out what tip you were working on?"

"That's what I'm doing," she said, still bitterly. "Unfortunately, he's gone all the way to Phrygia." She got up, preparatory to stomping off. "And don't ask me why we don't simply ultra-wave him. All-Planet Press, the Bureau of Investigation and who knows who else, would be listening in. Good-bye, Jerry!"

"Jimmy," Ronny said mildly. "Sure you wouldn't like another drink I was really beginning to enjoy our talk, about being inside and all."

Rita Daniels wasn't as much of a lightweight as his first encounter on the spaceline with her might have indicated. She avoided him for two days, then showed up at his table in the passenger's mess, while he was finishing off some fruit dessert.

He began to come to his feet, but she slid into a chair before he could invite her.

"Your name is Ronald Bronston," she informed him. "And you're an operative for Ross Metaxa in that Section G mystery outfit. In fact," she added snappishly, "you'r

52

one of his top hatchet-men. I must say, it's hard to believe."

He said calmly, "You Interplanetary News people have your resources, haven't you?"

"What do you want with me?" she asked flatly.

"Nothing," he told her. He didn't like this. If he hadn't been a flat, he would have let the girl alone. Evidently, she had an in with Baron Wyler, or, at least, Interplanetary News did, and she through that organization. Now the Baron would be informed that Agent Bronston was on his way, and the Baron didn't cotton to Section G.

"Then what are you doing following me?"

"I wasn't aware that I was, Citizeness Daniels. We're simply on the same vessel." He twisted his mouth ruefully. "Why don't we start all over again?"

"And you continue to pump me? No thanks. Do you deny that you're going to Phrygia?"

He thought about it. "No. I don't deny that. But, you know, I could reverse the question. Why are you following me?"

"Don't be silly."

"Well, we're on the same spacecraft and you don't deny you're going to Phrygia."

She stood again, abruptly. "I don't know why I was memorywashed, but, obviously, something big is in the wind and my job is to find out what."

He murmured mildly. "So that Interplanetary News will be inside, eh?"

She glared at him. "And, don't be too sure that Section G won't be outside."

He wasn't too sure at all.

A few hours before estimated coming out time, he approached the captain's private quarters and looked into the door's screen. He said, "Ronald Bronston, requesting an interview with Captain Henhoff."

The screen said, "The Captain is busy. Could you state your business?"

He brought forth his badge and held it to the screen "Important matters involving the Bureau of Investigation."

In a few moments, the door opened. Ronny stepped through.

Captain Henoff's quarters were moderately ample considering that this was, after all, a spacecraft. He was seated at a desk, going through reports, a junior officer across from him, taking orders.

The captain, frowning, said, "Citizen Bronston? What can I do for you? Frankly, I am afraid I've never heard of Section G of the Bureau of Investigation."

Ronny looked at the junior officer. "May I speak to you privately?"

The frown had become a testy scowl. However, the skipper said, "Howard, go on out into the corridor. I'll call you."

Howard got up, looked at Ronny, shrugged and left.

The captain said, "Well?"

Ronny laid it on the line. "We'll be coming out of under space and setting down at Phrygia in a matter of hours I'm on a special mission. I have reason to believe an attempt will be made at the spaceport to apprehend me I want to be smuggled off the ship in some manner."

Captain Henhoff leaned back in his swivel chair. "That' asking a lot."

Ronny said, "I suggest you get in touch with you superiors and ask whether or not you should cooperate with Section G."

Henhoff looked at him for long moment. He said fin

ally, "I suppose that won't be necessary." He thought about it. "They use pilots at Phrygia. Usually, three men pick us up in orbit and supervise setting us down. When we've finally set down, a spaceport auto-floated picks them up and runs them back to the spacepilot quarters, while the ship is still going through quarantine procedures. You can leave with them. I'll see that one of the men fixes you up in a uniform like the pilots wear to get you by. Think that would do it?"

"It should," Ronny nodded. "Thanks, Captain."

"You're not doing anything against the Phrygian government, are you? I don't want to get into trouble with that gang."

"Of course not. I've shown you my credentials. You don't think the Department of Interplanetary Justice goes about meddling in the affairs of member planets of UP, do you?" Ronny was very righteous.

"No. Of course not."

He left the liner in the spacepilot's auto-floater, as provided; the others couldn't have cared less. They probably figured he was some Tri-Di entertainment star, beating the fans out of an opportunity to give him the rush, when the regular passengers disembarked.

His precautions had been well merited.

At the foot of the spaceliner's disembarking ladder, he noted, stood three brawny, though inconspicuously dressed men. He didn't have to look at their feet to know their calling.

The Supreme Commandant's welcoming committee for visiting Section G operators. Citizeness Daniels was doing her best to make certain that whilst Interplanetary News got inside, the Bureau of Investigation didn't.

VI

The auto-floater left him off at the spacepilot's quarters, and Ronny Bronston started off up the street immediately. He wanted to get out of the vicinity of the spaceport as soon as possible. He imagined that it would take a half hour or so before the Phrygians realized that he had gotten through their fingers. He didn't know what their instructions were: Whether they had meant simply not to allow him to disembark, or whether he was to be picked up and questioned by Phrygian authorities. Probably the latter. Undoubtedly, they had their own version of Scop. Nobody, but nobody, stood up under questioning these days.

He had none of the local means of exchange, whatever it was. His instructions had been to go immediately to the United Planets building and get in touch with Section G operative Phil Birdman, who would check him out on the local situation.

The auto-floater he had been in with the spacepilots had been similar to those on Earth, and were fairly general on the more advanced planets. He assumed there were taxis, of some sort or another, and kept his eyes open for something resembling a stand, having no idea of how the locals summoned such a vehicle.

He was struck by a certain *sameness* about this city. It was, he knew, named Phrygia and was the capital city of the planet of the same name.

The sameness, he decided—even as he strode briskly up a shopping street—came from the fact that so many of the buildings, vehicles, signs, traffic indicators and what not, were those of Earth, Avalon, Shangri-La, Catalina and Jefferson—the most advanced worlds. Evidently, Phrygia was quick to pick up any discoveries and developments pioneered elsewhere. Well, that was commendable.

There was one thing though. The average person in the street seemed to have a drab quality. Not one person in a hundred seemed up to the styles and general appearances of well-being, that one would find on Earth or Shangri-La. Yes, a gray drabness that you couldn't quite put your finger upon. They seemed well-fed and healthy enough, however.

He came to what would seem to be a cab stand, and stood, for a moment, looking at the first vehicle in line. He wanted to avoid asking questions and thus branding himself a stranger.

Well, he could only try. If the cab weren't fitted to take instructions in Earth Basic, he would be out of luck.

He opened the door and slipped into a rear seat. He made himself comfortable, and said into the screen, "The United Planets Building."

No trouble. The vehicle started up and edged itself into the street traffic.

The UP Building, he found, he could have easily walked to. It was less than a mile from the spaceport.

There were two Space Marines on guard at the door. Ronny Bronston called out to one of them.

The marine marched over and scowled down into the car.

Ronny flashed his badge. "I just came from the spaceport and have no local exchange. Can you pay the cab off for me?"

"Oh. Yes, sir. Certainly. They use credit cards here,

sir." The marine brought one from his pocket and held it to the cab's screen. The door automatically opened.

Ronny stepped out and said, "Now, quickly, take me to Citizen Phil Birdman."

The marine blinked. "Yes, sir." He turned and marched off, Ronny following.

The suite of offices was lettered simply, *Interplanetary Trade.*

Ronny said, "Thanks. I'll have that cab fare returned to you."

"Not necessary, sir," the space soldier said stiffly. "We're on unlimited expense account." He did an about-face and was off.

Ronny looked after him for a moment. How does it feel to be a professional soldier, when there hasn't been a war for centuries? He grunted sourly. Perhaps the soldier would be practicing his trade before long.

He opened the door and entered into a reception room. He walked over to the screen and said, "Ronald Bronston, Section G. To see Phil Birdman."

A door beyond opened immediately and a very dark-complected man, in his mid-forties, well over six feet tall and with a startlingly handsome face, came hurrying out, hand extended.

"Come in!" he said. "Holy Jumping Zen, it's been two years since I've seen a fellow agent from Section G."

Ronny ignored the hand. He brought his wallet out and showed his badge. He touched it with a finger and the badge glowed silver.

Birdman laughed, said, "Okay, okay, if you want to play it formal." He fished his own wallet out and displayed his badge. He touched it with a finger, and like Bronston's it shone brightly.

Ronny stuck out his hand for the shake, grinning self-deprecation.

Birdman cocked his head on one side. "Something must be up."

"Yes," Ronny said. "Let's get out of here."

The tall dark man looked at him. "Get out to where? Come on in the office and we'll have some firewater."

Ronny shook his head impatiently. "I'm already on the run. They'll probably be here any minute. Surely you've got an ultimate hideout—just in case."

"Wait'll I get my shooter," the other clipped. He hurried back into the inner office, returned in moments, shrugging a shoulder holster into a more comfortable position beneath his jacket.

"This way."

He led Ronny through a series of doors and halls, finally emerging at the back of the building. There was a row of hovercars. Birdman slid into one, a speedy-looking model. Ronny slipped into the seat beside him.

"We're not going very far in this, are we?" Ronny growled. "If it's yours, it's spotted."

"Of course," Birdman grunted. "Who are you working with?" His hand maneuvered the vehicle out of the parking area and into the traffic stream.

"Directly under the Old Man," Ronny said.

"Oh? And Sid Jakes? How's Sid?"

"Chuckling his fool head off," Ronny said.

They spoke no more for the next fifteen minutes, during which time Phil Birdman put on a show of how to lose a possible tail and leave no possible trail behind, in a big city. They dropped his car after a few miles, sending it back to the UP Building. They took a cab for a time. Then they got out and walked. They took a rolling road for a time. They took a pneumatic. Then they walked some more.

Finally, in a residential area, they entered a house. It seemed deserted. They entered a closet. The closet was an elevator.

When they left the elevator, they were in a Spartan apartment, well-equipped from the Section G gimmick department, and from Communications and Weaponry.

Ronny looked about and whistled approvingly through his teeth. "Nice setup, considering you're only one man here."

Birdman nodded. "I'm going to have to brace Sid Jakes on that. We need a bigger staff. Phrygia is more important than they seem to think back there in the Octagon." He headed for a manual bar. "Now how about that firewater?"

"Firewater?" Ronny said.

Phil Birdman grinned at him. "Ugh, guzzle, you pale-faces call it. I'm from Piegan."

Ronny frowned in memory. "Oh, yes," he said. "Colonized by Amerinds. Mostly Blackfeet and Sioux. Diehards, who still wanted to get away from the whiteman and go back to the old tribal society. Setup, kind of a primitive communism, based on clan society."

"That's the way it started," Birdman nodded. "How about pseudo-whiskey?" At Ronny's nod, he added, "And water?" He finished the drinks and returned with them

Ronny was already seated. He took the drink and said, "How did it work out?"

"Piegan? Terribly. You can't go back, no matter how strong the dream."

"So what happened?"

Birdman grinned at him, wryly. "Section G happened

A few of the boys turned up and subverted our institutions. Best thing that every happened. We've still got an Indian society, but we're rapidly industrializing. Couple of more decades and we'll be at least as advanced as Phrygia, here."

Ronny drank half of the pseudo-whiskey down. "If any of us are around, a couple of decades from now."

The big Indian looked at him. "I knew it was something important," he said.

Ronny nodded and briefed the other operative on recent developments.

Their drinks were finished by the time he was through. His host got up to get new ones. "And now?" he asked.

Ronny shrugged. "My assignment isn't particularly important. Just one phase of the whole. Ross Metaxa wants me to take what steps I can and keep Baron Wyler from sounding off about the Octagon's plans to speed up the amalgamation of United Planets and all other human settled worlds. From what this mopsy, Rita Daniels, tells me, the Baron has been playing footsie with Interplanetary News."

"Footsie, yet," Birdman snorted. "Baron Wyler *is* Interplanetary News."

Ronny gaped at him. "What are you talking about?"

"I told you we need a larger staff here. There's a lot cooking that's going to have to come right before Metaxa's eyes. I'm working on the report right now. At any rate, Baron Wyler owns communications on Phrygia. All communications. And he also controls Interplanetary News. Who did you think owned it?"

"It never occurred to me to wonder. I realize, of course, that we've got every kind of socio-economic system ever dreamed up, through the centuries, at one place or another in United Planets; but I didn't think in terms of an organization as strong as Interplanetary News being privately owned. Certainly not by one individual."

"It's not exactly one individual," the Indian growled. "More like a family, and the Baron's the head of the family."

He made a face. "I'd better give you some background. You were right, when you said UP has every socio-economic system ever dreamed up by man, on one planet or the other. It also has a lot of crisscrosses."

Ronny frowned at him.

Birdman explained. "Take communism. We've got planets, such as my own Piegan used to be, that practice primitive tribal communism. Then we've got planets of 'purists,' who have attempted to build a society such as Marx and Engels originally had in mind back in 1848. Then we've got a sample or two of communism, as Lenin saw it; then, one or two as DeLeon adapted socialism to America; and, at least one on the Stalinist conception —that's a *real* honey—and one, I can think of, based on Trotsky's heresy. And Mao, the Chinese. And Tito, remember Tito?"

"No," Ronny said, "but you've made your point. There's a lot of confusion on just what communism is."

The Indian was nodding. "Yes. Well, the crisscross on this planet is a doozy. You might call it industrial feudalism. Kind of a classical capitalism gone to seed. Kind of free enterprise without either freedom, or, except for a handful, any enterprise. You see, they got to the point where the wealth of Phrygia is in the hands of less than one percent of the population. The means of production, distribution, communications, the farms, the mines, the whole shebang—all owned and controlled by comparatively few families."

Ronny grunted. "In any society, a good man gets to the top."

"Or loses his scalp trying," Birdman agreed. "If he can't, he tries to change the society. Well, they have one fairly workable way of getting around that on Phrygia. Any real stute that comes along, gets adopted into one of the big families. The Romans used to do the same thing; Octavius was an adopted son of Caesar.

"But to get on with it. There's evidently no end to the desire for wealth and the power it brings. A millionaire wants to become a billionaire and a billionaire wonders how it'd be to have a trillion. Far, far beyond the point where his own needs are completely satisfied, the stute with a power complex continues to accumulate more wealth, more power. It might not make sense to you and me, but there it is. Well, Baron Wyler has about outgrown Phrygia. He's looking for new worlds to conquer, and I've a sneaking suspicion he doesn't expect to allow United Planets to stand in his way. In fact, it didn't even start with the present Baron. The dream had evidently been in his family, and probably other industrial feudalistic families here, for several generations. Interplanetary News is just one of the projects designed to help pave the way."

Ronny was staring at him.

The Indian chuckled sourly. "Sounds unbelievable, eh? Well, in spite of the far-out nature of this super-loose confederation of ours, United Planets is still basically a republic. Whatever the home government of each planet, in the UP it has one voice, one vote, no more. But there's no particular reason why man, in his eruption into space, has to remain a republican. Given a strong enough ambition on the part of a few fellas like our good

Baron, and what's to prevent an empire from being established?"

Ronny was shaking his head. "To many would fight."

The other nodded in agreement. "That's what's baffled me. Something is going on. Something the Baron is counting upon to give him such an edge over the other strong worlds, which would ordinarily resist his ambitions, that he'd prevail."

Ronny Bronston thought about it for a long moment, staring down into his glass. He said finally, "I suppose it's about time I got in touch with this Baron Wyler. Have you got a Section G communicator handy?"

"Over there."

Ronny sat at the indicated desk. The device was about the size of a woman's vanity case, and was propped up now so that the small screen was immediately before the operative. He activated it.

"Ronald Bronston," he said. "I want to report to Supervisor Jakes, soonest."

He sat there, saying nothing, until Sid Jakes' grinning face appeared on the screen.

"Hi, Ronny." He chuckled. "On Phrygia, eh? How's that redskin coming along?"

Ronny said, "That redskin is evidently a one-man task force. He's dug up the fact that Baron Wyler controls Interplanetary News and is evidently prettying up a scheme to unite UP . . ."

"Well, isn't that what we want to do?"

". . . under his leadership. Possibly, I should say, under his dictatorship."

The supervisor scoffed. "Neat trick, if he could pull it off."

"Evidently, he has some reason to believe he can."

Sid Jakes looked at him thoughtfully. "Get a complete report on this, soonest, Ronny."

"Phil Birdman's just about got it finished. Meanwhile, would it be possible for you to put through an order making me a plenipotentiary extraordinary from UP to the Supreme Commandant of Phrygia?"

"Have you gone drivel-happy, old boy?"

"No. The Baron's got his heavies out looking for me. I want to face him, but not on the kind of basis he evidently has in mind. I want some weight to throw around."

Jakes thought about it some more. "All right. Within twenty-four hours, you'll be a special mission from the President of UP to Baron Wyler. You'll have to play it from there. Dream up your own idea of what the mission is. Wyler won't dare touch you, with such a commission." He grinned. "This oughta be a neat trick."

He faded from the screen.

Ronny turned back to his companion.

Birdman said, "I'm not sure I like this. Wyler's feeling his oats. He's getting near the point where he's ready to take action. I don't think he's afraid of the Commissariat of Interplanetary Affairs."

Ronny shrugged. "The way you brought me here, to this hideout, I couldn't find it again. So even though he slips me Scop, I can't betray you. For myself, I'm no big loss. If I don't get away from him, again, there's not much he can get out of me that he doesn't already know. Now, let's get about the job of outfitting me properly to be a plenipotentiary from the President to the Baron. Sid is going to radio through to Wyler that I am to appear."

VII

If Ronny Bronston had thought the surface buildings of the nadirscraper, which housed the Interplanetary News in Greater Washington, were ostentatious, he could only admit he had had little upon which to base his opinion—comparatively.

Baron Wyler's official residence was some ten kilometers outside the Phrygia city limits. At first, the Section G agent couldn't place the theme; but it began to come to him, when his limousine—driven by a United Planets Space Forces marine, in dress uniform, with another seated beside him—was stopped at a gate by a squad of men in an armor of yesteryear and in short linen tunics. They were armed with spears, swords buckled to their sides.

The driver said from the side of his mouth, "You're getting the full official greeting, sir. Ordinarily, we could've driven inside."

Six of the guards stood at rigid attention, spear butts grounded. An officer, his breastplate of gold, approached the heavy hovercar, and came to the salute.

He said, "Hail the Plenipotentiary from the United Planets!"

Maintaining his dignity, Ronny nodded.

The officer said, "If your Excellency will alight, you will be conducted to audience with the Supreme Commandant."

Evidently, his two marines were going to be left here at the gate. Ronny mentally shrugged. He was already in the Baron's hands. Let them bounce the ball. He left the car.

In a clatter and a small cloud of dust, a chariot, pulled by three enormous white horses, came speeding forth. Ronny blinked at it. He had seen chariots in illustrations, and in historic Tri-Di shows, but never in actuality.

The driver pulled the horses to a rearing halt, only a few feet from him.

The officer said, not a flicker of expression on his face, "If His Excellency will mount. . . ."

Ronny Bronston looked at his marines from the side of his eyes. They remained expressionless as well. He wondered vaguely if they would have pulled this gimmick had he been an eighty year old man. Well, there was nothing for it. He jumped up into the wheeled vehicle and grasped the edge, next to the driver.

They were off in a clatter.

The setting was beginning to come to him. The double-headed ax motif, the bulls in fresco and statuary. Once, as a boy, his father had taken him to the so-called Palace of Minos, at Knossos on Crete. Baron Wyler had obviously drawn upon the reconstructions of Sir Arthur Evans in building his residence. The British archaeologist had notoriously exercised his imagination in the reconstruction; but many a Cretean must have turned in his grave at this version of a palace of the four thousand year old civilization.

They clattered up a broad ramp, Ronny Bronston hanging on for life, and came to a rearing halt before an entrada flanked with highly colorful columns, which started narrow at the bottom and widened at the roof.

There was another guard unit, clad in the costume of Knossos, at the entry. A full twenty of them here. They came to the salute.

An officer stepped forward, came to attention.

"The Supreme Commandant sends greetings to His Excellency, the Plenipotentiary from United Planets."

Ronny stepped down from the chariot, looked at the driver bitterly. Inaudibly he muttered. "Do you have a license to operate that thing?"

"Thanks," he said to the officer. "I would like to see the Baron immediately."

"His instructions are to bring you to his quarters upon arrival, Your Excellency."

He turned and marched, stiff legged, into the building. Ronny followed.

As at the Interplanetary News building in Greater Washington, the resemblance to the ancient past fell off immediately in the interior. The officer's costume seemed doubly ludicrous among the hosts of guards, messengers, secretaries and officials, all garbed in modern dress.

Two guards, fish-cold of eye, stood before an elevator door, one behind a device of switches and screens. Ronny assumed he was being given an electronic frisk. Well, they'd find him clean. It would have been ridiculous to think he could approach the ruler of Phrygia armed.

The elevator opened and the officer accompanying him gestured. Ronny entered alone, the door closed and the car dropped.

Then the door reopened, and even before Ronny Bronston could step out, the tall, heavy-set man there— his face beaming—reached for his hand.

"Ronald Bronston!" he said heartily. "Your Excellency, I've been waiting for you!"

He was at least as tall as Phil Birdman, but would have outweighed the Indian by fifty pounds. He carried his weight well; gracefully, might be the word. He moved as a trained pugilist moves, or perhaps one of the larger

68

cats. His charm reached out and embraced you, all but suffocatingly. His face was open, friendly; his eyes, blue and wide-set; his nose, the arched Hapsburg nose, giving an aristocratic quality that only his overwhelming friendliness could dissipate.

He could only be, Ronny realized, *Baron Wyler, Supreme Commandant of the Planet Phrygia, and, were Phil Birdman correct, would-be dictator of this sector of the galaxy.*

Ronny let his hand be pumped, admittedly taken aback. He realized now that, although he had never seen even a photo of the Baron, he had built up a ficticious picture of him. *Yes, the picture,* he admitted in sour realization, *had nothing to do with reality.* Among other things, far from being middle-aged or even an elderly Prussian type, the Baron was little older than Ronny, himself.

Ronny Bronston hated to be touched by another man —other than perhaps a quick handshake—however, he suffered now his host to place an arm around his shoulders and lead him to as comfortable a room as the Section G agent could remember ever having been in. It was a man's room. A small but complete bar to one side. A number of large, well-used chairs and couches. Racks of books that, even at a distance, looked interesting and oft-handled. Good, well-chosen, not necessarily expensive, paintings on the walls. A fireplace.

A fireplace, Ronny thought. *At this distance down into the Earth's crust?* He wondered vaguely what effort must have gone into devising a manner of dispelling smoke and fumes.

The Baron was at the bar. "May I suggest this departure on the wines of the Rhine and Moselle? One of my ancestors imported the Riesling grape to Phrygia. Local soil conditions were somewhat different; but I trust you will find a lightness and bouquet not at all unpleasing." Even as he spoke, he was pouring from a very long necked bottle into two delicate crystal glasses.

Ronny found himself seated in one of the chairs, glass in hand. The Baron was across from him and now picked up a small sheaf of papers from a coffee table.

He read aloud. "Ronald Meredith Bronston, 32. Born in Luana, Hawaii. Parents, Michael L. Bronston, and Pauline Meredith. Studied, ummm, ummm, finished education at University of Stockholm . . . ummm, ummm, at age of twenty-six took position at New Copenhagen in the Population Statistics Department. Was discovered by Bureau of Investigation scouts and jockeyed into Section G. . . ."

Ronny stared at him. "*Jockeyed,*" he protested. "I applied for a position that would take me overspace and was lucky . . ."

Baron Wyler chuckled at him magnanimously. "My dear Bronston, no luck is involved in getting into our friend Metaxa's Section G. Not one human being in a million qualifies. Were you a bit more privy to the inner workings of your ultra-ultra cloak and dagger organization, you would know that at any given time at least a hundred of Metaxa's picked men are scouting out potential agents. You were probably selected as far back as when you were in high school."

Wyler's eyes went back to the report. "But to go on with it. Given first assignment with Supervisor Lee Chang Chu and, as a result, was made full agent. . . . Umm, umm, worked with distinction on the planets Kropotkin, Avalon and Palermo. Has become one of Supervisor Jakes' most trusted field men. Height, weight, ummm, fingerprints, eye pattern, skull measurements." The Baron looked up. "Some of these statistics come directly from Section G files."

"All right," Ronny said in resignation. "You've made your point. You have a rather complete dossier on me."

The Baron put down the report and turned on his charm with a smile. "So we can dispense with preliminaries and get to the point."

Ronny said, "The point being that the Supreme Commandant of the Planet Phrygia is ambitious to encrouch upon the sovereignty of fellow worlds belonging to the United Planets."

"Which is one way of putting it." The Baron nodded agreeably. "Tell me, Bronston, what is the eventual goal of this United Planets to which you have devoted your life?"

"The advancement of the human race!"

"Neatly summed up in but six words. But, my dear Bronston, man has made his advances down through the ages in a wide variety of methods. Your knowledge of history must be such that you recognize the contributions of strongmen who have arisen in time of need. The democratic principle does not always apply."

Ronny said sharply, "My studies have led me to believe that man makes his greatest advances under conditions of freedom."

"An example?"

The Section G agent groped for a good one. "The Athens of the Golden Age. The Athenian democracy nourished a culture such as had never been seen before, nor since."

Baron Wyler chuckled. "My dear Bronston, have you never heard of the strongman, Pericles? Besides, calling the Athenian society a democracy is somewhat stretching a point, is it not? For every Athenian citizen free to pursue the arts and sciences, there were a dozen slaves, or more, kept in complete subjugation. Come now, do you contend that if these slaves—who did the drudgery necessary to maintain the leisure of the Athenian citizens—had been given their freedom, been given complete equality, that the Golden Age could have been?"

Ronny looked at him. The Baron was obviously no fool.

The Baron got up, brought the bottle from the bar and refreshed the glasses. The Section G agent was no connoisseur of wine, but, admittedly, this was the most pleasant beverage he could remember drinking. He wondered if it was available on Earth.

The Baron said, "Let me use a somewhat more recent example of strongman versus the mob."

"I wasn't exactly advocating mob rule."

"Indeed? However, remember when the Egyptian Nasser seized power in his country, oh, somewhere about the middle of the 20th Century? His nation had been a backward one, dominated by the big powers, ignored in the world's councils. When he took over the Suez Canal, all prophesied that the waterway would soon be silted up and impassable. Instead, within a few years, traffic had doubled. Borrowing, begging, securing funds and techniques from every source he could find, he began to industrialize, to irrigate, to find new potentials in his desert country. His soldiers were sent out to fill up the wells in thousands of native communities, supposedly a crime beyond understanding in a desert land. They filled them up and forced the fellahin to dig new wells in places where the water would not be contaminated with sewage. He sent soldiers out and rounded up the children and forced them into schools. Children that otherwise would have been taught nothing further than a few

72

suras from the Koran. These were but a few things done by strongman Nasser."

Ronny was scowling at him.

The Baron twisted his mouth in deprecation. "At the same time, and on the same continent, the newly emerged nation, the Congo, seemed unable to find an equivalent of Nasser. Instead, in an atmosphere of pseudo-democracy, they went from one barbarism to the next, going backward, rather than progressing. Come now, Citizen Bronston, don't you think conditions sometimes call for a strongman?"

Ronny put his glass down. Thus far, he had been satisfied to hold his peace, if only to see just how the other was going to bounce the ball.

Now he said, "Interpreting history isn't my field. I do know this, as Metaxa said, the human race is in the clutch. This is not the time for would-be strongmen to try to seize control of worlds other than their own. We can't afford the time, nor the energies involved in interplanetary war. And, please don't attempt to put over the idea that you, or anyone else, could form an empire from the largely individualistic United Planets, without war. Baron Wyler, you saw that charred body of the intelligent alien life form. You heard what Ross . . ."

The Baron held up a hand to restrain him. He nodded, still agreeable. "Indeed I did. And I was surprised that the estimable Commissioner was in possession of it. However, we could have shown him better examples."

"Better examples?"

The Baron reached out and touched a switch on the coffee table. One wall of the room clouded, then became a giant screen.

The Baron fiddled with a small dial set into the table.

On the screen, there faded in an extensive laboratory. At least a dozen white-smocked men were working about an operating table. The Baron turned another dial, zooming in on the scene.

Ronny sucked in his breath. Those on the screen were dissecting two bodies of what were obviously specimens of the tiny life form Metaxa had deep frozen.

Another turn of the dial. A new room, more extensive than the last. At least several thousand men—technicians and mechanics—were working away at various benches, on various pieces of equipment: the nature of which, Ronny couldn't even guess.

The Baron said wryly, "They're trying to figure out the use of some of the devices, weapons or whatever, that we've gleaned from the alien planets." He snorted his deprecation. "What if you took a squad of Neanderthal men and set them down in a 25th Century laboratory in the midst of all the products that century produced? What do you think they might accomplish?"

Ronny, his eyes bugging still, said, "Is there that much difference?"

"At least," the Baron told him. "However, as our good Metaxa pointed out at the conference, this culture is not the one we must confront. This culture was destroyed by one beyond."

Ronny nodded. "That is the basic point, Baron Wyler. That is why the human race doesn't have the time to bother with ambitious men of the caliber of the Supreme Commandant of Phrygia. We know nothing at all about the culture beyond."

"Oh, I wouldn't say that," the Baron said easily. "A taste more wine?"

He had Ronny staring again. "What do you mean by that?"

The Baron waggled a finger at him. "You see, my dear

Bronston, we are far, far beyond Section G and its well-intentioned plans to preserve the race. Some time ago, long before the Space Forces exploration force located the alien planets, Phrygian cruisers had found them. Properly masked, of course, we were able to descend and explore. My laboratories have been working on the equipment, and even the bodies of the aliens, as you have seen. We found a few under conditions which had preserved them."

"But you said something about the power beyond."

The Baron nodded. "Yes. Our little aliens left enough in the way of photographs to indicate part of what we're up against."

"Photographs?"

"Both still photographs and also a tape that one of my more brilliant young men has been able to project. It would seem that our little aliens actually landed upon at least one of the beyond culture's planets."

For the last half hour the Baron had been throwing curves faster than Ronny Bronston found himself capable of catching. Now he blurted, "What in the world is the other culture like?"

"Fantastically advanced. Among other items, it would seem they have matter conversion units that can make anything out of anything else. It would seem they have fusion reactors, and, hence, unlimited power. Oh yes, an unbelievably advanced technology."

"What do they look like?"

The Baron paused. "Just a moment." He played with his screen dials again, said something into an order box. The screen clouded, went clear once more.

On it was an incredibly handsome man. He was dressed in nothing more than brief shorts and sandals. He had a golden-brown coloration, was of bodily perfection seldom seen, and then only among physical culture perfectionists who spend a lifetime achieving it. There was no indication that he was aware of being photographed.

"Who's that?" Ronny said blankly.

"That's one of your aliens."

"Alien! That's a *man*."

"Ummm," the Baron said. "There's just one thing in which he differs from man as we know him."

He paused for effect. "These aliens don't seem to be intelligent."

PART TWO

VIII

If Baron Wyler had suddenly metamorphosed into a gigantic butterfly, he could hardly have surprised Ronny Bronston more.

"Not *intelligent?*" he protested. "A moment ago you said they had an unbelievably advanced technology. Fusion reactors and matter conversion units aren't exactly the products of unintelligent minds."

The Baron looked at him strangely. "Can we be so sure? Have you ever considered some of the things insects accomplish? However, neither as individuals nor as units—such as beehives or anthills—do we think of insects as intelligent. But the analogy isn't too good. A moment, please."

He got up, walked over to a wall screen and said something into it, then returned.

"You noted, of course, how humanoid our Dawnman was?"

"Humanoid?" Ronny blurted. "That was a *man.*"

"Perhaps." There was still a strange element in the Baron's voice.

The screen on one of the room's doors said, "Academecian Count Felix Fitzjames, on orders to see the Supreme Commandant."

"Enter," the Baron said.

He made off-hand introductions, then said to Ronny

77

Bronston, "The Count has been specializing in this particular aspect of the matter. Undoubtedly, he will be pleased to enlighten you." He turned to the Count. "The matter of the nature of the Dawnmen."

"Dawnmen?" Ronny said.

The Academecian, who was an elderly scholar and somewhat nervous in the presence of his ultimate superior, said, "Undoubtedly, a misnomer, but one that has come into common usage among we who are working on the project. One hypothesis is that these aliens are the original *Homo sapiens*, that Earth was seeded from one of their planets."

Baron Wyler said affably, "Sit down, my dear Count."

The Count nervously sat, remaining on the edge of his chair.

Ronny said, "That's ridiculous. Earth is the origin of man."

The other nodded, apologetically. "Most likely, Your Excellency; however, there are those among us who think otherwise. You are undoubtedly aware of the theory that would evolve upon various planets. The fact that he stands erect, that his eyes are so placed, that he has a voicebox, so many of the other factors that go to make up the entity, man—all have good reason for having evolved, and given similar situations would evolve on similar worlds as on Earth."

"I've heard the theory," Ronny begrudged. "I haven't thought too much about it."

"Most authorities don't," the other bobbed his head agreeably. "However, there are certain factors that give credence to *Homo sapiens'* evolution elsewhere. For instance, we know that the earliest man-like creatures, *Zinjanthropus* and *Homo habilis* were in existence some two million years ago, and, utilizing very primitive tools and weapons. For two million years little progress was made. And then, almost overnight, in terms of history, modern man was on the scene. Some twenty or twenty-five thousand years ago, Cro-Magnon man bust upon us with his advanced tools, his weapons, his religion, his advanced art."

"Advanced art?" Ronny protested.

"The cave drawings and paintings of the Magdalenian period in the Upper Paleolithic—especially in such places as Altamira in Spain and Lascaux in France—are not primitive art, as so many seem to think. It is a highly developed art, and, without doubt, connected with their religion. Consider a moment, and you will realize that the very concept of religion is indicative of a sophisticated mind."

Ronny said impatiently, "I don't seem to get the point."

"The point," the older man said reasonably, "is that possibly Cro-Magnon man was not native to Earth, but was either seeded there, or was the result of an ages-ago spaceship crash."

Ronny looked at him. "But there is no proof?"

"Not as yet. Perhaps one day it will be found on the Dawnworld planets."

"Dawnworld?" Ronny said. Then, "Never mind." He looked at Baron Wyler who had been leaning back in his chair, quiet but beaming encouragement. "What's this got to do with this preposterous idea that the, uh, Dawnmen aren't intelligent?"

The Baron said, "Count . . .?"

The elderly scholar ran a hand back through thinning hair, as though unhappy. "Your Excellency, are you at all acquainted with the caste system of early India?"

"No." Ronny hesitated. "That is, not much. I understand that it was one of the reasons India never got very far."

The academician looked at him unhappily. "Well, that is debatable. From your name and your facial characteristics, Your Excellency, I assume you are of European extraction. Europeans seem to have arrived at the opinion that their efforts have predominated in man's development. In actuality, few, if any, of man's really great breakthroughs originated in Europe. Indeed, the Europeans came late on the scene and were largely brought into the march of civilization despite themselves. This particularly applies to the Northern Europeans who are even more prone than others to think of themselves as the undisputed leaders."

The Baron's chuckle encouraged the old man.

He went on. "When my own Nordic and Tutonic ancestors were wearing animalskins and tearing their food from bones before campfires, the Indians were developing such advanced concepts as the zero, in mathematics. I mention in passing that the Mayans of Yucatan used the zero even before India. While my ancestors lived in skin-tents or inadequate shacks of wood and bark, large cities were being erected at Mohenjo-Daro and Harappa in the Indus River valley. Elsewhere in Asia and Africa, the wheel, the domestication of animals, agriculture, mathematics, astronomy—I could go on—were being developed. And my ancestors, and yours, Your Excellency . . ."

"And mine," the Baron laughed encouragingly.

". . . were still in their animalskins. Why, the art of writing has developed, in different form, in various places about the world: in China, in America, in Mesopotamia, in Egypt. The alphabet we use today had its origins in

Asia Minor. But to my knowledge, the Europeans had to import writing, never striking upon it on their own."

The old boy was evidently capable of dwelling upon non-essentials indefinitely, Ronny decided. "All right, all right," he said. "So the Indians made great strides, in spite of the caste system."

The scholar pursed his lips. "Or perhaps, because of it?"

"Oh, now, don't be ridiculous."

Count Fitzjames looked apprehensive, as though he feared he had gone too far.

But the Baron nodded to him. "Go on, my dear Count. Tell us a bit more of the caste system and its origins. And why you think it analogous to the Dawnworld's culture."

The other bobbed his head. "Yes, Your Lordship." He looked back at Ronny. "The origins of the system are lost in the mists of antiquity, but it is usually thought that when the Aryans invaded from the north—destroying the earlier culture, or assimilating it—they realized that unless they took stringent measures, they would soon interbreed and merge with the more numerous conquered indigenous people. So they divided society into four orders: the *Brahmins,* who performed religious and scholarly pursuits, the *Kshatriyas,* who were the ruling class and warriors, and the *Vaishyas,* traders and businessmen. All these were composed of the conquering Aryans. Intermarriage between castes was forbidden—a deep religious matter. Below these three castes were the *Sudras,* which were composed of the original peoples and took over the laboring jobs. Beneath these were the Outcastes, the untouchables, who were consigned to the most menial tasks.

"Now, consider. This system prevailed for a thousand years, two thousand years, or even more. A man born into the Brahmin caste became a scholar or religious; a Kshatryas, a soldier or ruler, and so on. A man born into one of the subdivisions of the Sudras was a cobbler, if his father, grandfather and so on had been. It never occurred to him to seek education, beyond what was involved in learning to make shoes. However, he did learn to make shoes and make them very well indeed. On the other hand, it never occurred to a Brahmin *not* to be educated. That was the nature of things. It was inevitable. Indeed, did he fail in his studies and application of them, as he had a good chance of being ostracized from society. What family would wish their perfectly normal, well-educated, Brahmin daughter to marry a cloddy? There were exceptions, of course, but on an average and over a period of time, the outstanding scholar in the caste got the pick of the girls. I assume your knowledge of genetics leads you the proper conclusions."

Ronny was looking at him thoughtfully. "I think I begin to see your ultimate point."

"Indeed. Actually, man on Earth has seldom come up with the type of socio-economic system that developed in India. Oh, there have been some. The so-called Incas of Peru were one. You were born into your social strata and could seldom, if ever, leave it. The Inca clan supplied the warrior-priests, the administrators; other clans supplied artisans; but most were of the soil and automatically became farmers." The old man looked up. "It worked, by the way, surprisingly well. The average inhabitant of Peru, at the time of the conquistadores lived on a considerably higher level than did the average inhabitant of Europe."

"The anthill," Ronny said, an edge of distaste in his voice.

The Baron shrugged and smiled pleasantly. "Perhaps," he said. "We are not exactly advocating such a socio-economic system, my dear Bronston; however, it has its admitted advantages."

"From your ambitious viewpoint."

"Granted. But the point the good Count is making is that man can evolve along such a path. He need not automatically follow the more individualistic road we most often witnessed in Earth's early development. On the Dawnworlds, it would seem—if we interpret the information we've accumulated correctly—they have taken a path of specialization unknown even in caste system India."

"But what has this got to do with your claim that they aren't intelligent?"

"My dear Bronston, extrapolate a bit on the example the good Count gave you of the cobbler. Suppose that instead of being a cobbler for two millennia, he stuck to his specialty for a megayear or so. No need for education, no need for anything—except learning to make shoes."

"Yes, but such a cloddy doesn't invent a method of converting matter."

"Are you sure? Our cobbler doesn't invent a matter converter, obviously. His field is shoes. But as the centuries go by, and the millennia, a slight improvement in technique here, a slightly different tool put into use there, and you'd wind up with some very nearly perfect shoes.

Remember, by this time he *instinctively* makes shoes. Over the megayears, the inadequate shoemakers, the throwbacks, have been weeded out. It has become a matter of genetics. The child born into the cobbler—let's call it caste—can make shoes without training. In the same manner that the bee takes no training to collect honey, nor the soldier ant to guard the community."

"But the matter converter?"

"Obviously devised by some other caste. Some caste which has been at work in manufacture a megayear or so. Undoubtedly, a member of this caste is no more capable of making shoes, other than putting them into a converter and copying them, than the cobbler is capable of producing matter converters, or fusion reactors."

The Baron pursed his lips. "Actually, of course, I doubt if they have cobblers at this late date. With the matter converter, such as skills would disappear."

He looked suddenly at the elderly scholar, "That will be all, Count Fitzjames."

The Count scrambled hurriedly to his feet, put his hand over his heart in the salute he had made when he entered the room, and backed hurriedly toward the door through which he had come half an hour earlier.

When he was gone, the Baron looked at his visitor. "It's all rather mind shaking, isn't it?"

Ronny didn't immediately answer. Finally, he shook his head, as though to clear it, and said, "Frankly, I can't understand your reason for letting me in on all this. Surely, you must realize I'll simply report to Ross Metaxa."

"I hope not," the Baron said seriously, pouring the remainder of the light wine into their glasses.

All right, you've got it. Ronny thought. *Start bouncing.*

The Baron said judiciously, "Largely, what your commissioner reported to the chiefs of state, there at the conference in the Octagon, is valid. Man is face to face with his greatest crisis. Nothing can prevent our coming in contact with the Dawnworlds and their unique culture, sooner or later. Probably sooner than we would wish. However, where Metaxa and I differ is in the manner in which United Planets must be organized most efficiently."

Ronny said, bitterly, "You, the strongman, figure on enforcing union."

The Baron smiled and sipped his wine. "My dear Bronston, has it never occurred to you that your admired Ross Metaxa is a strongman himself?"

"He works within the framework of the United Planets Charter."

The other clucked deprecation. "Does he, indeed? I am afraid, only when it so suits him. His methods differ little from my own, in actuality. He is downright Machiavellian when he can achieve his purpose by no other means. For instance, in selecting his tools . . . his agents, such as yourself. I am sometimes surprised that young men of obvious integrity and idealism, remain on his, ah, team."

Ronny could see something was coming. Another curve ball.

Baron Wyler said decisively, his friendly eyes boring earnestly into the Section G operative's, "Bronston, we of Phrygia know the location of the nearest Dawnworlds. We are on the verge of sending an expedition there. We are of the opinion that it will be quite practical to land and observe sufficient of that culture to be able to duplicate some of their ultra-advanced devices." He twisted his mouth. "If not duplicate them, perhaps, ah, liberate one or two. It would seem that the matter converter is highly portable, for instance.

"I hardly need point out that the possession of such a device would put our planet into such a position of advantage that the whole of United Planets, even if they could be coerced into acting in full unison, could not stand against us."

The Baron came to his feet, and his personality seemed to fill the room to straining. "Reunited under the aegis of Phrygia, man, of all the three thousand worlds we have colonized, will march forward together. By the time the inevitable all-out contact between the Dawnworlds and our own is made, we shall be ready for these unintelligent—though highly advanced technically—antmen, beemen, call them what you will."

Ronny looked up at him, expressionlessly. "And where do I come in on this? Why have you told me about it? Why do you hope I won't report to Ross Metaxa?"

Baron Wyler smiled at him. "I would think that as sharp a man as yourself, my dear Bronston, would see what I have been leading to. I am as desirous of top operatives as is Ross Metaxa. I want you to join my forces, Ronald Bronston."

Ronny looked at him.

He came to his own feet. "I see. You want a man planted in Section G who'll keep you tipped off to the latest maneuvers of Ross Metaxa."

"Why mince words? Obviously."

The Section G agent's mouth worked. He said finally, "I'll have to think about it. Frankly, what's been said here in the past hour has set me back on my mental heels."

"Of course, my dear Bronston. Do not take too long, is all. Events are on the march. We must not be dullards."

He made his way over to the wall screen he had utilized earlier, and said something into it.

The same door, through which the elderly Count Fitzjames had come, opened again and Rita Daniels entered the room.

Ronny stared.

She said, a mocking quality in her voice, "Good afternoon, Citizen Bronston." He had noted the comparative drabness of the local women on the streets, here was the direct opposite. Not even in the most swank salons, in the most luxurious embassies in Great Washington, could he have found a more stunningly turned out young woman than this. No Tri-Di star could have equaled this slim blonde; no artificially manufactured sex symbol, the pert prettiness of this elfin girl.

The Baron beamed at the two of them "I understand you have already met my niece, Your Excellency."

Ronny Bronston closed his eyes in pain.

Rita said sweetly, "This was quite a little gimmick, getting yourself appointed a plenipotentiary from UP. Or do you maintain that you bore that rank before reaching Phrygia?"

Ronny bowed, wryly. "You seem to have a gimmick or so up your own sleeve, Citizeness Daniels," he said.

The Baron smiled his wide smile. "Whatever our friend's immediate methods, my dear Rita, he obviously can think on his feet, a desirable trait." He turned to Ronny. "My niece has been working, ah, incognito, with Interplanetary News, the better to learn the workings of our fellow worlds. However, I believe I shall, in the future, utilize her talents even more profitably. Had I known what Metaxa had up his sleeve, I would never have allowed her to try and penetrate that conference; I had no idea he would go to the extent of seizing and then memorywashing the poor girl."

He turned back to Rita, "And now, my dear, will you see our guest to his quarters? He has some important decisions to make."

IX

Rita took him up, by way of the private elevator, to the ground floor and through the pseudo-Minoan Palace to a hovercar ramp. As they progressed, silently, passers-by came to a quick halt. Civilians pressed their hands over their hearts in the same salute Count Fitzjames had given the Baron, soldiers came to stiff attention.

She looked at him from the side of her eyes, a mocking quality still there.

Ronny said dryly, "Like magic, isn't it? On Mother Earth, a lowly Interplanetary News reporter, sneaking into places she's not wanted. Being grabbed, manhandled, mauled, battered around, and then memorywashed. But now a veritable princess, the niece of the Supreme Commandant."

"What! Manhandled, mauled, battered around! Who dared?"

He looked at her as though in surprise. "Oh. That's right, you wouldn't remember."

She had stopped. Now she stood there, fists on boyishly slim hips, glaring at him. "You . . . you . . ." Then she caught his grin.

"Ha!" she snapped. "The last time you told me I had a bottle of guzzle, was drenched, and in trouble with a traffic coordinator."

He continued to grin, the mockery was in his face now.

She spun and marched on. "Someday, I'm going to find out what happened to me during that twenty-four hours," she snarled. "And when I do . . ."

They reached a wide entryway which led off toward the gates down the ramp. Rita snapped something to one of the guards, who then spoke into a screen set in the wall. In moments, a low slung auto-car approached them. It was a two seater, and Rita slid under the controls. She dropped the manual lever and took the stick, waiting for him.

Ronny got in beside her and they started down the ramp. He said, "I've got an official car waiting for me at the main gate."

"Let them follow. I want to talk to you."

"All right. My suite's at the United Planets Building."

When they passed the UP limousine with the marines, he gestured to them to follow.

Rita said, "What did you think of Uncle Max?"

"Uncle Max? Oh, the Baron."

"Maximilian, and a whole lot of other names and titles."

Ronny said warily, looking out over the countryside, "He surprised me." This whole area had been landscaped, all the way to the city. Phrygia evidently spared no expense in aggrandizing her Supreme Commandant.

She said, conversationally, "Have you ever noticed the extent to which man can delude himself when considering persons of whom he doesn't approve?"

"Such as strongmen?" he said dryly.

"Exactly. Evidently, few consider that men such as Alexander didn't stand alone. Actually, he was the leader of a team. A team of military and political geniuses so capable that they were able to pull down the world's greatest empire. Men like Parmenion, Ptolemy, Antipater, Antigonus, Seleucus and all the Companions. Can you see the charm he must have radiated, the strength, the ability to draw men of great capability into his service? He must have indeed been like a god. Or Napoleon. Can you imagine the personality that man must have had, the charm, to draw together his team? Men like Ney, Marat, Bernadotte, Lannes, Soult and Masséna."

She shook her head so that the ponytail she affected flounced back and forth. "No, Ronny Bronston, your strongmen of history weren't dark villains with a mean glint in eye and dastardly deeds in mind. They were men of exceeding charm and strength, and they became strongmen because of the superiority."

"How does Hitler fit into this theory?" Ronny said mildly.

"He's come down to us as the archvillain of all time. And I have no doubt that his victims saw him in that light. But his immediate team evidently worshipped him. Even men of the caliber of Churchill admitted his personal charm, his strength of personality. Without it, he would never have swayed the people as he did."

They were proceeding toward the capital city at full tilt now, the marines in the car behind having their work cut out trying to keep up with the speedy two seater the girl drove.

Ronny looked over at her, not failing to note the spray of freckles dusted over her slightly upturned nose. "You seem to have read up quite a bit on history, especially the history of strongmen." He paused, before adding, "Could it be because you see another strongman, Uncle Max, coming along?"

"Obviously, Ronny Bronston. And I want to be part of his team. Don't you?"

Ronny said, "I thought I'd think about it a bit. I don't change coats as easily as all that."

She slowed the car's pace a trifle and put a hand on his sleeve. She said, an element of inspiration in her voice, "Of course you don't. But man has come as far as he can, Ronny, along the path as it is now. We *need* a strongman. What a glorious race we could become, if under the banner of Maximilian Wyler, we united to march together into the future."

"What future?"

"Eventually, the complete domination of the galaxy, no matter what other life forms we run into as we progress."

"That's quite an order," Ronny said mildly.

"Don't be silly. I don't mean within our lifetimes. But only that can be the eventual destiny of man."

Ronny said, "Suppose I granted that the race could use a strongman along here, a man on horseback, as the term goes. What leads you to believe that Uncle Max is the man?"

She frowned at him. "But isn't that obvious? If he isn't, he'll never form his team, he'll never come to power. History is strewn with the wrecks of would-be strongmen, who didn't really have what was required."

He nodded agreement. "You're right, there. If Baron Wyler isn't the man he thinks himself, he'll land on the rocks, too."

She drew up before the UP Building and brought the vehicle to a halt, although without setting it down. Her hand was on his arm again.

"Think it over, Ronny. My uncle evidently wants you on his team."

"All right," he said. "I'm thinking. Thanks for the ride."

He turned and taking two levels at a time, started up the stone steps. He didn't turn when he heard her sporter whisk away from the curb.

In the small apartment which had been assigned him,

he immediately went to his bag. He brought forth a small object looking something like a woman's compact or a cigar case. He sat down at the table and propped it before him, activating it.

"Phil Birdman," he clipped out. "Soonest."

Birdman's mahogany face faded into the miniature screen. "I've been waiting for you to call."

"Get over here," Ronny rapped. "I'm at the UP."

"Right." The Indian's face faded.

Ronny said, "Irene Kasansky. Soonest."

Irene's perpetually harrassed face faded in, and twisted into her version of a smile, when she saw who it was. "Hi, Ronny, what's the urgency?"

"I've got to talk to the Old Man, immediately."

"No can do. Another big conference. He's browbeating fifty or more presidents, kings, patriarchs and what not."

"Give me Sid, then. And let the chief know I have to talk to him."

"All right, but Supervisor Jakes is busy, too."

Sid Jakes faded in, grin wreathed as usual. "Ronny! Plenipotentiary Extraordinary! Frankly, in spite of that imposing tag, I thought the Baron'd have you into his deepest dungeon by now."

"Knock it!" Ronny clipped. "This is highest emergency. Everybody, but everybody, has been underestimating Uncle Max."

Sid Jakes' eyes widened slightly and his grin was a bit less bright. Not even in the seemingly lax Section G did an agent customarily tell Ross Metaxa's right-hand man to shut up.

"Who?" he asked.

Ronny briefed him on what had transpired.

The feisty Section G supervisor ran a hand over his mouth thoughtfully. "Hmmm, I wonder how it'd work out if you told the Baron you're signing up with him? Then we'd have you on the inside of his organization."

Ronny said plaintively, "I keep telling you, this Wyler is no cloddy. The moment I told him that, he'd slip me some Scop, just to see if I was lying. Then, when he found out my passion for him and his ambitions wasn't exactly overwhelming, he'd see I had a few holes blasted in me."

Sid said, "Yeah. Possibly, we'd better pull you out of there, Ronny. When you turn him down, the Baron isn't going to be very happy about the fact that he's revealed so much to you."

"You can't pull me out," Ronny said. "There's nobody else here but Phil Birdman, and the Baron is about to send his expedition to the Dawnworlds. If it succeeds, and he gets some of those ultra-ultra devices the Dawnmen have, the fat's really in the fire. That matter converter. If I get a clear picture, with it he could duplicate himself a fleet of space cruisers that would outnumber everything UP has combined."

"You have no idea where these Dawnworlds—where in Zen did that name ever come from?—are located?"

"None at all. The Baron learned through some of the things his people found on the little aliens' planets."

Jakes muttered, for once unsmiling, "Without coordinates, it could take us a millenium looking." He looked up again. "Listen, I'll get to Ross. Call you back."

While he had been talking, Phil Birdman had entered the room. Ronny deactivated the Section G communicator and turned to his colleague.

The Indian said, "Well, at least, you're still with us."

"But how long that will be, I couldn't guarantee," Ronny told him.

The older agent sank into an auto-chair and dialed.

"Pseudo-whiskey?" he asked. "I have a sneaking suspicion I'm going to need a bit of firewater before I've heard all your story."

They'd got through two highballs apiece before Ronny had finished bringing him up to date.

When he had ended, Birdman grunted. "There's only one answer," he submitted.

"What?"

"Let's go down to the recruiting station and join up with Uncle Max."

"Oh great, you overgrown funker. Funnies, I get."

The communicator hummed. Ronny went over to the desk, sat down before it and activated the device. It was Ross Metaxa, at least as rumpled and weary as usual. He minced no words.

"That madman is taking a gamble, in his bid for power, that could destroy us all. Our big chance was to put off for as long as possible first contact with these aliens. To stall for time. Now he's planning to set down on one of their planets, right now—to make immediate contact. He's drivel-happy! Well, there's nothing for it. Ronny, find out where these damned Dawnworlds are located."

"Yes, sir. How?"

"How in the devil would I know? You and Agent Birdman are there. I'm not. The nearest other agents to Phrygia are a good week's trip away. It's all in your lap."

Ronny Bronston looked at him.

His ultimate superior looked back, his eyes level.

On an impulse, Ronny blurted, "Was my becoming a Section G agent an engineered deal, not of my own choosing?"

The moist eyes looked deeply into his own, without flicker. "Yes."

Ronny took a deep breath.

Ross Metaxa said, "Report through Irene as soon as you have anything." His face faded.

Ronny turned to Phil Birdman, who had come up behind him to listen in on the conversation, but had missed even the final sentences. "You better dial us another drink, Phil. We're going to need it."

Phil, his expression passive, got the drinks, then sat down across from Ronny Bronston.

Ronny said slowly, "Phil, the Baron's working on a full time basis on this project. That means somewhere, on or very near his person, is the information we need—the location of the Dawnworlds."

The Indian said nothing.

Ronny said slowly, "Phil, the Baron isn't quite as well informed on Section G as he'd like to think he is. There're a few little items that come out of the gimmick department that that—I'm willing to bet my life—he hasn't heard about."

Phil Birdman put down his glass.

Ronny said, "Phil, one of us has got to go in."

"You mean . . ." The older man ran his tongue over suddenly dry lips. He said, his tone a blend of protest and apology, "I'm forty-five, Ronny. There aren't many of the good years left."

"Metaxa would undoubtedly retire you immediately, on full pay, of course."

The other said slowly, "I don't want to retire. I like this work. Some day I look forward to making supervisor."

Ronny said, "All right. I'm only thirty-two."

Birdman looked up at him, his handsome Indian face working. "It's fifteen years off your life, Ronny."

Ronny Bronston nodded, a weary aspect in the gesture. "When I joined up with Section G, I figured I was expendable. This isn't as bad as copping a slug from some secret police goon on some backward planet, where we're trying to upgrade their government, or some such."

He thought of something and said, "By the way, Phil. How'd you get into Section G? What led you to apply?"

"Oh, I didn't. Sid Jakes looked me up one day while I was still living back on Piegan. I was in the local police. We jawed around a little and before I knew it, I was in."

"Kind of got jockeyed in, eh?" Ronny said bitterly.

Phil looked at him. "I wouldn't put it that way."

Ronny got up and went over to the order box on the desk. He said into it, "I want the biggest whale of a meal you can concoct. Very concentrated, rich food, high calorie content."

Later, they retraced the route the marines had driven him earlier in the day. Phil Birdman was driving now, his own speedy hovercar.

Ronny was pensive. He said, after a long silence. "How close do you figure we can get? That's important. It'll cut time."

Phil said thoughtfully, "On that diagram you drew: You know that ramp this Rita Daniels mopsy took you to, when you were leaving the palace?"

"Yes, sure."

"I can take you to the top of that."

"I think that's the private entry of the Supreme Commandant and his family."

"I know. As soon as I get to the top, they'll order me to drive down again. That's perfect for us. Every split second can count, Ronny. It could be seventeen or eighteen years, you know. . . ."

Ronny Bronston said nothing. For that matter, it had

been known to be twenty. Beyond that point, you inevitably died. You starved to death.

The hovercar bore diplomatic indentification. The guards did no more than present their spears in a salute as they roared through the palace gates. Phil Birdman kept up a good speed. Not so high as to be conspicuous, but fast enough that their faces were unlikely to be spotted.

They got to the foot of the ramp and started up.

"You'd better take it," the Indian said tightly, from the side of his mouth.

Ronny took a syrette from a small compartment in the dash and pushed it home in the back of his neck. He reached immediately for some of the energy pills.

Things were jerking frantically by the time they reached the head of the ramp and the entrada there—jerking frantically and already beginning to slow up.

A guard officer moved sluggishly toward them, more sluggish still. As he approached the car, his mouth, slowly, slowly, began to open. But before sound issued forth, he had stopped completely, one foot held in the air, his body in such position that it seemed impossible for him not to fall forward, out of balance.

Ronny Bronston vaulted over the side of the car and darted into the interior. He had done this but once before, in training, and had been under for less than ten seconds, pseudo-time. But this was the real thing. He darted a hand into his jacket pocket and gulped down more pep pills.

All was frozen.

He had no time to waste observing the utterly fantastic phenomenon. *The world had stopped.*

X

He retraced the route Rita Daniels had brought him along only a few hours earlier, dodging around the frozen statues that had—moments before—been soldiers and officials, clerks and secretaries, in all their bustling activities.

He came to the private elevator that led into the depths that housed the apartments of the Supreme Commandant. This was his first serious barrier. There was no manner in which he could operate the machinery, nor any other machine, save the equipment he carried.

He whipped out a laser gun, flicked the stud to cut and began beaming a hole through the elevator shaft door. Pure luck was involved now. He grabbed the door handle, and when he had largely cut the door away, pulled it toward him. It was a fantastically thick door. Evidently, Phrygia security took care that it was not easy to get at their Supreme Commandant.

Finally, the door began to fall toward him, slowly, sluggishly, but sped up by the effort he was exerting. It was as though he were pulling it through water, or even a thicker fluid. Before it had half reached the floor, he gave up his efforts and peered into the shaft beyond.

Luck was with him. Built into the metal wall of the shaft were ladder steps, obviously meant for repairmen, and possibly as a last method of emergency exit from the quarters below in case of some extreme disaster.

He vaulted over the falling door, now arrested in its drop, and scurried down the ladder.

Ronny tried to remember how long it had taken him to get down to the Baron's apartments, when he had been there before, and couldn't. This was the crucial thing. If the other maintained his rooms five or ten stories down, that was one thing. If they were a hundred stories, that was disaster. He would starve to death in this shaft.

Which brought his needs to mind. He darted a hand into one of his pockets for another handful of energy pills, even as he descended.

Luck was with him still.

His feet hit the top of the elevator cab.

He pulled the gun again, even as he gobbled pep pills, and cut a hole through the top of the elevator cage. He jumped on the circular, cut away a section so that it would fall. As soon as it had fallen sufficiently for him to jump off onto the elevator cage floor, he did so, and turned the gun to the door, cutting that away, too.

Ronny pushed hard against the great inertia, forcing the door inward into the room beyond. He wedged himself through as soon as there was sufficient way.

He was within the Baron's apartments. Now he needed fortune's kiss, indeed. Suppose the Baron wasn't here. Suppose, even though he was, he didn't have the information on him. Suppose he did have it, but in such form that it was impossible to decipher.

Suppose a lot of things.

He darted his hand into another pocket for a supply of the energy pills, and dashed into the room in which Wyler had invited him earlier in the day. It was unoccupied.

He headed for the door beyond, through which both Count Fitzjames and Rita had entered. Happily, it was open. He sped down the hall that was there, searching frantically. The living quarters of the Supreme Commandant of Phrygia were laid out in similar fashion—though utterly more swank—to any home of an extremely wealthy individual on a score of planets Ronny had visited. He had little trouble in guessing the layout.

From time to time, he would pass frozen statues in this dead world. Servants, guards, what were obviously secretaries or clerks, sometimes, if garb meant anything, evidently some high ranking Phrygia official.

Somewhere along here, Ronny thought, *must be some sort of audience chamber, some sort of conference room.* It was unlikely that Baron Wyler would be eating at this time of day, and certainly not sleeping. Ronny was gambling on the possibility that Wyler was at work in conference with underlings, and probably deep in the project for sending the expedition to the Dawnworlds.

The gamble paid off.

He came to a large door guarded by two huskies in elaborate uniform, muffle-guns at their sides.

He wrenched at the doorknob, miscalculated and ripped it completely off.

Ronny snarled an obscenity, stepped back and flicked his beam gun up again. He repeated the process of cutting a circular hole large enough to pass his body, and then pushed the panel through. When there was space to see, he realized he had found what he sought. The Baron Wyler, standing at a table, a dozen men, mostly uniformed, also about it.

He pushed harder on the slowly falling panel, finally had the space to squeeze through. The Baron was standing, mouth closed, looking down the arch of his aristocratic nose at one of his subordinates who was speaking, his finger touching a chart. At least, he had been speaking at the moment of the freeze—his mouth was open,

And remained so, though no sound issued forth during Ronny's stay.

Ronny Bronston darted to the table. He stared down at the paper the other was touching. It was a star chart, but not, he realized, the one that could possibly have helped in the location of the Dawnworlds. It was a chart of United Planets.

Ronny sorted through the papers on the table, frantically. On the face of it, these men were discussing the broad subject of the Baron's designs against UP. If so, the subject of the Dawnworlds was obviously in mind.

But there was no other chart. Plans, reports, graphs, diagrams of this, that and the other. But no further charts.

He stepped over to the frozen statue that was Baron Wyler and ran his hands over him. He went through every pocket, examined, however briefly, every paper. The other's body felt like clammy clay, there was a nauseating element in making physical contact with a living object under these conditions.

There was nothing pertaining to the Dawnworlds.

For the briefest of moments, he wondered if it were all a hoax. Was the wily Baron planting the idea that he was in contact with this fabulous unintelligent race with the idea of bluffing the UP into accepting him as supreme? But no, the bluff might work with some, but hardly with others. Such planets as Delos were going to have to be shown something tangible before knuckling under to a Baron Maximilian Wyler.

Ronny Bronston's eyes began to dart around the room, inspecting the Baron's underlings. Which, of them all, might be expected to carry a star chart, pinpointing the Dawnman worlds? He simply didn't have time to search them all. The only one he recognized was the self-effacing Count Fitzjames, who, characteristically, was back away from the others, as though not wishing to intrude.

He grabbed energy pills from his jacket and munched on them. He had to think. No matter how desperate for time, he had to think.

He had been in this room already so long that he could note a slight change in the Baron's eyes. They had begun to widen a merest trifle, the first indication of surprise.

Then, as though magnet drawn, the Section G agent's attention whipped back to Count Fitzjames. What was the other doing over there, away from the others? Something hadn't at first registered on Ronny's awareness.

Yes! The oldster was looking at a . . . a map. No! It was a chart, a star chart. Ronny whipped over. Attached there to the wall.

Phrygia was heavily marked, down in this corner. Over here, surprisingly near, were the three star systems of the originally discovered tiny aliens. And beyond, all those numberless stars in red! They could only be . . .

Whether or not he was right, Ronny had no more time. No more time. He reached out and ripped the chart from the wall. Swore at himself for tearing it badly. Carefully and slowly pulled it down, folding it, so he could carry it more easily.

He spun and dashed for the door he had blasted through, slowed somewhat by the resistance of the object he carried. He wedged himself into the corridor beyond. The panel he had cut out had not as yet dropped all the way to the floor; in fact, was not more than an inch or so lower than when he had finished shoving it.

In the corridor, the guards were beginning to react somewhat as had the Baron. Their eyes had begun to widen in shocked surprise.

He hurried down the hall, retracing his steps. To the

elevator. Through the roof of the cage, up the ladder. As he went he desperately swallowed his energy pills, desperately crammed them down.

The ground floor could be no more than a few stories up, but he felt himself tiring. He was weary with the activity. He had been moving at top speed since Phil had pulled the hovercar up before the entry. And he could feel it now.

At least, that is what he told himself he was feeling.

He refused the fear that was welling up inside. How long, how long?

He pulled himself at last through the hole he had burned in the heavy elevator door at the ground floor. He began to drag himself along the way to the entry, the ramp, Phil's hovercar and release. The star chart he carried grew increasingly sluggish, impossibly heavy.

And even as he went, he knew he wasn't going to make it.

The energy was draining out of him with every step. He had taken too much time. He had taken far too much time.

He went down on his knees, the star chart falling slowly from his hands, then remaining suspended in the air. He laboriously took it again. He had to make it to the hovercar. He stumbled forward. It was far too far.

He was too weak even to bring more pep pills to his mouth. The last few he had taken had had little effect, at any rate. His body had taken all the punishment it was capable of taking. He wasn't going to make it.

This, then, was the ultimate failure.

He looked up in agony, down the long corridor that ed to the direction of the ramp. The oocupants of the hall were still frozen in their movements. For him, they would always be frozen. But . . .

He saw movement!

Down the hall toward him came running Phil Bird man, his eyes going in all directions.

He spotted Ronny, grabbed down at him, hoisted him over his shoulder and started back.

Ronny held on to consciousness. He didn't understand but it was going to work out now. He held desperately to the chart.

They were back in the hovercar. The Indian operative dumped him into the passenger seat, hurried around to the other side and vaulted into the driver's position. His hand darted to the dash compartment and seized two syrettes. He pressed the first into his own neck, the second into Ronny's.

Things began jerking frantically. Things began moving sluggishly. The people. The guards.

The guard officer, who had been walking toward them when time had first stopped, began moving more natur ally, faster, and still faster.

Scowling, he barked, "What's going on here?"

Phil Birdman said apologetically, "Sorry, officer. I seem to have ascended the wrong ramp."

"You certainly have! This is the private entry of the Supreme Commandant! What's going on here? You men look suspicious."

The Phrygian stared at Ronny Bronston. "What've you got there in your hand? You didn't have anything just a second ago."

It was the star chart.

Ronny shook his head, weakly. "Nothing. I . . . I feel sick. Let's go on back, Birdman."

"Yes, get out of here," the guard officer rapped. He was scowling, obviously wondering whether or not to arrest this pair.

Phil Birdman had never dropped the lift lever. Now he applied pressure to the velocity pedal, tipped the stick to the left and back, and spun the vehicle to descend the ramp again.

Ronny fumbled for a sandwich, gobbled it. Got it down and felt like retching. There was a bottle with a score of assorted pills. He got them all down, drank deeply from a flask of water. He was dehydrated, weak, empty.

They were speeding toward the gate through which they had entered mere moments ago by straight time.

The gate was closing. The guards were milling about, anxiously. Four or five barred the way, spears raised.

Spears raised as though they were rifles, and it came to Ronny Bronston that appearances deceive. The Baron Wyler wasn't about to arm his guards with nothing more effective than iron tipped wooden shafts. Those spears were undoubtedly disguised weapons demanding of considerably more respect.

"Blast through!" Ronny clipped to his companion.

Phil shot a glance at him. "If I do, we'll have the paleface cavalry after us in moments."

"We've got them after us already. What d'ya think they're closing those gates for?"

The Indian's hand shot out, flicked a switch. Part of the dash fell away to reveal a pistol grip built into the car. Phil Birdman grabbed it, touched the trigger, slowly swerved the car right and left.

The gate and the soldiers that guarded it melted away into nothingness.

The two Section G agents felt nausea. It was seldom one took human life, even in the ultra-dedicated Bureau of Investigation.

They shot through what had once been the gate and down the road toward the city limits of Phrygia.

Ronny growled, "They'll be after us both in the air and on the road. Chances are, we'll never make it halfway."

"It's getting dark," Birdman muttered. "Not that that'll make much difference. You got the location of the Dawnman planets?"

"I think so." Ronny wolfed another sandwich. "Listen, how did you ever find me? What was the idea? How could you do it?"

Birdman grunted. "I pressed my syrette a split second after you did. I was gambling that my metabolism wouldn't be hit until you had already been gone long enough to do what you could. I figured that you'd probably keep going, long after you'd passed the danger point, if you hadn't found what we needed. I figured I'd be going into pseudo-time, just in time to come looking for you."

He added apologetically, "It was all I could do. Of course, I was in pseudo-time only a fraction of the duration you were. I doubt if it makes more than a year or two difference."

"You cloddy!" Ronny growled. "Well, thanks." He knew well enough Phil would have kept coming, looking for him, no matter how much time had elapsed.

"All for dear old Section G," Phil said cheerfully. "Listen, I can hear them behind us. We'll never make it."

"Keep going," Ronny muttered. "I'm beginning to feel the immediate after-effects."

"Oh fine," the Indian operative said. "You haven't got a communicator on you?"

"No, of course not. We couldn't take the chance of the Baron getting hold of one of us and finding the thing. He'd be able to tap Section G communications."

The dash screen lit up. There was the face, the icy face of an officer in the uniform of Baron Wyler's personal guards.

The officer snarled, "You have exactly two minutes in which to come to a halt and surrender. Otherwise, we blast. You are not going to be allowed to reach Phrygia city limits. The Supreme Commandant's orders."

Ronny flicked the screen off. "Two minutes to go," he said. "Can you think of anything?"

"All I can think of," Phil said expressionlessly, "is that we should have taken my earlier idea. Go down to the recruiting station and join up with the Baron."

"To late now." Ronny grunted. "We've taken our stand. Look out, here comes a car toward us from the city."

"Probably a civilian," the Indian muttered. "There hasn't been time for security guards to be coming from that direction."

"Wait a minute!" Ronny said urgently. "I know that car. Stop."

The Indian shot a quick glance at him, but jammed on deceleration.

Ronny waved at Rita Daniels.

"Hey!" he called.

She came to a halt, her high forehead furrowed.

"What're you doing out there?" she asked. "I thought you were in town thinking over Uncle Max's proposition."

He was feeling increasingly weak, but he climbed from Birdman's hovercar and made his way to hers, fumbling as he went for his gimmicked fountain pen.

He said, "Look, I want to talk to you. Come along with us."

Her eyes narrowed. She could hear the sounds of the pursuing guard vehicles. "Not likely," she snapped. "What're you up to?"

He lifted the stud of the device and turned to call weakly to Birdman. "Get the Baron on the screen. Soonest, damn it!"

He turned back to the girl. She was scratching her cheek where the tiny dart had struck her, and already her eyes were going blank.

"Come along with me, Rita," he ordered. Without bothering to see if she followed, he staggered back to the other hovercar.

Phil Birdman had managed to get through. Evidently, Baron Wyler had been stationed at a screen wating for a report from his guards on the progress of the chase. His face was on the screen.

Ronny Bronston slumped into his seat, the drugged girl climbed in next to him, the slim figure warm but unnoticed against his side.

He said weakly, "We've got your niece, Uncle Max. She's going with us into Phrygia."

The Baron's face was blazing with anger. "Have you supposed altruists of Section G stooped to abducting helpless women and using them as hostages to protect your miserable selves?"

"You have said it, friend," Phil Birdman said flatly. He kicked the acceleration pedal with his foot, switched off the screen again to prevent the other from following their conversation.

Ronny Bronston had been hanging on to consciousness with considerable effort. Now he gave up.

XI

Ronny came to, weakly, in the hideaway the Indian operative had made in the suburban housing area of the Phrygian capital. Evidently, Phil had just given him a draught of something highly stimulating.

"How'd you ever make it?" Ronny murmured.

Phil grinned down at him. Bronston was stretched out on a couch. "Ugh. Redman have no trouble shaking pursuing palefaces in confusion of big city traffic."

"Funnies, I get," Ronny muttered. "Where's the girl?"

"She's with us. Our strongman isn't as strong as he ought to be, if he's thinking in terms of taking over whole empires of planets. He should have figured her expendable."

Ronny said, before passing out again, "Get the Old Man."

Phil Birdman went over to the desk and set up the Section G communicator. He said into it, "Irene Kasansky, soonest."

Her tight face faded in, her expression worried. "Phil Birdman," she said, "what's going on?"

"Give me the Chief, Irene. Absolutely soonest."

"He and Jakes are waiting for your report."

Metaxa's acid sour face faded in. "Birdman!" he growled. "What's happened to Ronny Bronston?"

The Indian said, "I've got him here. He's out." He had an edge of bitterness in his voice now. "He took your orders literally, of course. The only way of getting that information was for him to go into pseudo-time."

109

Ross Metaxa stared at him, unblinkingly. "How long was he under?"

"Evidently maximum. He probably set some sort of record."

The Section G head allowed himself to close his eyes for the briefest of seconds. He took a deep breath and said, "Did he get the information from that funker?"

"I think so. He brought a star chart away with him." Phil Birdman cleared his throat. "We also have a hostage. The Baron's niece."

Ross Metaxa assimilated that, not bothering to ask for details. He said, finally, "Have you any manner of getting out into space?"

Birdman hesitated. "UP has a small craft assigned to it. But if we utilize that, I have no doubt that the Baron will lower the boom on all UP personnel, the moment we're gone. He's got a reputation for ruthlessness, when he gets excited about something."

Metaxa shook his head. "They'll have to take their chances. You and Ronny and the girl get yourselves out. There's a Space Forces cruiser heading at top speed for you. They'll be there in five days, Earth time."

"Then what do we do?" Birdman said, though he could see it coming. "Return Ronny to Earth for whatever treatment he can get?"

Ross Metaxa looked at him bleakly. "The Baron is going to head immediately for those Dawnworlds. You take off after him. In a week's time, Bronston will have recovered."

The Indian said flatly, "Ronny Bronston will never recover, as you well know, Commissioner. He's lost at least twenty years in that jazzed up phoney-time he went into. Five years from now, he'll look and be twenty-five years older than he is today."

Metaxa said evenly, "He knew what he was doing, Birdman. He did what he had to do. He wouldn't have been Ronald Bronston otherwise. He'll recover within a week. As you know, the age doesn't come immediately, but over a period of time. For awhile, it won't effect him. When he has recovered, give him the story and make your way immediately after the Baron."

The Indian operative scowled. "How do you know the Baron, personally, will go out to the Dawnworlds?"

"Because when men like Maximilian Wyler really get in the clutch there's nobody they dare trust. He could never be certain that his closest right-hand man wouldn't take over the reins, given some of those gismos the Dawnmen evidently have. No, you can be sure that the Baron will go himself."

His face faded from the screen.

Birdman looked at the now opaque screen for a long moment. "So everybody's expendable, including the complete UP staff on Phrygia. The party's getting rough."

Ross Metaxa had been right. By the time the four man Space Forces cruiser reached them, Ronny Bronston was in his old shape. Good food and rest had done it. He felt the same as ever. All except, deep within, he knew that he had thrown away at least twenty years, the good years, of life. A few Earth years from now and he would look and be as old as Metaxa himself. It wasn't the happiest of prospects.

No effort whatsoever was being made to apprehend them. The Baron's regard for his niece evidently precluded any attempt by the Phrygian spaceforces to find and destroy their craft.

It occured to Ronny Bronston that if the girl were as close as all that to the would-be dictator, perhaps she had information about the man that might be of use in later developments. As he rested in the small space vessel that they had taken over from UP, he tried to pump her, though with precious little luck.

To the extent she could, in the confined space allotted to her nd the two Section G operatives, she tried to ignore them. From time to time, though, temper flared and she allowed herself to be drawn into argument.

The time, for instance, that she snapped out of a clear sky, "I don't see why you don't recognize that UP needs a leader such as Uncle Max."

Ronny said mildly, "Perhaps it does."

"Then why are you trying to hinder him? Why don't you join him?" she demanded.

Ronny looked at her wryly, "He hasn't proven to my satisfaction, as yet, that he's the man he thinks he is. Perhaps history will prove otherwise. As you pointed out the other day, it is strewn with the wreckage of would-be strongmen, who didn't make it."

"My uncle will make it!" The girl's natural attractiveness was accentuated in anger.

"Meanwhile"—Phil Birdman grinned at her—"there are a few of us who don't think so."

Ronny said, "Many aspire to supreme power, few are chosen. Take those examples you gave me the other day: Alexander, Napoleon, Hitler. They each supply a lesson.

"Alexander, for instance. He conquered the biggest empire known up to that time, but died at about my age from his inability to conquer himself. And when he died he left precious little. His immediate family, including his son, were killed off. That wonderful team of his fell apart, each trying to seize absolute power. Of them all, Ptolemy didn't do so badly; he and his descendants got

Egypt as their chunk of the pie. But the next fifty years and more was spent by the Macedonians trying to find another strongman, and failing"—Ronny twisted his mouth—"Their energies might have been put to better use.

"Or take your other example, Napoleon. He had his absolute power for awhile, but he was still in his forties when they kicked him out and he wound up his life there on St. Helena. And his team? They didn't do so well, either. Some turned traitor on him, when the bets were down. Some were shot. Of them all, Bernadotte, who became king of Sweden, was about the only one who came out ahead of the game.

"And Hitler . . ."

"Oh, he's the best lesson of all." Phil laughed. "That's the fella who taught me to believe in strongmen."

Rita Daniels was flushing, and on her it looked remarkably good, Ronny Bronston decided. However, something came to him and he brought himself up. As a man in his early thirties, he could consider a girl of Rita's age and weigh her in the balance as a potential life companion. But as a man past fifty, as he would be, all too soon, it wasn't in the cards. If Ronny Bronston were ever to consider marriage, he'd better steel himself to the fact that he had better begin looking at widows in their middle-forties, not frecklenosed girls in their twenties—no matter how provocative their ponytail hairdos.

Rita said snappishly, "The end of the strongman isn't always disaster. Ghengis Khan and Tamerlane founded dynasties. And though Alexander died a young man, and didn't leave one, still, it was through his efforts that Hellenism emerged and the Greek culture was spread from the Mediterranean to India. And Napoleon. When he stepped onto the scene, Europe was almost entirely feudalistic. When he left it, there was a new and more progressive socio-economic system."

Ronny continued to needle her. "Whether or not Hellenism was an advance over the Persian culture can be debated, my dear. The Greeks wrote the history books, since they won the war, but there are some doubts about just how progressive they were. If Hitler had won his war, you can be sure that the villains who came down to us would have been Churchill, Roosevelt and Stalin—not Adolph the Aryan, who would have been properly deified, as was Alexander before him."

Phil Birdman snorted and went over to check the control screens. "This waxes too intellectual for me," he complained. "I'm simple at heart. I just don't like guys in a position above me to make arbitrary decisions. Sometimes it hurts—me."

"Sometimes we need men with the ability to make quick, arbitrary decisions," Rita snapped.

"Yeah," Phil agreed over his shoulder. "But I like to be in a position to help decide who it's going to be. Any of these stutes with big ambitions will tell you they've got super abilities and you ought to let them make the decisions. But if those abilities of theirs aren't really so super, then I'm the cloddy who winds up crisp."

Ronny added mildly, "Our friend Hilter was a good example. He let the German people know he was the superman to end all. And they believed him."

"Oh, you're both flats!" Rita flared.

Ronny said, "Well, your Uncle Max is evidently making his play. I hope we're alive to see whether or not he succeeds."

Rita said scornfully, "If he makes it, my friend, I doubt if you'll survive long enough to enjoy the advantages of his guided political system." But even as she said it, her facial expression changed, and she looked at Ronny anxiously.

Phil, from the controls, laughed. "Touché. She's got you there, Ronny." He looked into a zoom-screen. "Hey, I think our Space Forces cruiser is coming in."

They considered, briefly, releasing the girl and allowing her to return to Phrygia in the small spacecraft they had taken over from the UP, which had been their home for the past week.

In fact, they called the UP Building with the intention of discussing her release, in return for leniency toward the United Planets personnel.

The only response was from a uniformed Phrygia security police colonel, who informed them coldly that there were no longer any UP personnel in the building and that he was not free to discuss the situation. He inquired after the health of their prisoner, but showed no emotion when he was told that it was excellent.

Phil Birdman looked at his colleague. "We'd better take her."

Ronny didn't like it, but he had no valid argument against continuing to keep an obviously valuable hostage. Whatever force the Baron had taken to the Dawnworld's with him, always assuming that their guess was correct and he actually was on his way, was most certainly more than this tiny space Cruiser with its crew of four.

He said unhappily, "There'll be six of us in that small ship as it is. She'd make it seven. Besides, who knows what trouble she might kick up? She's fanatically for her Uncle Max and might try to blow us all up, just on the off chance that it might help him."

Phil Birdman looked at him questioningly.

Ronny said, "We'd have to have her under guard for the whole trip."

Phil said reasonably, "Why not put her into cold for the duration? We can arouse her as soon as we want her awake. It won't hurt her."

Ronny said grudgingly, "I suppose we could do that."

The skipper and the three junior Space Forces officers of the little cruiser were taken aback by the fact that they were to have a feminine fellow passenger, and a pretty one. And not to speak of the fact that she was the kidnapped member of the royal family of Phrygia.

This particular vessel, the Space Cruiser *Pisa*, had been the nearest to Phrygia when the crisis arose. Ross Metaxa had thrown his weight around and quickly had the *Pisa* diverted to the trouble spot. The instructions were to put ship and crew at the service of the two Section G operatives. Captain Gary Volos and his three juniors hadn't the vaguest idea of what the assignment was to be.

Rita Daniels didn't help matters any.

At the first opportunity, and before Ronny could hardly more than begin his explanations to the Space Forces skipper, she had yelped, "I am being detained illegally. I am the Countess Rita Daniels Wyler, niece of the Supreme Commandant of the member planet Phrygia of the United Planets, and these criminals are violating Article One of the United Planets Charter. I demand to be returned to my uncle's palace on Phrygia immediately."

Captain Volos was shocked. His eyes went from her to the two Section G agents in disbelief.

"Some squaw," Birdman muttered.

Only then did it come to Ronny Bronston that he had been concentrating so long on the present emergency

116

that he had forgotten that not one person in a billion, in the overall population of the United Planets, knew that the emergency existed. The average member of the human race had no knowledge of the existence of the original little intelligent alien life form, not to speak of the Dawnworlds and the Dawnmen.

He rapped, "Captain, your orders are to place your ship and yourself and men under the command of Agent Birdman and myself. We'll hold you to that."

Volos, staring, retorted, "My superiors made no mention of my condoning the breaking of the United Planets Charter. Do you deny this citizeness' words?"

Ronny shook his head wearily. "Substantially, she is telling the truth. However, the circumstances are drastic."

"Drastic!" one of the junior officers retorted. "How can anything be so drastic that the UP Charter be violated? Why, that's the reason for the existence of the Space Forces. That's why I joined it. To preserve the United Planets Charter—with my life, if necessary."

"Oh fine," Phil muttered. "A flag waver. Just what we need."

"You're going to have your chance to die for United Planets," Ronny snapped back, impatiently. "This young lady's uncle is attempting to subvert it. Right now, he's on his way to some newly discovered planets with a type of man far in advance of the . . . well, the human race. He hopes to get ultra weapons and techniques that will enable him to take over complete control of every planet, United Planets members and otherwise, which our species has colonized. That's why you were sent out here: To help us stop him."

The four spacemen were staring at him as though he had gone completely around the bend.

117

Rita saw her opportunity. "See?" she demanded. "He'
out of his mind."

"Obviously," the flag waver said, his eyes wide.

"Knock it, Richardson," his captain ordered. "I'll tak
care of this." He turned back to the two Section G agents
"I don't know what's going on here, but I'm going t
land and check with the local delegation of Unitec
Planets."

"That'll be a neat trick, as Sid Jakes would say," Bird
man muttered. "The local delegation of UP has eithe
been shot or thrown into the cooler."

"I keep telling you," Ronny said, trying to maintai
reasonableness in his tone, "Phrygia is in a condition o
armed aggression against her fellow members of UP an
in revolt against the UP as a whole."

"You mean to tell me," Captain Volos demanded un
believingly, "that this planet wants to take on all thre
thousand worlds of the UP and conquer them?"

Rita laughed mockingly.

Ronny Bronston closed his eyes in pain. He openec
them again.

He said, "Phil, cover them!"

A Model H gun flowed into Phil Birdman's hand.

XII

"Captain," Ronny said mildly, "your orders are to put yourselves and your cruiser under the command of Agent Birdman and myself. We are going to insist you observe them."

The skipper's eyes went down to the gun. He recognized the competent manner in which it was being handled. He also recognized the weapon and its potentialities. He checked his three juniors with his eyes. Even Richardson avoided the question in his commanding officer's face.

Captain Volos said coldly, "I am acting under coercion, Citizen Bronston, and wish the fact to be entered into the *Pisa's* log."

"Very well. Within a short time, I'm going to prove to you what we've tried to put over. You don't seem to be a flat. When the proof is obvious, then Citizen Birdman and I will expect more hearty cooperation on the part of you and your men. Meanwhile, here is a chart. We are to head for the first of these sun systems marked in red."

The four hesitated for a long moment.

Birdman jiggled his gun, meaningfully.

The captain took the torn chart, scowled at it, took it over to his navigating table.

"Where'd you get this?" he asked grudgingly.

"It's a long story," Ronny told him. "Once we get underway, I'll tell you at least part of it. Suffice to say, for the moment, that I liberated it from our friends on Phrygia, who are trying to take over control of every human being alive."

The captain looked with continued disbelief at him then turned down to the chart.

Phil Birdman said cheerfully, "I think we'd better chil the squaw here, like I suggested. She's already caused enough trouble in just these past few minutes. What could she accomplish working on our cloddy friends, here over a period of a couple of Earth weeks, or so."

Rita looked at Ronny. "You plan to put me in cold?"

"Can you think of something better to do with you?"

"I refuse!"

He didn't bother to answer her.

"That's illegal!" one of the other junior officers said belligerently. "Illegal, without the permission of the subject."

The Indian laughed. "Friend," he said, "you're probably going to see one hell of a lot of illegality in the next few weeks, so you might as well start getting acclimated to it." He looked at Ronny. "You realize we're going to have to take this in shifts, don't you? We aren't going to be allowed to both sleep at once."

Ronny sighed and nodded. "Now let's see about this girl's shot."

The trip to the Dawnworlds went with little incident.

Ronny Bronston and Phil Birdman made no effort to interfere with ship routine and Captain Gary Volos' prerogatives. They conducted themselves as passengers with but one great difference.

They stood alternating eight hour watches. Never was there a time when both slept. Never was there a time when their weapons weren't immediately to hand.

They had taken measures, the first day, to put the

Pisa's small arms under lock, and remained the only men aboard with guns.

Largely, they spent their time playing battle chess with young Richardson, or with Mendlesohn or Takashi, the other two junior officers. The skipper himself refused to associate with the Section G agents beyond what was necessary to operate the spacecraft.

Ronny had thought he was making some progress with Richardson and Takashi, at least. Since they were going to be as exposed to the dangers of the Dawnworlds as anyone, he could see no reason for not giving the others all the information he held himself. This included a complete rundown on the true nature of United Planets and of Section G. It included the information about the little aliens, and the further information that this species had evidently been wiped out in their entirety by the Dawnmen.

He told them about the desperate efforts being made by Ross Metaxa and other ranking officials of the Octagon to bring complete unity to the United Planets, in order to prepare men for the eventuality of the touching of the two cultures. And he told them of Baron Wyler's ambitions and his present expedition to the Dawnworlds.

He had thought he had been making progress and was disillusioned the seventh Earth day after they had left the vicinity of Phrygia.

Phil Birdman had been playing battle chess with Mendlesohn, by far the best player aboard, which irritated the Indian since he rather fancied his own game. At this point, Birdman's double line of pawns were in full retreat before the other's strong armor attack. And Phil was muttering unhappily to himself, even as he tried to fight a delaying action until he could bring up his own heavier pieces.

Richardson, seemingly about nothing more importan[t] than crossing the small mess hall lounge for coffee, sud denly launched himself on the Section G agent's back.

Birdman, with no time to unholster his weapon, fell t[o] the floor, the other clinging desperately to him, an[d] tried to roll out. Mendlesohn, his eyes wide, scurrie[d] about the two threshing men as though not quite sur[e] whether to throw his inconsiderable weight into the fray.

From the doorway, H gun in hand, Ronny snapped "All right. Break it up. Richardson! On your feet, or I'[ll] muffle you."

The aggressive ensign stood up, panting, his face un repentant.

Phil Birdman sat there for a moment, shaking hi[s] head ruefully. "Why'd you stop it?" he growled at Ronny "Now I'll never know if I could have clobbered th[e] young yoke."

Ronny said, "You're too old to be rolling around on th[e] deck."

"Huh," Birdman snorted, pushing himself erect. "Loo[k] who's talking. It won't be long before . . ." He cut himse[lf] short.

Ronny Bronston looked at him bleakly.

"Sorry," Phil said. "That's the trouble with wisecrack ers. A supposedly smart quip gets out before you re alize it's jetsam."

Ronny said to Richardson, "What was the idea?"

The other glowered resentment, in spite of the levele[d] gun. "What do you think it was? You've taken over th[e] ship at gun point. I was trying to recapture it."

The captain entered from the compartment entranc[e] opposite the one Ronny occupied. "What's going on?" he demanded.

"This cloddy here is making like a hero," Ronny said mildly. "I'm afraid we're going to have to ask you to put him in cold, Captain Volos."

"He's a necessary member of my crew!"

Phil Birdman muttered, "He's about as necessary as a coronary."

Ronny Bronston, still holding the gun, said, "So long as we're in underspace, you could handle the ship single-handed, Captain, as you well know."

"I refuse to put a man into cold without his permission."

Ensign Richardson glared defiantly at the Section G agent.

Ronny said mildly, "Then I'll have to shoot him. I can't afford to take the chance of having him loose. Next time, he might succeed."

"Not if he tried it on me," Birdman said nastily.

Ronny looked at Richardson, then the skipper. "The fat's in the fire, gentlemen. One man's life isn't very important."

Richardson said tightly, "Captain, I think he means it."

Captain Gary Volos rasped, "Very well, but I insist that this, too, be entered in the ship's log."

"That log is going to be plumb full before this trip's over." Birdman grinned.

Afterwards the two agents sat in the lounge alone over hot drinks.

Ronny growled, "It was lucky I couldn't sleep."

"Aw, I could've scalped that molly," the Indian grumbled.

"Not if Mendelsohn would have got around to slugging you on the back of the head."

Birdman chuckled. "Two down and only three left to go. You think we'll ever get there without putting them all in the cold? The party gets rougher and rougher."

Ronny asked suddenly, "Phil, why'd you join Section G?"

"Who, me?" Phil seemed embarrassed. "I don't know. Better job than I had. Chance to see a lot of the different planets. Get out of the rut. That sort of thing."

Ronny Bronston went on, as though he hadn't really heard his companion. "When I was a kid I had the United Planets dream but good. Man exploding out into space, carrying our species to the stars. Going every which way, trying every scheme ever dreamed up from Plato's Republic to Howard Scott's technocracy. Trying out every proposed ethic. Trying out a hundred methods of improving the race, by breeding in this, or breeding out that. Planets colonized by nothing but Negroes, others by only people over six and a half feet tall, others by Zen Buddhists, others by persons with I.Q.s of over one-fifty, others by vegetarians, and on and on."

Phil snorted, missing the earnestness in the other's tone. "How about Amazonia? A few thousand feminists. No men at all, at first. Artificial insemination. Then when boy kids came along, they enslaved them."

Ronny said impatiently, "Sure, a lot of them are purely from jetsam, but they're balanced out by those that are finding new paths, new truths, and really advancing the species. The United Planets dream. An opportunity for everybody to try anything. But what's the ultimate aim? What's the goal? To dominate the whole galaxy, the way Rita sees it?"

Phil looked at him questioningly. "Does there have to be a goal?" He was beginning to catch the other's mood.

"That's my point. I wonder if there should be. I wonder if the dream wasn't going better before the Octagon stepped in and decided that UP needed direction."

"Well, you know how the Old Man would answer that. It was fine to let mankind take off in all directions back when we had no reason to believe there was other intelligent life in the galaxy. But when we ran into those little fellows, then we had to get underway."

Ronny's expression was strange. "But underway where? A comparatively small group of men, of Ross Metaxa's type, decided it was up to them to steer. But of what are they composed that they should know best? Why should Ross Metaxa, and his various supervisors such as Sid Jakes and Lee Chang Chu, be allowed to decide that the government of this planet Amazonia, for instance, should be overthrown and a bi-sexual regime encouraged? Perhaps the matriarchy they're experimenting with is superior."

"Yeah." Phil grinned. "And perhaps not. Especially for *me*."

"Yes, but my point is, who is Metaxa to decide? There are tens of billions of members of the race. What makes him so special that he can throw Section G into a local situation on some planet colonized by this opinion group, or that, of their own free will and conscious of what they were going into?"

At long last, Phil Birdman turned thoughtful. "Maybe I don't know the answer," he admitted. "And maybe my decision was a wrong one. But I'm in my mid-forties now and I took my stand quite a time ago. I'm not going to change it now." He looked at Ronny. Are you?"

Ronny grunted self-deprecation. "I wouldn't know what to change it to."

Ronny Bronston came up behind Captain Volos, who

was standing watch in the *Pisa's* control compartment. He said, "What's wrong?"

The skipper was bug-eyeing into a zoom-screen. "A spacecraft! I've never seen another ship in underspace before. But . . . but that's not it. It's the size. It's as large as a medium-sized satellite."

Ronny said, "Let me see."

The captain grudgingly made room for him.

"I don't see anything," Ronny said.

The captain scowled at him and bent over the horizontal screen again. "It's gone!" he blurted. "It can't be gone!"

"We seem to be approaching the Dawnworlds," Ronny said dryly. "From what little I know about the Dawnmen, shortly, we're going to be witnessing a good many things that simply can't be."

Gary Volos was still gaping into the zoom-screen.

Ronny said, "How far out are we?"

The captain at last stood erect. "Not very far," he said. "I can't be too sure. I have no references except that chart you gave me. Possibly the coordinates are off. However, we should be coming out of underspace before long."

He looked at Ronny Bronston with puzzlement in his face, and also a touch of accusation. He said, "That craft I just saw was far and beyond anything that could be built on any United Planet's world."

Ronny said mildly, "I told you that the Dawnworlds are evidently fantastically beyond us, technically."

Volos shook his head. "I didn't believe your story. I didn't know what your game was, but I didn't believe this tale about other intelligent life forms."

"Well, Captain, you'd better start thinking about it.

The more cool minds we've got around, when we come out of underspace, the better off we're going to be. We have only one small bit of evidence that these critters won't crisp us immediately upon our materializing."

"What's that?" Volos asked, a shade of apprehension in his tone now.

"Those little aliens had photographs, both still and movies, on them. That would indicate that the little fellows actually landed on at least one of the Dawnworlds and were allowed to use whatever camera devices they had and then leave again."

He indicated the chart on the navigation table. "And that star chart. It shows hundreds of star systems in red. I've assumed that those are all Dawnman settled. The little fellas must have sent out various expeditions to compile that extensive a chart. Which means, in turn, that the Dawnmen allowed them to do it."

"Didn't you say that the atmosphere of the planets the little aliens were on was changed to what was poison for them?"

"That's right. Eventually, they must have done something to irritate these Dawnmen; but before they did, they must have done considerable exploring about the Dawnmen domains."

Ronny thought for a moment, then said, "I suppose you might as well start the process of reviving Rita Daniels and young Richardson. We're not going to be in any position to remain divided among ouselves after breakout from underspace."

"All right," the captain said nervously. He spoke into an order box.

Ronny said, "Look. This trip hasn't been any too happy, thus far, which isn't surprising. But now that we're here,

I want to let you know that so far as the operation of the *Pisa* is concerned, Agent Birdman and I want to co-operate. You're the captain. We'll follow orders."

Volos looked shamefaced. "My instructions were to put myself and command under your orders. I'm sorry I got around to following them so tardily. Very well. I captain the *Pisa*, but the overall decisions are yours."

His eyes flicked to the control panels. "We're coming out." He reached over and threw an alarm.

Within moments, Birdman and Lieutenant Takashi hurried into the compartment.

Takashi, his characteristically bland face showing un-oriental-like excitement, said, "Mendlesohn's bringing the others out of the cold."

The captain said, "We're emerging."

They came out in the planetary system of a sun remarkably like Sol, and within reasonable distance of a planet most remarkably similar to Earth.

The captain muttered, "The coordinates were as perfect as any I've ever seen. Much better, in fact."

Phil Birdman said, "We told you, those little aliens were far and gone in advance of us. Evidently in inter-planetary navigation as well as elsewhere."

Rita Daniels and Ensign Richardson, both looking a bit green about the gills, came into the compartment, cups of some steaming broth in hand.

The captain, his eyes magnetized to the large screen which took up a full half of one control compartment wall, threw a lever. Richardson put down his cup and slid into a control chair, so did Takashi.

The captain said to Ronny Bronston, "Well?"

Ronny shrugged. "Why put it off? Let's go closer." He had an afterthought and said, "You people have some method of detecting any craft down below using nuclear propulsion, haven't you?"

"Of course. It's part of the equipment utilized to locate possible wrecks of spacecraft, which have crashed."

"Could you locate the Baron's ship, or fleet, as the case may be?"

Volos frowned. "Why do you think he's here? There are hundreds of star systems on that chart."

"I'm not sure he is," Ronny told him. "But this is the nearest of them all. Why should he go further, if he's in a hurry?"

Rita snapped, "I demand to be put in instant communication with my uncle!"

She was universally ignored, even by young Richardson.

"We can detect him easy enough," Volos said. "But can we tell if it's him, rather than one of these Dawnworld craft? Although I suppose it's possible that they no longer use nuclear power."

Richardson turned and stared at him. "Has he talked you into believing that jetsam, sir?"

"I saw a starship at least a thousand times larger than anything in United Planets," his skipper told him without inflection. "Mr. Richardson, and you others, consider yourselves under the command of Citizens Bronston and Birdman. Countess Wyler, if that is your correct name, you attempted to confound me. Please keep in mind that I am captain of this vessel, no matter who your uncle may be. I expect the respect and cooperation of everyone aboard."

It was half an hour later before he spoke again.

And then it was to say, "On the face of it, below we have one of your Dawnworlds. It could be nothing else."

Below them was a world that was a park.

XIII

It was as though you took a planet, approximately the size of Earth itself and transformed the whole into a landscaped garden. As though you made of the whole, a cinema set portraying the Garden of Eden, the Garden of Allah, the Promised Land, the Islands of the Blest, Zion, the Elysian Fields . . . what will you, for Paradise.

Rita Daniels hissed her breath in.

Takashi said shakily, "I can detect a nuclear powered ship. Only one. Seemingly larger than our own size."

Rita said, unthinking, "Uncle Max's yacht. It's the fastest . . ." Then she clammed up.

Ronny said, "Try to pinpoint it, Lieutenant." He looked at the captain. "No radio contact? No nothing?"

The captain shook his head. "I would think there would be some sort of patrol. Some sort of defense mechanism. But there doesn't seem to be. I can't even pick up any radio waves."

"Possibly they don't use radio waves any longer," Birdman muttered.

Richardson looked at him in disgust. "You've got to use radio waves," he said. "You can't run an advanced technology without radio waves."

Phil Birdman said, "You mean, you can't run *our* technology without radio waves."

Richardson blinked. "Just how far ahead of us are they supposed to be?"

Nobody answered him.

Ronny said to the captain, "What do you say we orbit her a few times, coming closer slowly?"

Several hours later, it was Rita who said, mystified, "But there aren't any cities."

And Phil Birdman said, disbelief in his own voice, "Maybe they don't use cities, either."

Takashi said, "There are a few worlds in United Planets that don't have cities."

"Yes," the captain muttered, "but the most backward of all. Places like Kropotkin, the anarchist experiment, and the planet Mother, with the Stone Age naturalists. By the looks of this world, the whole thing has been landscaped. That's not exactly within the capabilities of either anarchists or nature lovers, who refuse to utilize any inventions more complicated than the bow and arrow."

Ronny said thoughtfully, "Early man didn't have cities. They first came in as defense centers for the new developing agriculturalists, against rading nomads. Later on, they became centers for trade, and when social labor came in, large numbers of people had to live close together to work in manufacture."

"What are you getting at?" Rita asked.

"Well, perhaps these people, if they actually have matter converters, no longer need manufacturing or trade. No longer have to live in each others' laps."

The captain muttered, "I can't even make out individual houses. Or, for that matter, any sign of agriculture."

Mendlesohn said, awe in his voice, "Do you think that this could be a whole planet just devoted to being a park? Possibly their other planets are so built up and crowded that they've kept this one just for the sheer beauty of it."

Phil Birdman said, "Look at that herd of deer, or whatever they are!" His voice tuned low. "The Happy Hunting Ground."

"What?" Ronny asked.

"Nothing. How long does it take to breed out of a people, the instinct of the chase?"

Takashi said suddenly, "There. There's a city for you. And it's not too far from where I detected the nuclear powered spacecraft."

It was an area of possibly a square mile and the buildings were unique, even at a distance.

The captain looked at Ronny Bronston.

Ronny thought about it. "Let's drop closer," he said. "From all we know, if they'd wanted to crisp us they could have done so long before this. A race that could produce a spaceship as large as the one you saw, would have weapons to match."

They hovered over the complex of buildings, descending slowly, until the screens could pick out considerable detail.

"There in the center," Richardson said, "a pyramid. It looks like a Mayan pyramid."

"What is a Mayan pyramid?" Rita asked. Her voice held the same awe of this strange world as did the others.

Ronny said, "Your Earth history has been neglected, my dear. You spent too much of your time reading up on the strongmen. The Mayans were an early civilization in the southern part of North America. They . . ." He broke off suddenly as something came to him. "This isn't a city. It's a complex of religious buildings. Maybe schools, things like that, too. But it's not a city. Not in the sense of large numbers of persons living in it."

"There's one thing for sure"—Phil nodded—"there aren't

a good many people down there. What's that, on top of the pyramid?"

The skipper focused the small zoom-screen, quickly flashed if off again, his face pale.

"What's the matter, Captain?" Richardson asked. "Why didn't you throw it up on the large screen for the rest of us?"

Volos said to Ronny tightly. "Didn't you tell us that these so-called Dawnmen were sort of a copperish color?"

"That's right. Great, beautiful physical specimens. Rather a golden color."

The captain fiddled with his small zoomer again, finally located something and switched it to the compartment's large screen for all to see.

It was a small group of the Dawnworld people, both men and women. All were dressed in no more than loin cloths, or short kilts. All seemed approximately twenty-five years of age. All were in obvious sparkling health.

"These, eh?" the captain said, his voice strange.

Ronny looked at him. "Yes, of course. Those are the Dawnmen. They don't look particularly hostile or aggressive, do they?"

Volos said very slowly, "That wasn't a Dawnman on the top of the pyramid."

Ronny said, "If Baron Wyler is in the vicinity, it means two things: No matter how much of a headstart he got on us, he hasn't managed to get what he came after, as yet. Which means, in turn, that we've got to get a move on."

All the others looked at him.

"Well, what's the program?" Birdman asked.

"The Baron—if that's his craft we've detected—is on the ground," Ronny said thoughtfully. "We're going to have to land, too. Skipper, what say that you edge over a mile or so, beyond the limits of this city, or whatever it is, and drop one of us to reconnoiter?"

The captain turned to his control panel, silently.

He drifted the *Pisa* to the north, brought it down carefully in what was seemingly an isolated glen, devoid of life.

Ronny went to the hatch, Birdman and Takashi accompanying him, the others remaining in the control compartment, glued to the screens.

Lieutenant Takashi eyed the scanners built into the bulkhead over the hatch. "Almost identical to Earth atmosphere, Bronston," he reported.

Ronny said, "Well, here goes nothing, then."

The captain came up behind them.

"Citizen Birdman, Lieutenant, would you leave me with Citizen Bronston for a moment?"

Phil's eyebrows raised and he looked at Ronny, but then shrugged, and following the junior officer, went back into the control room.

Ronny asked, "What was it you saw at the top of the pyramid?"

"That's what I came back to tell you. I thought perhaps you'd just as well not alarm the girl—and the balance of the ship's complement, for that matter."

Ronny looked at him.

The captain cleared his throat. "It was what seemed to be an altar, and on it, a man."

"A Dawnman?"

"An Earthman. Or, to be more accurate, I suppose, a Phrygian. But, at any rate, a member of the human race, not a Dawnman."

Ronny sucked in air. Finally, he said, "All right. Drop me. Then take off again. I'll keep in touch, through

Agent Birdman. If anything happens to me, he's in command."

"Right," Volos said. There was a certain respect in his voice now, which had hardly been there in his early dealings with the Section G operatives.

When Ronny Bronston had gotten a good thousand yards from the *Pisa*, he turned and waved; and seconds later, it lifted off. He watched it fade away, upward and out.

He turned and looked about him.

It was still a park. A garden.

He shook his head in disbelief.

And not ten feet from him, some sort of door opened in empty space. For the briefest of moments, he could see into what seemed to be living quarters of a man-type being. Chairs, tables, decorations. . . .

But then a body blocked his view. A Dawnman came out and began walking toward him. The door, or whatever the opening was closed again.

Ronny was gaping, his jaw sagging. He shook his head for clarity.

The Dawnman, walking briskly and looking to neither left nor right, passed him by no more than three feet.

He could have stepped off a pedestal in a Greek temple devoted to the god Apollo. He was approximately six and a half feet tall and would have weighed approximately one hundred and ninety. His skin was golden, his hair dark cream. His eyes were blue and very clear, and there was the slightest of smiles on his lips.

He wasn't ignoring Ronny Bronston blindly, he was ignoring him enthusiastically, avidly, even vigorously, if that made sense.

He walked right on by and went about his business.

Ronny stood there for a long moment, blankly.

Perhaps the other was blind.

No. Ridiculous. A man didn't stride along as carefree as this young man was doing, without benefit of sight. He was about to top a slight hill, and would be lost to view. On an impulse, Ronny ran after him.

He called, "Say!"

The Dawnman either didn't hear, or didn't bother to answer. He strode on. Back from him floated a trill of song. Well, not exactly a song. Sort of a happy cross between song and whistle. It had a beautiful lilt.

Ronny called, realizing that the use of Earth Basic was ridiculous, "Wait! I want to talk to you!"

But the Dawnman passed over the rise and, by the time Ronny Bronston got to the top of the hillock, the Dawnman had disappeared.

Ronny looked about him, bewildered. There was no place for him to have gone in such short order. But then he remembered how the Dawnman had emerged from what had seemed open space. Without doubt, he had disappeared into another such . . . such . . . What was it?

And even with these thoughts in mind, Ronny walked full into . . . what was it? He smashed, at full pace, into an invisible barrier. He sat down, abruptly, his hand to his nose, which he at first thought, must be broken. It wasn't. In a couple of minutes, still sitting, he got the nosebleed under control.

Then he stared accusingly at . . . at what? At nothing. Immediately before him seemed a beautifully kept lawn leading to a small grove of trees. Beyond the grove he could see a stream of unbelievably clear water.

He reached a hand forward, tentatively.

He could feel . . . what? A glass-like substance? He supposed so. He traced it from the ground up as far as he could reach, and then he walked slowly along it, ever feeling.

Seemingly, it was a wall. But he could see through it perfectly. No matter how close he brought his eyes, he could not see it, however.

He could hear his communicator hum in his pocket. He took it out and flicked open the lid. Phil Birdman was on the screen.

He said, anxiously, "For a minute, there, we thought we saw one of these Dawnmen right near you."

"You did."

"Well, what happened to him?"

Ronny said sourly, "He evidently came out of one house, walked down the street aways and into another."

Phil said, "Are you all right?"

"Except for a busted nose, I'm all right. This planet isn't depopulated. They evidently just don't like the idea of cluttering up the scenery with a lot of buildings, so they camouflage them. For all I know. I'm in the middle of a big city right now. No, I guess I couldn't be, or I'd see more people out here in the open."

"Camouflage? We don't see any camouflage."

"Oh, knock it," Ronny told him. "It's *perfect* camouflage, of course, you can't see it. Have you got in touch with Earth?"

"Right. I talked with Sid Jakes. He said to play it by ear."

Ronny grunted. "Tell him I'm playing it by nose, instead." He flicked the communicator off.

With no other idea of what to do in mind, he walked the direction of the city, or religious buildings, or whatever they were.

He rounded a bend and came upon what could only

be a picnic. A group of the Dawnpeople, about ten of them, were seated on the bank of a stream. There were both men and women, all seemingly somewhere between the ages of twenty and thirty: All absolutely perfect physical specimens. If anything, the perfection was its own drawback. They were, Bronston decided, too perfect.

Not a woman nor a man among them that wouldn't have met the highest standards of Tri-Di sex symbol back on Earth, or any of the other planets that continued the fan system of theater. No Greek goddess could have rivaled a single of these women in pulchritude. Paris would have had his work cut out, choosing whom to give his apple.

Ronny hesitated. Obviously, these people were at their leisure, enjoying themselves. He disliked to intrude.

But then it came to him, that given fusion power and matter converters, they must have considerable in the way of leisure. Besides, they would be interested in him as a complete alien. He might as well take the plunge.

He stepped nearer and said, "I beg your pardon," feeling like a flat at the words, but the ice had to be broken somehow. He assumed that a race this advanced would have some method of communicating with him. Some technician who . . .

But then, Baron Wyler's words came back to him: *these Dawnpeople are not intelligent.*

Nonsense! On the face of it . . .

But on the face of it, they didn't even see him.

He stepped closer.

They went on with their picnic, if that's what it was. They ignored him, completely, enthusiastically. He stepped so close that they couldn't possibly have missed his presence.

And it wasn't as though they were blind. He could see them performing actions that obviously required the coordination of hand and eye.

One of them, an absolutely perfectly formed girl wearing nothing but sandals and a colorful kilt, picked up a handful of sand and gravel from the stream's bank and turned with it to a low table. There was, on the table, a device that reminded Ronny of nothing so much as a primitive coffee grinder he had once seen in an Earth museum. She poured the dirt into a funnel-shaped hole on the top and touched a switch or stud.

She opened a small door and brought forth what was seemingly a piece of fruit, though unrecognizable as to type by the Section G agent. She began to munch it.

Ronny Bronston closed his eyes in surrender.

He said, in sudden exasperation, "Look, won't somebody give me a steer?"

They still didn't notice him.

He looked at the gathering more closely. There were several of the coffee-grinder devices. Evidently, they were in continual use. Some of the Dawnpeople were drinking from intricately shaped glasses, some eating various unidentifiable foodstuffs. They laughed. One or two sang, from time to time, in that strange trilling manner Ronny had heard earlier from his first contact.

They were obviously having one whale of a time.

He stared at the devices.

With unbelievably good luck, he had stumbled, within a half hour of the first landing on the Dawnworld, on one of their matter converters. They were paying no attention to him. He might as well have not existed. Suppose he took one of the things up. What would they do? It was hard to believe that any of these people were apt to resort to violence. And most certainly they carried no weapons.

But that gave him pause. Given the occasion, who could say but that they were capable of pouring a handful of sand into one of their gismos and bring forth a pistol to end all pistols?"

But this was his obvious chance. For whatever reason, the Baron was evidently still on this planet. His expedition, thus far, had failed. If Ronny could acquire one of these working models of matter transformers, Section G's technicians could possibly take it apart, duplicate it, come up with larger models.

He went so far as to tentatively reach forth a hand toward the nearest. They continued to ignore him. By not a flicker of eye did they admit to his presence.

Ronny drew his hand back.

He wondered wildly if he were invisible to them. But no. Obviously these people were human. Perhaps not exactly of his genus, but most certainly they were of the species *Homo*. This world of theirs had obviously been landscaped to please their own taste. It pleased his as well. They saw what he saw.

He stared at the matter converter. There it was. There was victory over the Baron and his plans to dominate.

Something kept him. Intuition? What? He didn't know. He was disgusted with himself. Why not snatch it up?

His communicator hummed. Impatiently, he snatched it from his pocket. It was Birdman again.

"What is it?" Ronny snapped.

"Baron Wyler," the Indian said urgently. "He's made contact with us."

"Oh." Ronny paused. The Baron's space yacht was considerably larger than the four man United Planets Space

Cruiser. Ronny had no doubt that it was armed with the most efficient weapons the Baron could find.

He asked, "What does he want?"

"Help."

XIV

For the moment, he didn't allow himself to dwell further on that. He snapped, "Tell the skipper to get down here and pick me up."

"Right," Phil said, and faded.

Ronny Bronston went back to the grove in which the *Pisa* had set him down such a short time before. His mind was in a whirl. He held in abeyance Birdman's information about the Baron, and tried to find some rhyme or reason about his own discoveries.

Wyler and Fitzjames must have been right. These people were not intelligent in the sense of the word that *Homo sapiens* implied. *Intelligent, somehow,* he supposed. *But with a different intelligence.* He shook his head in exasperation.

The *Pisa* came gently to rest, and he went over to it as quickly as was safe.

The captain and Birdman were at the lock when he entered.

Ronny snapped, "What's all this . . .?"

Phil Birdman said, "Wyler took the initiative. I suppose he picked us up as quickly as we did his yacht. At any rate, he contacted us. He says he wants help."

"Help from what?"

"He didn't say."

They went back to the control room and joined the others.

Ronny said, "It's a trap, he's trying to suck us in."

Captain Volos shook his head. "I don't think so. On

the screen, he looked like a broken man. Obviously, he knows you'll place him under arrest. That all his plans are shot."

Phil Birdman said, "Listen, let's leave him in whatever juice he's stewing in. If it's a trap, we won't spring it. If he's really in trouble, it couldn't happen to a nicer guy."

Rita held a small fist to her mouth.

Ronny shook his head. "No," he said. "Let's get over there. No matter what, he's our people, and we're all in a strange land." He grumbled, "A damnably strange land."

While the captain and his crew turned to their ship's controls, Rita looked at Ronny Bronston. She said softly, "You're not the worst person around, young fella."

Ronny chuckled wryly. "The term is *old man*, not young fella." He turned to the others and gave them a quick rundown on his meagre adventures.

He earned their disbelieving stares.

Phil Birdman blurted, "Why didn't you slap one of them across the chops? That would have got a rise."

Ronny looked at him. "I didn't think of that." He paused. Then, "You wouldn't have, either. Somehow, there's a no-touch feeling in the air."

"Why didn't you put the lift on one of the converters, or whatever they are?"

Ronny scowled, "I don't know. The no-touch atmosphere entered into that, too."

Takashi said, "There is the Phrygian ship."

They brought it into the large screen.

"No sign of a fight, or anything," Phil Birdman said.

The space yacht was at rest in a lovely dell.

Volos looked at the Section G operatives.

Ronny took a breath and said, "All right. Set down next to them." He looked at the *Pisa's* three junior officers,

143

finally deciding on Richardson. He said, "If I give you a gun, do you think you can keep from shooting me with it?"

The young ensign was embarrassed. "Yes, sir. Sorry about our earlier difficulties, sir."

Ronny said, "Richardson and I will go over and case the situation. I'll keep my communicator on, and in constant touch. Anything goes wrong, you take off. Birdman will be in charge. Does Wyler know that Citizeness Daniels is aboard?"

"I talked with Uncle Max," she said worriedly. "Can't I go with you?"

"Not yet," he said apologetically. "I'm afraid you're still a hostage. I doubt if he'll attack the *Pisa* as long as you're aboard."

Rita shook her head. "He wouldn't attack it, anyway. Something terrible has happened."

"We'll see," Ronny said. "Come on, Ensign."

Takashi saw them through the lock, and closed it behind. They crossed the seemingly neatly trimmed grass to the other craft. Ronny looked it over. A luxurious, highly powered yacht, probably as fast as anything UP could produce. And, obviously, well-armed to boot.

He had expected to be met by well disciplined, nattily uniformed spacemen of the Phrygian space forces, but instead, Count Fitzjames was the only one at the lock to greet them.

Ronny made a brief introduction, not hiding the fact that he was holding his communicator up. His right hand was ready for a quick draw.

Count Fitzjames said, the usual worry in his voice, "The Supreme Commandant is in his lounge. This way."

Baron Wyler was indeed in the lounge. He was sprawled, as though exhausted, in a deep chair. His eyes were wide and unseeing, and there was despair in his face.

Ronny stood before him and he looked up.

There was no more of the hail-fellow-well-met tone of voice. No friendly projection of personality, no all-embracing charm of the born leader of men.

Ronny and Ensign Richardson had seen no others on their way through the ship. It came to Ronny that whatever had happened, this was no trap. Neither Wyler nor Fitzjames were shamming. Somehow, their expedition had become a cropper.

"All right," Ronny said. "What happened? What did you mean when you radioed us for help?"

The Baron said wearily, "I can't navigate this craft, nor can the Count. We have no way of getting back."

Ronny stared at him. "Where's your crew?"

"They've evidently been sacrificed to the gods—or something along that line. Cutting the heart out with what looked like an obsidian knife!" a spasm of horror went over the former strongman's face.

The Baron didn't seem to be particularly coherent. Ronny sat himself down and looked at the scholarly Count. "Suppose you bring me up to date."

"I am not sure I can, in complete detail; but I have a theory."

"All right, take your time. Richardson, take a look through the ship."

Richardson left.

The Count said unhappily, "I am not quite sure where to start." He looked into Ronny's face. "Citizen Bronston, has it ever occurred to you that perhaps primitive man, say Cro-Magnon man, might have been more intelligent than modern man?" He hurried on before getting an answer. "Don't confuse intelligence with accumulated knowledge. You can take a man with an I.Q. of ninety and fill him with a great deal of accumulated knowledge. Keep at it long enough and you can get him a doctor's degree. On the other hand, you can take a man with an I.Q. of 150 and place him in the right—or rather, the wrong—surroundings and he'll wind up with very little education at all. He'll be smart, but will possess little accumulated knowledge.

"In primitive times, if a man was slow in the head, he died. The race needed better brains and bred for them. But as we solved the problems of defense against other animals and against nature, and we learned to feed, clothe and shelter ourselves, the need became less pressing. Our less intelligent survived, and lived to breed. Finally we achieve to the point where there was an abundance of everything for all, and the need of having superior brains fell away. No longer were the most brainy in the community given the best food, the best women—the best the community could offer in all desirable things. They were no longer at a premium."

"What in Zen are you driving at?" Ronny asked impatiently.

"One of my theories is that these Dawnmen are the end product of having an abundance for all for a megayear or so. They don't *need* intelligence."

Ronny took a breath. "All right, and what are some more of your theories?" Through this, the Baron was sitting, staring into emptiness again.

Fitzjames said, "If I am correct, in the Dawnworld culture, the form of their early industrial revolution differed from ours on Earth. Remember my using the example of the caste system in India? Well, on the first Dawnworld, wherever it was, automation didn't finally take over, conformity did. What it became was a very high industrial level, beehive-type culture. The individual workers are genetically predisposed to particular kinds of endeavor, and very readily and rapidly learn that specialty . . . but can't learn anything else.

"They're a contented people, a happy people. Everybody is happy—or he's a genetic defective, and disposed of. Because he *is* a genetic defective, or he'd be happy."

Ronny was staring at him. The scholar cleared his throat and went on. "They are evidently not aggressive or warlike. But they're insect-like in the all-out-and-no-counting-the-casualties defense of their territories and their ways of doing things. They probably can't be aggressive, because they're one hundred percent ritualistic, and they have no ritual for aggression, nor for exploiting a new planet. Their expanding to new planets probably ended megayears ago.

"We were at first amazed, when we landed, that they ignored our presence. But they couldn't do anything else, because they don't have any rituals that acknowledge our existence. They haven't any rituals that take strangers, whatever their business, into account at all."

The Baron looked up. He sighed deeply and said, "Tell him, Fitzjames. I grow weary of your pedantic talk."

The count hurried on. "They do have rituals that concern treatment of criminals. Steal something from them, and you come under those rituals and your classification as *stranger*—to be ignored—is superceded by the new classification *criminal*, and that, they do react to."

"Tell him," the Baron said petulantly.

"Their defectives are killed in a human sacrifice ceremony, which must have religious aspects going back to the very dawn of their culture."

Ronny looked from one of them to the other. "You sent

out your men to grab any of their devices not nailed down."

"Yes," the Baron said.

The count continued. "My theory is that the little aliens, whose planets were destroyed by changing their atmospheres, did much the same. They took a longer time. They charted a considerable number of the star systems the Dawnmen occupy. They photographed. They operated very slowly, evidently fascinated. But then they took their steps and tried to appropriate some of the devices these Dawnmen use. Perhaps they tried to trade for them, buy them, loan them, or whatever, but there was no possible way to do so. The Dawnmen are simply not interested in any contact whatsoever with any alien race. So the little aliens finally resorted to theft—and that was their end."

Richardson came back into the lounge. He said to Ronny, "There's nobody else aboard."

The Baron said, "We watched it all, the Count and I. The men were taken one by one to the top of the pyramid. It was an elaborate ceremony. It must go back to a period when they were on the level of the Aztecs. They cut open the chest cavity and pulled the still throbbing heart out. The Count and I watched from an altitude of about one hundred feet. There was nothing we could do. It was obvious to us that if we attempted to use weapons, they would have destroyed us in split seconds."

"Had we interfered," the count said, "we, too, would have become criminals. As it was, we were the only ones who had not attempted theft, and hence were left alone."

The Baron ended the story. "I can operate this craft well enough to take off and land, but I am no navigator. I request that one or two of your officers be sent to help us."

Ronny opened his mouth to answer, but, at that moment, a new element entered into the lounge of the spacecraft.

From nowhere a voice came into the consciousness of each of them.

You are at last correct, Maximilian Wyler. You must return to the planet which our researching of your mind tells us you think of as Mother Earth. There is naught for you here.

Ronald Bronston, we detect that your motives for landing upon this . . . Dawnworld . . . were not criminal in intent, nor have you committed depredation upon us. It is our custom to send warning to stranger worlds —who are potential depredators—by the way of strangers who have landed among us, but have committed no criminal act. You are such. However, our researching your health indicated that your life span has been so altered that perhaps it would not encompass the period required to spread the warning. Hence, we have made certain rectifications so that your span of years will equal that of a normal lifetime as we know it to be—some two and a half of what you call centuries.

Ronny Bronston sucked in air.

"Who are you?" Count Fitzjames blurted.

Researching your own mind, Felix Fitzjames, brings to our attention that in attempting to analyze our culture, you compared our society to the caste system of your India. Indeed you had elements of correctness. But why did you forget about the Brahmins amond us? Why did you assume that the equivalents of the sudras with whom you have come in contact, were the sum total of our race?

The voice addressed them as a group again.

Go back to your Mother Earth. Do not be afraid of the Dawnworlds. Felix Fitzjames was correct to this extent: We are not aggressive. We have no designs against you. So long as you have none against us, our cultures need never conflict. Farewell. . . .

"Wait!" Baron Wyler cried out. "Why should I go back to Mother Earth? Why not to my own planet, Phrygia?"

You would find it difficult to breath, Maximilian Wyler. When our people are interfered with, they trace back to the planet from which the criminal element came so as to preserve themselves from additional predators in the future. The atmosphere of Phrygia is now composed of methane, ammonia and hydrogen. To the extent that Ronald Bronston succeeds in his mission of warning, a like fate will be saved your other worlds. And now we will communicate with you no longer. Farewell. . . .

And suddenly there was an emptiness in the space yacht's lounge.

At long last, Ronny Bronston looked at the aging Count Fitzjames. "Are you still so sure they aren't intelligent?" he asked wryly. "At least on the highest level, we can expect cooperation. Where there's logical intelligence, you can communicate."

But Felix Fitzjames, his lips pale, was shaking his head. "Is a Brahmin less castebound than the lower castes? Does a queen bee have any more freedom of will than a worker?"

Ronny, and, to a lesser degree, Baron Wyler, were scowling at him.

The aged scholar was still shaking his head. "Perhaps the voice we just heard came from those who think of themselves as intelligent; but if it's gone through two megayears of this culture, it must live by pure ritual, too. Because its rituals are somewhat different and more complex than the lower castes', it possibly believes it isn't a pre-programmed mechanism."

"I'm not sure I get what you're driving at," Ronny muttered.

Fitzjames was feeling it out, even as he talked. "One of the early problems of the cybernetic researchers was the fact that—to be intelligent, an entity must be capable of inconsistent behavior. But that means not to be logically predictable. This brings the frustration that an intelligent-inconsistent machine—which would be capable of exercising judgment—cannot be reliable in the sense of predictable. That is, the closer they come to a truly intelligent cybernetic device, the more it approaches the unreliable performance of a living organism."

The Baron shifted in his chair, as though not following. He had remained silent, in shock, since the revelation of the end of his ambition, his dream . . . his very world.

Fitzjames turned his full attention to Ronny. "Ants are very reliable living organisms, an entymologist can predict exactly what a particular ant of a particular type will do. It's genetically pre-programmed. The voice we just heard is a part also of a genetically pre-programmed system; it must be just as reliable and, therefore, invariable as the lower castes. An anthill, termitarium, or beehive is a true totalitarian state—and in a true totalitarian state, the Führer, Dictator, Caesar, or whatever, is just as much controlled by the rituals and taboos as every other member of the state. This Dawnworld culture would not have been stable for such a period, if its Brahmins had not been just as rigidly unintelligent as every other entity in the system."

He shook his head once again, an element of despair

in the movement. "I am afraid we can look for no hope of eventual understanding between our cultures to these supposed intelligent elements in the Dawnworlds."

The two Section G agents, Rita Daniels, and Lieutenant Takashi moved from the *Pisa* to the Baron Wyler's space yacht for the trip in return to United Planets.

For the first few days there was little communication between them. No desire for words. There was a pervading atmosphere of mental lassitude, ennui.

It was toward the end of this period that Ronny Bronston found himself alone in the lounge with Rita Daniels. They had not been avoiding each other, it was just that they had failed to contact.

He brought her a drink from the bar and one for himself.

"What are you going to do?" he asked.

She looked at him thoughtfully. "I suppose I'll stick with Uncle Max. He . . . he needs someone now."

"The last member of the team, eh?"

She looked to see if there was bitterness in his face, but it was neutral.

"I suppose so," she said. "I believe Count Fitzjames plans to offer his services to the Octagon. After all, he is the nearest thing to an authority we have on the Dawnworlds."

Ronny said, "Don't worry about your uncle. The Wylers in life make out all right. Through his power hunger, in one fell swoop, he was the cause of the deaths of more people than Ghengis Kahn, Tamerlane, Stalin and Hitler all rolled into an unhappy one. But he'll make out."

She said lowly, "You hate my uncle, don't you?"

He shook his head at her. "I don't hate anyone. I'm rapidly coming to the conclusion that the more you learn about the workings of individuals, cultures and even the ultimate destiny of the species, the less possible is it to hate anybody. As I recall, you were particularly interested in the ultimate destiny of the race."

"I *was*," she said wryly. "Now, I'm not so sure about it."

AFTERMATH

After all reports were through, Ronny Bronston came to his feet and reached in his pocket for his wallet. He tossed it to the desk of Ross Metaxa.

"My badge," he said.

Metaxa and Sid Jakes looked at him.

The Commissioner of Section G said, "What are you going to do?"

"First, I'm going to ask a girl I've met recently to marry me. Then I'm going to migrate to Shangri-La. You can turn over to United Planets the job of spreading the warning against bothering the Dawnworlds."

Sid Jakes chuckled. "Shangri-La? What's there, my disillusioned friend?"

"The hedonistic ethic."

"Eat, drink and be merry, for tomorrow we die, eh?"

"Something like that."

"Great," Metaxa growled. "But it's hardly a teaching to be followed by a whole species."

"Oh," Ronny said. "Why not? But what I do know is that the purpose of Section G is gone. The pressing need to hurry man toward his final destiny no longer appeals to me. I have seen his final destiny, and it has little appeal."

Ross Metaxa, moist of eye as always as though from too little sleep or too much alcohol, looked at him wearily. "You haven't thought this Dawnworld threat through to its conclusion, Ronny."

His resigning agent grunted amusement. "There is no threat. We leave them alone, they leave us alone."

The Section G head grunted contempt of that opinion.

"Do you know the legal doctrine of the *attractive nuisance*? Swimming pools are classified as 'attractive nuisances,' for instance. It's a legal doctrine based on the proposition that something like a swimming pool is a natural, inevitable attraction to small children—children, who simply aren't old enough to be competent to take care of themselves; and who aren't old enough, either, to be wise enough to realize they can't. Children simply can't be fenced in at all times, so they can't wander into neighborhood swimming pools and drown. So the 'attractive nuisance' laws make the owner of the swimming pool liable, which forces the pool owner to put a fence around the pool, instead of saying—all the children in the neighborhood should have fences built around them.

"As I recall, the classic case that started that legislation rolling was a company, in the old days, that had a beautiful 75 x 125 foot concrete-lined pool on company property. One weekend, when operations were shut down, some kids sneaked onto the company land and dove in. The first two were in before they discovered that it was the company's sulfuric acid storage vat."

Ronny was getting the point.

Metaxa said, "More than one of the member planets of United Planets are in the 'children' category. Some of them will have populations with hysterical reactions to the existence of our passive-but-appallingly-deadly-threat Dawnworlds. They'll want to provoke war. Then there'll be, inevitably, the crooks who want to steal some of those magnificent gadgets, that magnificent science. Baron Wyler was an example. There'll probably even be religious cranks, who'll want to send missionaries."

Ronny said, "So we still need a Section G, to act as a

fence around this 'attractive nuisance.' Is that your point?"

Ross Metaxa growled, "You once asked me if you'd been conned into joining Section G. The answer was 'yes.' It also would have been 'yes,' if you'd asked the question about Sid, here—or, about myself, for that matter. The job's to be done, we have to take what measures we must to do it. The question is asked, 'am I my brother's keeper?'" He looked deeply into the other's eyes. "The answer, Ronny, is 'yes.'"

Sid Jakes chuckled. "Meaning, of course, that a keeper is one who cares for and controls the actions of one who is incompetent, irresponsible or insane."

Ronny looked at Sid Jakes. "I know of a girl you ought to get busy on, recruiting into Section G. She'll make a top agent." He slowly reached down to take up the wallet, which contained his badge.

But Metaxa anticipated him, picked it up and dropped it into a desk drawer.

Ronny looked at him.

Metaxa brought forth another wallet and tossed it over. The badge inside gleamed gold at Ronny's touch.

Ross Metaxa growled, "Recruit this girl yourself, Bronston. If necessary, using whatever dirty tricks are required to rope her into our service. That's one of the prime duties of operatives of supervisor rank."

ANDRE NORTON

....	022756	Android at Arms — $1.25
....	051623	Beast Master — 95¢
....	078956	Breed to Come — $1.25
....	092676	Catseye — 95¢
....	123125	The Crossroads of Time — $1.25
....	137968	Dark Piper — 95¢
....	139931	Daybreak 2250 A.D. — 95¢
....	142331	Defiant Agents — 95¢
....	166470	Dragon Magic — 95¢
....	166702	Dread Companion — 95¢
....	223651	Exiles of the Stars — 95¢
....	272278	Galactic Derelict — 95¢
....	337022	High Sorcery — 95¢
....	354225	Huon of the Horn — 95¢
....	358408	Ice Crown — 75¢
....	415521	Judgment on Janus — 95¢
....	436733	Key Out of Time — 95¢
....	471623	The Last Planet — 95¢
....	492363	Lord of Thunder — 75¢
....	541029	Moon of Three Rings — 95¢
....	577528	Night of Masks — 95¢
....	634113	Operation Time Search — 95¢
....	638221	Ordeal in Otherwhere — 75¢
....	668327	Plague Ship — 95¢
....	675553	Postmarked the Stars — 75¢

Available wherever paperbacks are sold or use this coupon.

ace books, (Dept. MM) Box 576, Times Square Station
New York, N.Y. 10036
Please send me titles checked above.

I enclose $................Add 20¢ handling fee per copy.

Name ....

Address ....

City..................... State.............. Zip........

24J

FRITZ LEIBER

Frank Herbert

.... 172627   Dune — $1.50
.... 302620   The Green Brain — $1.25
.... 909267   Worlds of Frank Herbert — 95¢

URSULA K. LEGUIN

.... 107029   City of Illusion — 95¢
.... 478024   Left Hand of Darkness — $1.50
.... 669531   Planet of Exile — 95¢
.... 732925   Roncannon's World — 95¢
.... 900761   A Wizard of Earthsea — 95¢

Samuel R. Delany

.... 045914   Babel 17 — 95¢
.... 045225   Ballard of Beta 2 — 60¢
.... 196816   Einstein Intersection — 95¢
.... 205716   Empire Star — 95¢
.... 226415   Fall of the Towers — $1.25
.... 390211   Jewels of Aptor — 75¢

A.E. VAN VOGT

Science Fiction
THE GREAT YEARS!

Science Fiction
THE GREAT YEARS!

45